Life on Fire

a novel by Jenetta Bradley
and *Karen D. Bradley*

Ambrosia Sands Publishing
Dolton, Illinois

Life on Fire Published by:

Ambrosia Sands Books
PO Box 827
Dolton, IL 60419
www.ambrosiasands.com

Trade Paperback ISBN: 978-0-9833560-6-6
Digital ISBN: 978-0-9833560-7-3
LCCN: 2015901605

Cover Art by: J.L. Woodson www.jlwoodson.com
Interior Design by: Lissa Woodson www.macrompg.com
Manufactured and Printed in the United States of America

Life on Fire

✦ Dedication ✦

For those who seek to soar,
Remember you must have a mindset that allows any failed attempts to make you better. Don't let the mistakes made and the chances that did not work out become the locking mechanism that grounds your flight. Instead, let those things be pavement on the runway that you use to take flight. If you can do that, you will soar.

✦ Acknowledgments ✦

The writing journey is always better when you have special people to help you along the way. This was the first time we had a traveling companion to share the journey from beginning to end. Collaborating on this novel has been a blessing.

Michelle Chester, lady you are appreciated more than you know and thank you is not enough. Many thanks to Ebony Walker, Tonya R. Briggity and Joelle Kirk, you three are aces in a deck with no jokers. With you in our corner we have a winning hand. Thanks to Janice Pernell for challenging us to take our writing to the next level and making this novel better. A special thanks to J. L. Woodson and Lissa Woodson (Naleighna Kai), we truly appreciate your time and efforts in helping us put the finish touches to this novel.

Finally, to the friends, family and readers who have supported and encouraged us as individual authors and now as co-authors, we are grateful, thankful and feel blessed because of you.

Chapter One

Memories of him, what was and what could have been stalked Brooklyn Saunders as she sipped her almond chai latté. The thoughts haunted her like a ghost. She was seeing shadows of him out the corner of her eyes. When she turned to look, he was not there. She would turn down the music because she thought she heard his voice, but there was only silence. It was the haunting of a love that could never be, yet it could have been so sweet. Last night, she thought she felt his breath on her neck. But, as she waited for his arm to slide around her waist, her heart dropped when she realized that it was only the wind from the window she'd left cracked. The writing was on the wall. The picture was so clear. She did not want to accept it. The imagery was so obvious, but she tried to change the interpretation of what was before her. Brooklyn thought, sighing, *Isn't that what art is, the artist's work and the individual's interpretation of it? Can my interpretation of what's before me really be wrong? Is it an accurate depiction of who we were and what we are? I hope not.*

The memories of the two of them were etched in her heart. Brooklyn didn't want them to be history, even though they were history long before they were officially over. They were doomed from the start. His words stayed with her like a song on repeat. *Dammit! Why do I do this to myself?* Distracted by the thought of him, she was barely functioning. She couldn't stop asking questions she already knew the answers to.

Why am I torturing myself? He's been out of my life for a while. I should have adjusted by now. This called for something stronger than a latté. Putting her mug down, she called a cab because she would definitely be in need of a designated driver later. She went to her room to change into tight jeans and red high heels, a combo that always commanded attention on her killer body.

Around the time the cab was due to arrive, Brooklyn grabbed her coat and wallet then went outside. Her high heels clicked on the pavement as she did a quick trot to get into the cab. She gave the cab driver the location, then leaned back in the seat and responded to all the texts she had been ignoring. It was a 'do not disturb' kind of Thursday night. But she knew that if she didn't at least reply to the texts from her friends, one of them would be at her house in a heartbeat.

When the cab pulled up to her favorite spot, she paid and took his business card so she could call when she was ready to go. A long line of people waited to get in the club, but Brooklyn did her catwalk right past them and up to the door. The bouncer opened it to let her in. She smiled, lightly touching him on the arm as she entered, ignoring the evil looks the people waiting in line threw at her.

"BK, who are you trying to hurt tonight?" a deep, sexy voice whispered in her ear as she pulled her coat off and got in line to check it.

Brooklyn turned to see a familiar face. "I could ask you the same, Hunter." Checking out the tall, muscular brother of Black and Cuban descent, she teased, "Mmm hmm, if Sophia didn't have you on lock down …"

He grabbed her coat, handed it to the attendant, then gave Brooklyn the ticket he was given. "You'd better be careful," Hunter warned while peering at the ample breasts revealed through her white shirt cropped in the front to showcase her flat abs. "You may be the one I'm hurting tonight—since I'm back on the market." He lightly touched her lower back as he led her to a booth with a reserved sign on it and smiled as she sat down.

"So what brings you in on a weeknight?" he asked, sliding next to her in the booth. "It's rare that I see you in here any other day but Friday or Saturday."

"It was an 'I need a drink' kind of night," she stated, waving at some familiar faces walking by. "Besides, dancing with some handsome men will do wonders for my attitude."

"Well, drinks are on me as usual. But try to stay out of trouble tonight. I got to get back to work, but I'll be stopping by throughout the night." Hunter slid out of the booth as the waitress brought one of Brooklyn's favorite drinks to the table.

"Thank you," Brooklyn mouthed to Hunter and the waitress as she lifted her glass and took a sip. He was good—she hadn't even seen him motion to the bartender to order her drink.

"Don't thank me yet," he warned. "I'm working on being your stress reliever after you leave this place."

"We'll see if you're saying the same thing when the night is over and all the single chicks have fallen at your feet."

He bent down, kissing her on the cheek then giving her a wink.

Brooklyn had just finished her drink when a light-skinned guy approached the table. Though he was of average stature and looks, he had a lot of swagger. She stood, taking him up on his offer to dance. Three songs in, her shirt was soaked and she was dancing with two gentlemen—one in front, one in back. She couldn't stop laughing as the guy in front somehow ended up between her legs. He moved under and through her legs as if she was a limbo bar. The guy dancing behind her circled around to the front. She didn't even know when the third guy came up.

She leaned in towards the guy in front of her and shouted over the music, "Sorry, it's time for me to take a drink break." She then got a pink lady from the bar.

This was just what I needed, she thought as she went back to her booth and slid into the leather seat. Not too many minutes later, she was back on the dance floor with a short, Hispanic guy showing her his moves. When he spun her around, Brooklyn noticed her ex through the crowd. She had been having such a great time drinking, dancing, and laughing, that she didn't notice when he walked in. It caught her off guard. Slightly tipsy, she stumbled and her dance partner steadied her.

She leaned down near his ear. "I think I'd better sit this next one out." He escorted her through the crowd on the dance floor and back to her booth, where Hunter was waiting. She graciously thanked her dance partner as she got into the booth, then motioned for the waitress, mouthing to her to bring a bottle of water and another drink. She scanned the crowd again checked to see if she had really seen her ex. The crowd was thick but his face wasn't among them.

"BK? BK? Brooklyn, are you all right?" Hunter called out as she took one more look around the room.

"I'm sorry. I'm having a rougher night than I thought. I could have sworn … Never mind." Not even the alcohol in her system could eradicate him from the forefront of her thoughts. Brooklyn smiled at Hunter. "So, Mr. Sexy, what happened with you and Sophia?"

"Let's just say she has pulled her last jealous stunt with me." Hunter took a swig of his beer.

"She didn't throw a drink on a girl again, did she?" Brooklyn laughed at Sophia's antics.

Hunter lifted the beer bottle to his lips just as the waitress brought Brooklyn a bottle of water and a pink lady. "Had that been the only thing she did, we'd still be together."

"She didn't hit anyone, did she?" Brooklyn sipped her drink, trying to focus on Hunter and not the thoughts running through her head.

"Worse. She slashed the tires of my cousin's rental car."

"No! I thought she got along with all your people." Brooklyn gave him a confused look when another waitress brought a platter of hot wings to the table.

"I figured with all the drinking you were doing, you needed something solid in your stomach," he stated.

"You always take such good care of me," Brooklyn sighed as she grabbed a wing. *Why am I so attached to a guy who is clearly not interested in going the distance with me?* she thought, scanning the crowd one last time for him. "So back to your story. Whose tires did she slash?"

"Idaliz." When she scrunched her eyebrows in confusion, he added, "You remember her? My cousin from Cali." Hunter checked his watch then grabbed a hot wing.

A very bottom-heavy African girl in a micro-miniskirt stood near the booth on Hunter's side. Her butt cheeks were two seconds from peeping out from under her hem. The girl glanced back to see if he was looking. He wasn't. Brooklyn laughed, returning her attention to Hunter as she devoured another wing.

"This whole tire-slashing incident happened because Idaliz hasn't visited since I started dating Sophia. So when Sophia saw her hug me and kiss me on the cheek, instead of coming up and making her presence known, she waited till after I had Carlos bring Idaliz's car around." Hunter checked his watch again then finished off his drink. "That's when she sliced her tires." He grabbed a napkin to wipe buffalo sauce off his hands, then offered one to Brooklyn, but she shook her head and licked the sauce off her fingers.

His eyes were glued to her lips. "You better watch yourself tonight," he commanded. "Between that nearly-sheer shirt from you sweating on the dance floor, to you licking that sauce off your fingers, I'm damn near ready to take you to my office and show you what I'm working with." Hunter slid out the booth.

"That's exactly why Sophia's behind was constantly throwing drinks on girls, tripping them, and slicing tires." She dipped her finger into the sauce, then lifted it up to her lips and slowly licked it off her finger.

"Stay off the dance floor until that shirt of yours dries a little, okay?"

Brooklyn gave him her best seductive look. "Or what?"

"Or I'll actually make you pay the bill for all you drank tonight." Hunter leaned down and wiped the extra sauce from her lips with his finger.

"I'll stay off the dance floor for thirty minutes tops, but if a fine guy asks me to dance, all bets are off and I'm going to have to set up a payment plan with you." Brooklyn laughed when she noticed that his eyes lit up. "Behave, Hunter."

"Only if someone scoops you up before I'm officially off the clock." Hunter tilted his head at her while giving her a sly grin. "And slow down on the drinks. I don't want you passing out on me before the real fun begins."

"Whatever." Brooklyn smirked. "Get back to work and keep the drinks coming," she commanded as he walked off.

Chapter Two

Brooklyn, stop thinking about your ex, she thought as she scanned the crowd for his face again. She couldn't have possibly seen him. It was probably someone who reminded her of him. She motioned to the waitress to bring her another drink thinking, *My high tolerance for alcohol is working against me tonight*. It was clear that she had either danced off the effects of her previous drinks or still hadn't drank enough to relax her mind. When the waitress came, she asked, "Hey, could you just make me a pitcher of the pink lady? Because by the time you make it back to the bar, I'll be asking for another one." Brooklyn downed the drink she just received to prove her point.

The waitress grabbed the empty glass. "It's a good thing we know you can handle your liquor, otherwise we would have cut you off long ago."

"Well you'll be happy to know I have no intentions of driving tonight," she sassed.

A few minutes later, Brooklyn was looking down at her watch when the waitress came back to her table. At least, she thought that's who it was until she looked up and saw *him* sliding into the other end of her booth. Her heart stopped as her eyes went from his chiseled, handsome face to his broad chest and well-cut arms that made his short-sleeved button down shirt look like it would not contain all his glory.

He stared at her and she looked away. "So you're not going to speak?" he asked.

Brooklyn turned and glared at the man who was the reason she had to get out of the house tonight in the first place. "You're the one who sat your behind in my booth without saying a word."

"I've been waiting for a moment of your time." His grey eyes seemed to change colors as he spoke.

"Dante Nines, what on earth are you doing here?" Brooklyn was glad to see the waitress had arrived with her pitcher.

"Are you sharing?" Dante asked with a devilish grin.

"No." Brooklyn poured herself a drink. "What are you doing here?"

"It's like that, huh?" He leaned forward, resting his arms on the table. "I love your hair pulled back like that."

"Here. You can have it." She pulled her phony ponytail off, pushing it over to him. "Now give it to your girl and have a nice night."

Dante pushed it back towards her. "I prefer it on you."

"You've said, hi. Now it's time to say bye." Brooklyn put her ponytail back on. *Remember what he did. Don't be a wuss this time!* She was grateful they were in a club full of people. Her brain stopped working properly when she was alone around him. She downed her drink, picking up the pitcher and pouring more into the glass. Being there with him was trouble and she knew it.

"Fine, Brook." He stood up, and Brooklyn's shoulders relaxed. This was not the night for her to do battle with Dante Nines over their complicated, nonexistent relationship. She had to do a double take when he sat back down beside her, close enough for their shoulders to touch. "Don't be too relieved," he warned. "I think I'll just stay here and block your path so you can't run. We need to talk."

"There's nothing to talk about. Your actions said everything. You didn't contact me for months, after you claimed you would." Brooklyn moved to her right and laid her left thigh on the seat to force some distance between them. "What was that line you gave me? 'Brook, baby, give us a chance. I have to wrap up a project, then I'll be back and we can see if we can go the distance.'" She scanned the crowd, looking for Hunter so she could give him the S.O.S signal. She poured herself another drink.

"How about we go back to my place and talk about it?" Dante touched her thigh but seemed to take no offense to her knocking his hand away and scooting further back.

"Like I stated, we have nothing to talk about." Brooklyn put her drink up to her lips, emptying the contents of the glass.

"You look absolutely gorgeous. I like how the red bra under your white shirt matches your shoes. Had you not been working it on the floor, I would have missed out on that beautiful sight." When he smiled, that damn square chin and 'I want you' look in his eyes had her flashing back to old times.

"Dante, you can leave now."

He reached for her hand. "I miss you. Come on, at least give me a chance to explain."

She snatched her hand away, refilling her glass then picking it up and downing the contents. "Explain what, Dante? That the project didn't allow you to reach out via phone, text, email, or even social media?" Brooklyn had been so busy drinking and pouring that she hadn't even realized she had gone through the whole pitcher. She did not want to have this conversation tonight of all nights. Once the clock struck midnight, it was officially the anniversary of the day that their lives became entangled all those years ago.

"The project went over. I had—"

"Don't lie. I waited an extra three weeks after the date you told me the project would end before I sent that nice and nasty email. I don't want to hear it. It's been years since you told me that there should be an official 'we'. Whenever you resurfaced, I still let you back in my life as long as I was single. And every time, you'd fall off the face of the earth afterward. I emailed to see if you were okay. I didn't even get a reply to my email or a phone call to explain things." Brooklyn was trying not to be affected by him, but foolishly, she still loved him.

"I know you, Brooklyn. As mad as you are, you want answers. Come back to my place and"—he reached, grabbing her waist and pulling her to him then whispering in her ear—"get reacquainted. Don't say no. Even when you're mad at me, you're always up for a little fun."

"Dante, no!" Brooklyn took a deep breath. *Don't do it! You know better. It never ends well for you. Be strong!*

"Your mouth is saying no, but your body is saying yes." He leaned in and kissed her.

Dammit! Automatically, she kissed him back. Brooklyn missed him and their crazy entanglement.

Hunter cleared his throat. Brooklyn and Dante broke apart and she looked up sheepishly at Hunter. "I think it's time for you to call that cab for me."

Dante sat with a smug look, as though he was waiting for her to introduce him. When she didn't, he stated, "Hey, I'm Dante, her ex." He sized Hunter up with his eyes.

"Nice meeting you." Hunter nodded as Brooklyn gave him her S.O.S. signal by pulling her earlobe twice.

"Come on, BK, I need you to sign off on your check before you go. I'll get Carlos to call you a cab." Hunter nodded his head for her to follow him.

Brooklyn nudged Dante to move out of her way and gave an impatient, "Excuse me," when he stayed put.

He turned to her, giving her a big grin. "This conversation's not over," he promised, standing at the edge of the booth to let her out.

Brooklyn had finally reached her drink limit. Downing that last pitcher that fast was probably a bad idea. She didn't know if it was the gin or seeing Dante again that had her legs all wobbly as she eased herself up. Not wanting her unsteadiness to make her look weak and vulnerable, she jutted her chin out and proclaimed in a defiant voice, "I would say it was nice seeing you again, but that would be a lie. Take care of yourself."

As she sashayed over to Hunter, she heard Dante call out, "We're not done by a long shot. I'll see you later."

Hunter slid his arm around her waist and led her through the crowd to his office. Once behind closed doors, he rounded his desk and picked up the phone to have Carlos get her a cab. "I guess we won't be enjoying each other's company tonight, or shall I say this morning," he commented.

"It never seems to be the right time for us," Brooklyn replied. "It's a rare occasion that we're both single at the same time. Now we are, and …"

"And your ex pops up, wanting to reconnect. By the lip lock I found you two engaged in, you're clearly not over him." Hunter leaned onto his desk and pulled her to him.

"As if you're over Sophia," Brooklyn whispered, resting her hands on his chest as he wrapped his arm around her back.

He pulled her closer to him. "I should have pulled you back here and swept the desk when you first came through that door tonight. I don't know how we remained friends so long without crossing the line."

Brooklyn linked her arms around his neck. "I've been waiting for your fine behind to be single, but the line to get to you is always too long."

"Hell, I was planning to spend more time with you tonight, but you were rarely without company. Look what happened when I left to wrap up for the evening so I could." Hunter's cell phone buzzed. He took a quick glance at it. "It looks like your cab has arrived."

Brooklyn tipped forward, kissing him on the cheek. "You're too good to me. You know that?"

"I'm surprised Sophia never spilled a drink on you," Hunter teased as he released her.

"It's only because when you met her, I was with Max. I was absolutely no threat to her." Brooklyn stood straight.

"If you haven't gotten back with your ex by tomorrow, roll through the club and we can decide if the time is right for us to find out if there's any real magic behind our attraction." Hunter stood, walking with her out of the office and to the exit.

"That's if I'm not dead to the world tomorrow night from being out until two-thirty in the morning then trying to make it to work by seven a.m." She yawned as she followed him to the coat check. Hunter helped her put on her coat then walked her out to the waiting cab.

"Hey, make sure you text me and let me know you made it safely home." He pulled her into a quick hug before opening the cab door.

"Yes, sir." Brooklyn slid into the cab. Hunter shut the door and waved as the cab pulled off.

A flash of Dante's face saying they were not done entered Brooklyn's mind. She knew that devious expression too well. As she leaned forward to give the cabbie her address, she thought, *Dammit Dante Nines. What are you up to?*

Chapter Three

Brooklyn started surfing the Internet on her phone for anything that might keep her mind off of Dante. It wasn't working. She started thinking about one of the times she had reached out to him after they had let too much time pass. If he was with another woman at the time, it made her question whether she was the real reason they never really got it together. Her attempt to focus on his negatives to calm down the excitement that ran through her tonight wasn't working either. The only thing she could think of was how he created an environment that made her feel protected, empowered, supported, and loved. That was the reason she had a hard time staying mad with him. The natural high she got from being with Dante was something that she couldn't replicate with any other man. Even when he wasn't active in her life, the words he spoke to her over the years inspired, encouraged, and strengthened her during some of the most challenging times.

The cab began slowing down and she noticed that the meter wasn't on. When he pulled over, Brooklyn looked out the window. The area was familiar, but it wasn't her neighborhood.

"Excuse me, sir, I think you must have misheard the address. I need to be taken to—" Her eyes widen as her door flew open.

Dante took a very shocked Brooklyn by her upper arm and wrist, to half-assist, half-pull her out of the cab. "He brought you to the right place."

"What are you thinking? I have to go to work in a couple of hours." Brooklyn wished she had driven tonight.

Dante moved her out of the way, closed the door, and waved off the cab. "While the cabbie waited for you to come out of the club, I made arrangements to drop you off here. It cost me a pretty penny."

"You know this is foolishness. I need to get home and get some sleep before I head to work." She put her hands in her pocket, searching for the business card she'd gotten from the cab driver that took her to the club a few hours earlier.

Dante took her by the shoulders and turned her towards his townhouse. "Sweetie, I know from experience that you can function relatively well on only thirty minutes of sleep."

She put on brakes as soon as she found the card. "What don't you understand about no?" she fussed, taking her phone out to call for another cab.

Dante grabbed her phone out of her hand. "I don't take no for an answer. Give me thirty minutes, Brook, thirty minutes." He put her phone into his pocket then walked to the door, opened it, and waited.

Brooklyn stood there awhile, staring at Dante on the porch. *Don't do it, Brooklyn! You can't be alone with him. You tend to cave every time you are around him.* She looked down the street, debating her options. *Just take the two-block walk to the hotel around the corner, catch a cab there, and take your behind home. You can get another phone tomorrow. Just say it was stolen.*

"Brooklyn," Dante stated, sounding convinced that he'd have to drag her into the house.

"Fine, thirty minutes." She glanced down at her watch thinking, *You're playing with fire, young lady.*

As she walked slowly up the stairs, Dante watched her like a hawk, as if he was waiting for her to bolt at any second.

She turned her body sideways and tried to skim past him at the door without touching. Dante stepped back, giving her room to get past. After he locked the door, he led her to the living room.

"Would you like some coffee?" Dante asked, motioning for her to sit on the love seat.

"No, thank you." Brooklyn figured she'd be safer sitting in the chair. "How about you say what you need to say so I can get my phone and go?"

Dante sat on the sturdy mahogany coffee table directly in front of her. "Look, Brooklyn, I know I screwed up. I had signed a confidentially agreement and couldn't speak about the project I was working on."

"That's bull crap. I wasn't asking you about the project. I was asking when you'd be back and if you were still interested in pursuing a relationship with me." Brooklyn leaned back in the chair when Dante moved forward.

"I made a mistake by not letting you know the project was taking longer than we originally thought." Dante slipped off the table and onto his knees in front of her, sliding his upper body between her legs. He took her hands. "You know we're good together."

"Dante, we had our chance and you blew it. Twice I might add." She snatched her hands from him.

"Can I at least have a goodbye kiss?" Dante pushed off his knees but only raised himself high enough so that his mouth hovered just over her lips.

Brooklyn put her hand on his chest and pushed him away. "I need to go." She stood as he sat back down on the table. He pulled her to him, pushing her coat open and planting a kiss on her exposed stomach.

"Don't do that! I've been sweating all night." She attempted to step back, but with his hands interlocked behind her, it didn't do her any good. Before she knew it, he went from sitting to lifting her up by her thighs as he rose to his feet. Quickly moving her back against the closest wall, Dante gave her a heated kiss. Their tongues did a seductive tango until she couldn't think straight. *Oh Damn! Here I go again,* she thought as she kissed him back, started grinding into him, and unbuttoned his shirt.

"Brook, baby, you don't know just how much I've missed you. But, I plan in the next few hours to show you." Dante carried her toward the bedroom, kissing her all the way there.

"Ah, I see you brought me home a playmate," chimed a soft, feminine voice from the bed.

Brooklyn immediately broke the kiss and looked at the beautiful, slender Asian chick laying in Dante's bed, wearing nothing but one of his white, button-down shirts.

"Really, Dante? A threesome? Didn't we fall out about this once before? Put me down and give me my damn phone." Brooklyn was kicking herself in the behind for caving in to him once again.

Dante put her down, looking from her, to the woman in his bed, and back to her. "Brook, I—"

"Hey, you two can have at it. You always have a pinch hitter in your back pocket. Let whoever she is"— she glanced down at the woman on the bed—"serve your every need and fantasy." The woman simply rolled to her side and propped herself up on her elbow. "Enjoy," Brooklyn hissed to her. "Dante, I want my phone!" she demanded as she stormed out of the room.

"Brook, give me five minutes and I'll give you your phone." He looked into the living room to see Brooklyn walking to the door.

"Now, Mr. Nines!" Brooklyn stood by the door steaming and snarling at Dante, who stood by the open bedroom door.

Dante looked back at the woman in his shirt. "I'll be right back." He exited the bedroom. Walking over to Brooklyn, he grabbed her phone out of his pocket and slowly handed it to her. "Brook, we'll continue this next time." He tilted his face close to hers as he opened the front door.

"There won't be a next time, Mr. Nines." Brooklyn walked out, quickly trotted down the stairs, and headed for the hotel.

Chapter Four

Brooklyn fingers were crossed that there were still a few cabs around the hotel. Glancing back, she could see Dante standing on his steps, watching her.

"Hey, Hunter, I'm sorry," Brooklyn answered after her cell rang and she saw it was him. She tucked the cell between her ear and shoulder as she tightened the belt on her coat.

"I didn't get a text from you. I just wanted to make sure you made it home safely." Hunter's concern reflected in his voice.

"My ex rerouted my cab to his house. It's a long story. I'm heading home now." A couple got out of a cab a few yards away from Brooklyn and she walked swiftly over to the cab to catch it before someone else did. Glancing back, she saw Dante reenter his building in the distance.

"Do you need a ride?" Hunter asked.

"No, I walked to the hotel near him and got a cab." She gave the cabbie her address. As he pulled off, Brooklyn looked one last time at Dante's place before it faded into the distance.

"Well, I'll stay on the phone with you until you get home."

"I don't know if I want to talk to you." Brooklyn searched for her apartment keys.

"Why?"

"Because in a few hours, you'll be sleeping while I'm working." Brooklyn rummaged through her coat pockets. Her keys were nowhere to be found. "Shit, it's just that kind of day." She exhaled her frustration. "Hunter, I'm so sorry to do this to you but I need you to meet me back at the club." Brooklyn leaned forward to give the driver the new address.

"What happened?" Hunter questioned.

"I think my keys fell out in the club." Brooklyn noticed that the cab driver adjusted his rear view mirror so that her chest was showcased every time he looked in it.

"You're sure you didn't lose them at your friend's place?" Hunter asked in a way that let her know he wasn't pleased that she'd been with her ex.

"I didn't take off my coat. I guess I could have lost them when I sat in the chair." Brooklyn hoped beyond hope that that wasn't the case.

"I'm on my way to the club, but I'll call ahead and see if anyone is still there to let you in if you get there first," Hunter spoke with urgency in his voice.

"Thanks!" Brooklyn replied as she hung up.

"Can't find your keys?" the eavesdropping cabbie asked.

"Yes, but I didn't lose my wallet, so you don't have to worry about getting your money." She fished her wallet out almost as confirmation.

"I wasn't worried. Any person that has the power to get one of the most popular clubs in the city to open back up after hours just so she can retrieve her lost keys has the power to get me paid." The cabbie smiled, taking a quick peek in his rearview mirror.

Brooklyn laughed.

Hunter's ringtone started sounding off. "Hi, what's the verdict?" Brooklyn sat up as they neared the club.

"Everybody's gone. Ask the cabbie if he minds staying till I get there. There's an extra hundred in it for him."

"That's not necessary," Brooklyn insisted, pulling out her wallet.

"Dammit, Brooklyn, ask! I don't want you standing out there by yourself." Hunter kept a lot of security on site when the club was opened.

The club was in the Ivy City area of Washington, D.C. but with mostly warehouses around, it was not the best neighborhood for Brooklyn to be waiting in alone. "Brooklyn, ask him."

She leaned forward. "Would you mind terribly waiting until my friend gets here? We can keep the meter running."

"That's fine." The cab pulled in front of the club.

"Thank you. Did you hear that? He'll wait." Brooklyn relaxed back on the seat.

"All right. See you soon." Hunter hung up.

While the cabbie answered a call, Brooklyn began playing with her phone to kill time. A gentle tap on the window alerted them to Hunter's presence.

Hunter shook his head, looking at the black sedan sitting in the distance. Neither Brooklyn nor the cab driver had been paying attention to their surroundings. The cab driver unlocked the doors. Brooklyn pulled the money out of her wallet.

"BK, you know I got this," Hunter insisted, holding the door open for her. The cabbie rolled down the window and stuck his hand out. Hunter shut the door, then slipped some bills in the man's hand.

Smiling from ear-to-ear, the cabbie beamed, "Have a good day," then pulled off.

"Did you see his crazy grin?" Brooklyn asked as they walked towards the club. "How much did you give him?"

"Two hundred dollars." Hunter glanced down at her chest. "But he's probably grinning from staring at your girls."

"Whatever," Brooklyn smirked as she walked towards the coat check.

Hunter caught her by the back of her coat. "Hey, where are you heading?"

"To look for my keys." Brooklyn gave him a confused look.

"How about we check the lost and found before we search the coat room? If one of the attendants saw them, they would be there." In the lost and found room, he grabbed the log. "It looks like you're in luck. A set of keys was logged in. Now let's just hope they're yours."

"Fingers crossed, 'cause if not, we're taking a trip to my ex's house to pick them up." Brooklyn shifted in her four-inch heels.

"Are these yours?" He held up the set of keys.

"Yes." She grabbed them then hugged him.

"Let me grab one more thing, then I'll take you home." He signed out her keys then locked up the room.

Brooklyn sat on a bench near the door. "What size shoes you wear?" Hunter called out from down the hall.

"Nine, why?" Her heels had reached their expiration date. She wanted so badly to take them off, but she knew that if she did, she wouldn't be able to get them back on.

"Take these," he ordered, stepping out and tossing something at her. Brooklyn caught it and the corners of her mouth curled up when she looked down and saw the ballerina slippers in her hand. "Sophia was crazy to let you get away," she responded as she slipped off her heels and slid her aching feet into the soft flats.

"You used to bring your own." Hunter locked the display case. "That's what gave me the idea to stock them here at the club. They're big sellers every night."

Brooklyn stood, grabbing her heels. "My feet thank you." She followed him through a doorway and exclaimed, "Sweet!" when he led her to his black Audi A8. "When did you get this beauty, Mr. Big Shot?"

Hunter laughed. "I've had it for three years. You would have known if you'd ever accepted my offers to hang out outside the club." He unlocked the car, got in, and threw his wallet into the cup holder.

"Ooo la la," Brooklyn moaned, sinking into the soft leather seats and pulling her seatbelt around her.

Hunter started the car then opened the garage door. Brooklyn was amazed as they pulled into the club's parking lot. "Wow, as many times as I parked here I never noticed this door."

"That's the point," Hunter stated as he waited to make sure that the door closed completely. He crept into the street. "So what happened with you and your ex?"

"Let's just say you can't disappear for an extended period then expect me to engage in a threesome." Brooklyn was still mad at herself because the only thing that had kept her from being entangled in the sheets with him was the fact that there was another woman in the bed.

Hunter chuckled. "Well you've always liked bold men."

"There's a difference between bold and disrespectful. He can't bother to call, but he can ask for a threesome. I will not be treated like some street walker or common whore."

"So if I treat you like a special whore it's all right?" Hunter glanced over at her.

She punched him in the arm. "You're stupid."

"In all seriousness, I need to ask you a question." Hunter looked in his rearview mirror again.

"What?" Brooklyn asked with a frown.

His facial expression turned really serious. "What kind of trouble are you in?"

"None. What are you talking about?"

"So you're not going to tell me why there's a black sedan following you?"

Brooklyn looked at him as if he was crazy. "No one's following me."

"You didn't notice the black sedan parked a half block down the street from the club while you were in the cab waiting for me?"

"No." Brooklyn flipped down the visor, trying to see the car in the mirror without turning around.

"Well it's been behind us since we left the club, which is why I took the long way to your house." He drove past her apartment building. "There's no way I'm dropping you off here."

"What do you suggest?" Brooklyn tried to think of who could be following her and why. "How do you know it's not Sophia following you?"

"Because the car was already parked on the street when I got there. Sophia knows my schedule well enough to know I would have been at home by that time. If she was scoping out my house and followed me when I left, how'd she get to the club before I did?" Hunter changed the radio station. "Do you think it's your ex?"

Hunter stopped at a red light noticing the black sedan had dipped into a parking spot down the street.

"I left him with his other woman. I would be very surprised if he'd have enough time to hit that and follow me to the club." Brooklyn nervously played with her apartment keys. "Once again, I ask what do you suggest we do?"

"We'll test our theory. Let's go get a bite to eat from our favorite 24-hour joint in Adams Morgan and see if our black sedan stays with us," Hunter stated, heading out of her southwest neighborhood. "If it does, you're staying with me. Do you still keep clothes at work?"

"Yeah."

"My building has security plus a doorman. I'll let you borrow my black hooded jogging suit. In a few hours when it's daylight, you'll head out of the building and go straight to work. I'll take a morning drive and let them follow me, thinking you're in the car."

Brooklyn smiled as they pulled into a park near the diner. "You came up with that plan just like that," she stated, snapping her finger. "I thought I knew you well enough, but I guess there's a lot more to learn about you, Hunter Torres."

Hunter laughed as they exited the car. He locked the door and waited for her to come around it before saying, "He's the same Hunter you've always known and loved."

She slid her arm through his and Hunter gave her a sly grin as they walked to the front door of the diner. He held the door open, looking down the street both ways before entering. There was no black sedan. Maybe he was wrong. They ordered their food to go and ten minutes later stepped out of the diner, laughing and talking.

Hunter noticed a black sedan parked down the street. He continued their light conversation as they neared his car. Before unlocking the door, he glanced around, then they quickly got into the car and headed to the main street.

Brooklyn lifted the bag to her nose. "Mmm, the food smells so good."

Hunter drove a couple of blocks, constantly glancing at the rearview mirror. He smiled. "It looks like you'll be spending time with me at my place after all."

Pretending to get something out of the back seat, Brooklyn turned around and looked out the back window. The black sedan followed in the distance.

"Maybe it's a different black car," Brooklyn stated, turning back around.

"Except that once again it's taking turn for turn with me." Hunter paused. "If you still want me to take you to your apartment, I have no problem dropping you off."

"Nope. You've got a guest for a couple of hours. I need to get some sleep to be able to function at work." Brooklyn glanced in the side view mirror. "I won't be able to rest at home because I'll be constantly looking out the window for a black sedan."

"I suggest that in the morning you don't get your car. Take public transportation, and go straight to work. I'll pick you up when you get off."

"Why can't I go home and get my car?" Brooklyn asked, now taking him seriously.

"If they follow you, would you rather they know where you work or where you live?"

"Okay I see your point, but is it a good idea for you to pick me up if they're following your car?" she questioned.

"BK, trust me. I'll get to you without being followed." Hunter glanced over, giving her a sly smile.

Brooklyn looked over at him then simply uttered, "Mmm hmm."

"Thanks for the vote of confidence. To ease your mind, I must remind you that this isn't the only car I own." He winked at her.

She shifted the bags of hot food on her lap and asked, "Then why can't I just borrow one of your cars to go to work?"

"I've seen your driving. I'm not ever letting you behind the wheel of any of my cars."

"You're not still holding that against me, are you?" Brooklyn remembered the incident where road rage had gotten the best of her and they ended up in an accident.

"Yes." He winced as Brooklyn popped him on his arm.

"That was an isolated incident."

Hunter's laughter resounded through the car. "I can't believe you said that lie with a straight face."

He pulled into the front of the garage and swiped his access card and waited until the door came completely down before heading to his parking spot.

"I wish I had gotten real food instead of breakfast," she stated as she followed him to the elevator. "At least then I could have nibbled on a couple of fries on the way over here instead of simply being tortured by the aroma."

"What time do you have to be at work?" Hunter asked when they exited the elevator and walked a few feet to the door.

"Seven a.m. on the dot." She leaned on the wall, waiting for him to open the door.

"No wonder it's tough to get you out Monday through Thursday." Hunter held the door to let her in, then relieved her of one of the bags of food after he'd locked the door.

"Most of our crew works the second or third shift, so partying until the wee hours of the morning doesn't have the same effect that it does on your work day."

Hunter plopped on the couch, pulling his food out of the brown paper bag. He grabbed the plastic utensils that were in the bottom of the bag, then sat the Styrofoam container on top of the bag. Brooklyn followed his lead, handing him a straw and one of the drinks out the bag.

"So I guess I shouldn't be offended when you don't go out with us. It's just that back in the day you used to kick it." He dug into his food.

"Things change. I told you not to take it personally," Brooklyn replied, putting a fork full of Cajun omelet in her mouth.

"What really brought you out tonight?" Hunter took a gulp of the orange juice.

"I was having a moment and was in serious need of a distraction." Brooklyn still couldn't believe that after all this time, Dante still affected her as if they'd just parted ways.

"So you called your ex and had yourself followed?" Hunter teased.

"Ha ha, funny. My ex was the reason I needed a distraction. As far as being followed, I don't know what that's about." For the rest of the conversation, Brooklyn switched from one subject to the next to keep her mind off of Dante.

Hunter stood, holding out his hand to her when they'd had their fill of their late-night breakfast. "Hey, come back to my room."

"Hunter, ummm." Brooklyn searched for the right way to say she didn't think it was a good idea to explore their chemistry.

"BK." He grabbed her hand, pulling her up. "We're going to my room so we can finish this conversation while I search for the black jogging suit."

"You know it's going to look like it swallowed me alive," Brooklyn joked, following him to his room.

"It shouldn't. I accidentally shrunk it but didn't have the heart to throw it out since my aunt gave it to me. It was one of the last gifts she gave me before she died." Hunter searched through the back of the closet.

"Oh great! Now I get to feel bad if anything happens to it." Brooklyn sat on his bed and leaned her back on the headboard.

"Did you want a shower before or after your nap?" Hunter tossed the sweat suit to her.

Brooklyn stood. "I probably shouldn't be sitting on your bed all sweaty and funky."

"Yeah especially since you aren't planning to get sweatier and funkier with me," Hunter teased. "Sit down. I'll go get you a towel." He grabbed an oversized t-shirt out of his drawer and flung it at her. "That's just in case you don't want to sleep in your tight jeans."

"Don't be getting any ideas and trying to get in the shower with me," Brooklyn ordered, watching him exit the bedroom. She leaned back on the headboard again. Her eyelids began drooping and she nodded off before Hunter could even return.

***

Dante reentered his townhouse to see the woman that just blew his plans with Brooklyn to shreds coming out his bedroom. "Liang, what are you doing here? And why were you in my bed? And half-dressed at that!"

"I'm here because we have a problem. I had no clue you would have company, since you just got back into town. This was the best idea I could come up with in the spur of the moment to explain my presence here without going into the real reason." She grabbed her bag that was leaning on the back of the chair.

Dante buttoned his shirt back up, thinking about what he had only been a couple of seconds away from making happen. "Your timing couldn't have been worse."

"I should be asking what you were doing. I thought you were working tonight, which is why when you didn't answer my phone or text, I let myself in." Liang took a seat on the couch.

"I was mixing business with pleasure. I was planning to do a little information digging while I revisited what I had with an old friend. Thanks to you, that is going to be much harder to do now."

"Well, after I heard you two while I was in the bathroom, I didn't want to have to explain who I am and why I was here." Liang tilted her head at him as if to say what do you expect. "This was the best cover that I could think of where she would ask no questions and you would have to provide no answers."

Dante sat in the chair across from her and asked, "What if she was up for that threesome you mentioned?"

"You would have been in for a night you'd never forget," Liang explained smugly.

He watched Liang dig into her bag and pull out paperwork. "You really could have called or texted to let me know you needed to see me."

"Like I said, I did. You didn't pick up or respond, hence the reason I'm here." She flashed him her cell phone as if to say check yours.

Dante grabbed his work cell to see all the missed calls and texts. "So what was so important that you showed up here?"

"Someone pulled your information before you got back in town." Liang flipped through her paperwork. "It looks like our case isn't a simple missing person."

Dante stood and went into the kitchen, grabbing two bottles of water. "That is not urgent enough to use the key, Liang."

"No it wasn't until you didn't answer any of my calls." Liang found what she was looking for; she placed the rest of the papers back in her bag. "When I got here, I noticed a suspicious black sedan half way down the block."

"Yeah, I noticed while waiting for Brooklyn's cab to arrive," Dante stated.

"Well, when you didn't answer I came through the back way to make sure you were okay." Liang took the bottle of water Dante extended to her.

"I took the license plate number down but you know it could be someone visiting one of my neighbors."

"I ran the plates and it's not here visiting a neighbor. The plates led me back to them," she explained, handing him the sheet of paper she had pulled from her bag. "Not being able to get you on the phone had me concerned they were doing a little more than just watching."

Dante's eyes scanned the paper. "Why in the hell are they watching me?"

Chapter Five

Sometime during the early morning, Brooklyn woke up and found herself snuggled comfortably into Hunter's back. She glanced over his shoulder at the nightstand clock. There was still a little time before she had to get up, so she snuggled a little closer and went back to sleep.

It seemed like only seconds after she fell back to sleep, she heard Hunter calling her name. "Brooklyn, time to meet the sun. If you want to have time to shower before you head in to work, you need to get up now." He stood over her, sipping a cup of coffee. He was already dressed.

Brooklyn sat up reluctantly. "Thanks, Hunter." She threw her legs over the side of the bed, stood up, and plucked the cup of coffee out of his hands. As she walked past him, she grabbed the towels and sweat suit he had laid out for her on the dresser earlier. "I won't be long," she called to him as she entered his bathroom.

"Change of plans," Hunter reported as Brooklyn entered the living room fifteen minutes later. "I'm actually going to drop you off at the office today."

"That's great," she beamed as she parked herself on the couch to put her flats back on. "I wasn't in the mood to ride public transportation anyway. Why the change of heart?"

"It dawned on me that I could just take one of my other vehicles now instead of taking the Audi and switching cars later to pick you up from work. If they stick to parking down the street, they'll still be looking for the Audi." Hunter slipped on his jacket and grabbed his keys.

"I just need a bag to put my stuff in, then I'm ready to go," she stated, standing and grabbing her coat off the couch. She followed Hunter down the hallway and back towards the room, where he handed her a black messenger bag. Brooklyn gave it back to him. "Umm, I was thinking a plastic bag or maybe a shopping bag to carry my dirty clothes in."

"Sorry. Unless you want to go digging in my garbage can, this is the best I got." Hunter tossed the bag at her. "You got sixty seconds, Miss. I need to drop you off, then come back and get some sleep before I find myself heading out to pick you up." He walked out, leaving her to stuff her clothes into the bag.

Inside the parking garage not long afterward, Brooklyn was climbing into Hunter's Cadillac Escalade. "It'll be hard for them to spot us in this gigantic thing," she joked sarcastically.

"Don't forget they aren't looking for this, Ms. Smarty."

They both checked the street for any sign of the black sedan as he exited the garage. It was nowhere to be found.

"Maybe it was just a coincidence last night and they weren't following us at all," Brooklyn declared.

"Doubtful," Hunter replied, checking the rearview mirror again. Fifteen minutes later he rolled past the entrance of her office building.

"Hey, you missed my building." Brooklyn pointed out.

"No, I didn't. We just passed the black sedan from last night. It's parked on the corner. They're watching your building. Maybe you should take today off until we figure this out," Hunter suggested, with a concerned look on his face.

"I have to go in today. Go around the block and we can come through the alley so you can drop me off at the delivery entrance."

"All right, but make sure you call me when you're ready for me to pick you up later on. I'll tell you what ride I'll be pulling up in. And make sure you meet me at the delivery entrance. Let me see what else I can figure out in the meantime." He pulled up to the delivery entrance and waited for her to get into the building safely. He backed out of the alley the same way he came so as not to tip his hand.

* * *

Hunter drove back around the block and parked a few spaces down and across the street from the sedan. He pulled out a pen and piece of paper from the glove compartment and jotted down the license plate number. He picked up his cell and dialed.

"Vince, I need a favor," he stated, looking down at the number he'd written.

* * *

Brooklyn badged into the building from the delivery door and greeted the guards by name. This wouldn't be the first time she used this entrance, so it wasn't anything that caused extra attention on their part. She rode the elevator to the tenth floor, where her company's office resided. Walking past the empty receptionist's desk, she hurried to her office and grabbed one of the three suits she left there in case of emergency. She slipped into the ladies washroom and changed quickly.

Back in her office, she pulled up the files to the latest acquisition her company was consulting on. As the Senior Financial Analyst in charge of mergers and acquisitions, she had a knack for spotting bad deals and seeing opportunities others did not. Her latest project was her biggest and greatest opportunity to show her bosses why she deserved an Assistant Vice President position. She pulled out the financial statements of the company her client was planning to acquire and began to review them.

Immersed in her work, Brooklyn didn't realize lunchtime had arrived until Denise, a fellow analyst and friend, arrived with two sandwiches and lattés. "You know if it wasn't for me, you'd never have lunch, right?" She sat the food and drinks down on Brooklyn's desk.

Brooklyn reached for a sandwich. "I do and I appreciate you for it."

"Are you working on the Bevik Media acquisition?" she asked.

"I am. I need to get an initial take on the viability of this acquisition. TriVision Media is our client. I'm looking over some information they just sent over this morning."

"Well let me know if you need any help or a sounding board." Denise took a seat in front of Brooklyn's desk.

"Most definitely, but enough about work." Brooklyn moved aside the papers she was working on. "I'd rather hear about the new guy you met last week."

"He was a jerk, and it's over," Denise grunted, shaking her head. She rehashed the quick and dirty story to Brooklyn over the rest of lunch.

Chapter Six

When Hunter came back to pick Brooklyn up later that evening, his chariot was a blue Mustang. Her cell phone rang, "Are you going to come out or what?" Hunter asked.

"I'm here at the door and I don't see you." Brooklyn looked up and down the alley again.

Hunter laughed. "I'm in the Mustang, woman."

"I thought you told me you were going to call me and let me know what you would be driving." After she got in, he backed out of the alley for the second time that day. "I have some information for you. I found out who owns the sedan that's following you."

"You did? How?" Brooklyn inquired.

He glanced at her. "You should be more interested in who. Do you know anyone who works for TriVision Media?"

"They're my new clients. Why would they be following me?"

"I was hoping you would be able to tell me," Hunter answered, frowning when he looked in his rearview mirror and spotted the black sedan.

* * *

Dante Nines walked down the alley until he approached a black door with no marking. He knocked and the slit in the door moved back. A pair of eyes gave him a once-over before unlocking the door. Dante entered and proceeded to the end of the hall to a room they called the library. There were wall-to-wall books on various subjects, and two long wooden tables with plenty of chairs in the center of the room. Near the entrance of the room, a chaise, coffee table, and love seat sat across from a desk with several bins and office supplies on it. Dante took off his jacket, threw it over the chaise, then went to get the report that Liang told him was in the bin. He walked over to one of the long wooden tables and pulled out a chair to review the report. When Liang walked in about twenty minutes later, he was still sitting there.

She placed another file over the report he was reading. Dante shook his head when he read the words on the pages. Liang leaned on the other long table across from him and watched without saying a word until he closed the file.

"Sweetie, you unintentionally opened Pandora's box." She pulled a chair out, sitting in it backwards. "They tracked down your girl last night."

"What? Why?" Dante opened the file to see if he'd missed something.

"It's not in there. You went to the club to find out if Hunter was still in touch with any of the guys from his old block. What you didn't know is when you decided to use your ex to get information on Hunter was that she was handling the acquisition of Bevik Media."

"Damn." Dante thought about the implications of being with Brooklyn last night. "When did they track her down?"

"I'm thinking that it happened after she stormed out of your place. I red-flagged her in our system after leaving your townhouse. By the time I woke up, they had looked into her background."

"It's no longer a question of if TriVision Media is trying to acquire only Bevik Media's legit business." Dante balled his fist on the table in front of him, trying to control his emotions.

Liang stood and pushed the chair back into place. "The fact that it was a representative of TriVision Media that tracked your girl down after you two parted ways indicates that they're trying to acquire Bevik Media's entire business, legit and otherwise."

"Let's concentrate on finding our client's daughter and bring her home to them so that we can get out the middle of whatever is going on." Dante stood, leaning both hands on the table. "We need to work harder to find Ryan." He and Liang had thought all along that Ryan had taken their client's daughter, Megan, because she tripped over proof that Bevik Media was shipping out something other than entertainment materials out.

"Maybe we should contact his brother, Levi." Liang leaned on the table.

"Contacting Levi is our absolute last resort. Based on the information we have on him, he may make the situation even more complicated."

"You're right. Since TriVision Media pulled your information shortly after your visit with Ryan's partner, I thought maybe we needed to back off and keep a low profile for a while." Liang kept silent while Dante's eyes scanned the file she'd given him. "Unfortunately, you brought Brooklyn back to the townhouse where they were waiting for you. They clearly stopped watching you and started trailing her."

He handed it back to Liang. "How in the hell did they find out who she was? They couldn't dig up information on her without knowing her identity."

"My best assumption is that they recognized her. After all, she is the senior financial analyst working on their deal." Liang opened her sling bag and put the file in it. "I'm sure someone in TriVision Media met her at least once or twice."

"I think we've been looking at things the wrong way. We always assumed that Megan was missing because Ryan took her." Dante walked over to the desk near the door, grabbing a sheet of paper and a pen off the desk. "What if it was TriVision Media that grabbed her? What if it's not just Megan missing, but Ryan too?"

"Damn, if that's true, it's a game changer." Liang watched him as he wrote. "How are you going to play this? They're going to be looking at your girl sideways."

"We've got to put more info into their hands. Put my P.I. info out there for them to find with a little extra digging or we need to find a way to discreetly drop the information in their lap. I'll explain to Brooklyn that I was checking out the companies that she's currently working out a deal with. She'll have a fit and threaten to rip me a new butt hole about why I'm interfering in her business and why I never told her I was a private investigator. But it'll get her off the hook with them." Dante handed Liang the paper he'd been writing on, then grabbed his jacket off the chaise.

"How?" Liang asked as she started reading over the sheet.

"If they bug her office and hear her fussing at me about it, as I suspect they will, it should work. I just need to make sure that argument happens over the phone or in her office." Dante put on his jacket and headed into the hallway, with Liang following. "With her connection to Hunter, me, and TriVision Media, I need you to find out everything I never wanted to know about my ex and fast." He tilted his head at the paper in Liang's hand.

"You never did any digging into her background before?" she inquired as they strolled down the hallway.

"I met her before I upgraded to high risk jobs. We've been off and on for years, occasionally flirting with the idea of a real commitment. Brooklyn always accepted me and my job as-is, no questions asked. She knew I had to travel a lot and she was cool with it for the most part." Dante started staring off into space, thinking about the times they had together.

Liang paused at the door in the middle of the hall. "So what happened?"

"I started taking the extremely confidential cases. I had to go dark for extended periods. The first few times I was able to smooth talk my way out of getting in trouble with her, but I had to keep extending my stays and taking longer to get in contact with her. She started making assumptions, and the fact that I couldn't really answer the few questions she did have didn't help."

"You must have been very smooth with that tongue, considering how many times it happened." Liang looked at him as if she thought it would be a challenge to talk his way of out it.

"Let's just say I'm extremely talented when it comes to using my tongue." He chuckled, giving her a devilish smile as naughty thoughts ran through his mind. He could only stay away from Brooklyn for so long before he found himself reaching back out to her or she was reaching out to him. Always hoping, wishing, and praying he could figure out how to have both loves of his life—his job and Brooklyn. "Anyway, when those periods of distance got longer, I became concerned about the effect it would have on her. Brooklyn not asking questions doesn't mean she's not seeking answers." Dante leaned near the door.

Liang smiled. "So you expected she would try to verify your story by showing up wherever you told her you'd be?"

"Don't let those suits that she wears fool you. She works hard and plays harder. She's a bit of a wild card. You never know what she might do." Dante smiled as he thought about the time he challenged her to go skinny dipping. When she stripped and jumped in the water, it took a while before the shock wore off and he joined her.

"Interesting," Liang stated, pulling out her key.

"She's a little like you." Dante laughed.

Liang raised one of her eyebrows, giving him her 'huh' look. "How so?"

"Anything is possible if you catch her in the right mood." Dante winked at Liang.

"How is that like me?" Liang unlocked her office door and held it open while waiting for his answer.

"I don't know, Miss you-would-have-been-in-for-a-night-you'd-never-forget." He smirked and began walking down the hallway.

"Whatever! It seems she's never in the mood for a threesome," Liang fired back.

"Maybe I just haven't caught her in the mood. When I do, I'll give you call," Dante replied in his sexy voice.

"I'm done with you." Liang laughed, shaking her head. "I'll call you when I get the information or if anything else pops up." She retreated behind the door.

Chapter Seven

Hunter and Brooklyn entered a restaurant in Georgetown. It was a popular fusion restaurant ran by a guy that used to be his college roommate. The hostess greeted Hunter as if he were VIP. Brooklyn glanced around the restaurant, taking in the mix of bright colors. Calculating the number of people they passed on the way to the hostess booth, she guessed they were probably going to have to wait an hour for a table. All Brooklyn wanted was to go home to sleep, but Hunter insisted they grab a bite to eat first.

"BK, come on," Hunter called out, oblivious to the glaring stares of the other patrons.

Brooklyn shook her head as she followed him. "You can take me wherever you want to go, Mister Big Time." She laughed. "I've tried to get in this restaurant several times. The lobby is always this crowded, but here you go strolling up and getting seated immediately."

"Hey, I can't help that I know people that know people." He smiled as they were seated at a table in the back. "The downfall to knowing people that know people is that you don't get to order your own food sometimes. When I want something specific, I have to call ahead and order it. Otherwise I'm out of luck."

Brooklyn glanced around the restaurant. "Could you tell me why I'm here instead of kicking my shoes off and falling into my bed?"

"For the same reason we grabbed something to eat last night, or should I say this morning." Hunter watched the door as people came into the restaurant.

"Really? You think someone's following us. I didn't even know you'd be in a blue Mustang until you called, so how'd they know?" Brooklyn's phone rang. She opened her purse, glanced down at the screen, and cut her ringer off. Dante had called her several times today. She had no desire to talk to him right now. "Which brings up the question, how many freaking cars do you own?"

"Enough," he responded as he sat his smart phone on the table in front of him.

"I knew you were doing well for yourself, but ..." Brooklyn stopped talking as the waitress brought an appetizer that looked like shrimp on bruschetta to the table.

The woman's olive complexion turned red with embarrassment. "I'm sorry, Hunter. When they said to bring food out for you and a guest, I assumed they meant Sophia."

"It's okay, Tonya," he responded.

Tonya sat the dish and two small plates on the table as she gave Brooklyn the onceover. "Sorry, I would have come over to confirm that there were no allergies that we should be aware of if I knew someone other than Sophia was here with Hunter."

"Not a problem," Brooklyn answered, grabbing an appetizer and popping it in her mouth. "I have no known allergies. I can eat whatever is being served up."

Tonya turned her attention towards Hunter. "Would you like anything to drink?"

"Yeah, two sangrias. I'm thinking red tonight." Hunter looked at Brooklyn. She nodded in agreement.

"Done," Tonya stated, smiling at Hunter then walking off.

"What were we talking about before she brought this delicious dish over? Is there mango in this?" Brooklyn asked as she grabbed another appetizer.

"We were talking about the fact that the black sedan was behind us briefly until he turned off on the street that I would have turned on if I was taking you home," he explained as he grabbed an appetizer.

"Hunter, I never knew you to be such a worry wart." Brooklyn grabbed three more appetizers and placed them on her plate, leaving Hunter only two.

"If the black sedan is nowhere near your apartment building when we get there, I'll gladly accept the title of worry wart." Tonya returned with the sangrias and more appetizers.

Brooklyn touched Hunter's arm. "Look, while this meal is great, my late night, early morning, and full day at work are catching up with me. I appreciate you looking out for me, but between my lack of sleep and this sangria ..."

"Maybe I should take the night off to keep an eye on you." He raised his eyebrows repeatedly.

"If you want to watch me sleep and listen to me snore, then go right ahead." Brooklyn laughed as he shook his head then raised his glass to her.

Hunter and Brooklyn were pretty much full by the time the entrees came. They continued talking and laughing as they ate. Despite the conversation, Brooklyn was having a hard time keeping her eyes open. Hunter motioned to the waitress to let her know he was ready to depart. Tonya nodded her head to let him know she'd seen him.

"Do you normally get dessert too? If you do, we need to get it to go," Brooklyn spoke between yawns.

Tonya walked over and smiled, leaving a plastic bag on the table. "Hunter, Mr. Ramos sends his regards."

"Thanks, Tonya." He pulled out a hundred-dollar bill and laid it on the table as he stood. Though the owner was picking up the tab for the dinner, Hunter, unlike some of the others who were comped, took good care of the staff who waited on them.

"You drop hundreds like they're singles," Brooklyn declared as they stood. "I know the girls at the strip club love you." She watched Tonya grab the money and disappear into the back.

"Since the meal is free, I usually tip what I think the meal is worth. Twenty to twenty-five for drinks, twenty to twenty-five for appetizers, and fifty for the entrees." Hunter grabbed the bag before escorting Brooklyn to the door. "It's only fair."

"One day when I grow up, I want to be just like you," Brooklyn teased as they headed to the car.

"I think you've grown up enough," he chuckled.

When she caught him watching her behind as she rounded the car heading to the passenger side, she sassed, "Grown enough for what, Mr. Torres?"

"Grown enough to have me throwing hundreds at you in a strip club," Hunter replied once they were in the car.

Brooklyn smiled at him but said nothing as she leaned her seat back and closed her eyes.

* * *

Dante tried calling Brooklyn again. TriVision were watching her building but hadn't bugged her apartment. If Brooklyn found out that he'd broken into her home and gone through her things, she'd strangle him. Liang had pulled Brooklyn's information; he'd requested to only know facts pertinent to the case. He thought about digging into her past several times through the years, but he wanted an authentic and real relationship. It felt like it was an invasion of her privacy. He wouldn't want someone he was dating to do it to him, so he refrained from doing it unless she raised red flags. She had never given him a reason to dig into her past. Brooklyn was one of the few people whose history he wanted to find out the old fashioned way.

Besides her connection with Hunter and TriVision Media, there was nothing in her background that would cause additional complications. While he wanted to talk to Brooklyn, he knew that for her safety he would have to wait until Monday to force a face-to-face. His cell phone rang. It was Liang.

For the last few years, she had been working administrative duties.

However, with a shortage of women on the payroll, their boss had occasionally put Liang on a case. It always took some prodding, but Dante knew part of her missed working out in the field. He was confident he knew her pretty well. They had previously been roommates for a few years. He wished their boss hadn't insisted that Liang work on this case. It reeked of all the elements that could bring to the surface the issues Liang was fighting.

"Liang, did you work your magic?" Dante inquired.

"Yes, but I'm not happy about being on clean-up duty all weekend," she replied in a frustrated tone.

"Hey, welcome to my world." Dante knew all too well about changing personal plans because of work.

"I know what your world is like."

"Yea, but you're now a visitor where I normally live." Dante treaded lightly. He knew that even after all these years she continued to fight those demons.

"Yeah, yeah. I'm sending the information you requested to your smart phone." She huffed, then disconnected the call.

Dante knew tracking down Ryan was more important now than ever before. There could be another reason why both Ryan and Megan were hard to find. He just hoped for Megan's parents' sake that she was still alive. Dante's goal was to bring their daughter home, not to find her body.

* * *

Hunter whizzed past the parked cars, glancing over occasionally at the sleeping beauty reclining in his passenger seat. The music and Brooklyn's soft snoring filled the car. He shook her awake as he passed her apartment. Brooklyn opened her eyes as they rounded the corner at the end of the block. He pulled the Mustang into an empty spot on the street.

"Well, Brooklyn, you have company."

She sat her chair up. "I figured that much when I woke up and we weren't parked in front of my building." Brooklyn wiped the corners of her mouth to make sure she hadn't drooled in her sleep.

"What do you want to do?" Hunter asked as he turned the car lights off.

"Let's park in the back of the building. You can only be parked there for thirty minutes or they'll tow you." Brooklyn pulled out her keys, searching for the one to the back door.

Hunter went through the alley to the back of the building. He parked in the only empty spot in the back. Brooklyn grabbed the black messenger bag as she got out. Hunter grabbed a dessert box out of the bag from the restaurant and followed Brooklyn through the door. When they arrived at Brooklyn's floor, she handed Hunter the keys and took the box out of his hands. She waited outside as he checked her apartment. After a few minutes, he opened the door, stood back, and nodded for her to come in.

"The coast is clear."

"Thank you for playing my protection detail for tonight. I'm tired, so don't be offended that I'm not inviting you to stay for a drink," Brooklyn spoke as she kicked her shoes off and threw her coat haphazardly over the coat rack. "Don't call to check on me while you're at work either, because I'll be sleep." She took her suit jacket off and flung it on the couch.

"Understandable. Just make sure you lock up after me and put your dessert in the refrigerator. Trust me, you'll be mad at yourself later if you forget about it." He leaned down, kissing her on the cheek before he exited.

Brooklyn locked the door before heading to the kitchen to put her dessert up. She debated keeping her cell phone ringer off, then decided to put it on do-not-disturb mode instead, so that only the people she'd designated as favorites could contact her for the time being. She entered the bedroom and fell across the bed, not bothering to take her clothes off.

Chapter Eight

A couple of hours later, Brooklyn's cell phone woke her up. She glanced at the caller ID, thinking she should have known better than to include her wild friend Alexis in the favorites list. Brooklyn silenced the ringer and decided she'd call her back in the morning. As she rolled over to go back to sleep, her home phone rang. No one used that number unless they were trying to be buzzed in. She scooted toward the night stand, wishing she'd turned the home phone ringer off too. She looked at the clock. At one in the morning, no one should be requesting to be buzzed in. She looked at the caller ID and shook her head.

"Alexis, what is it?" Grogginess plagued Brooklyn's voice.

"I'm sorry, Brook. I need your help," Alexis whispered into the phone.

Brooklyn sat up in the bed. "What kind of foolishness have you gotten yourself into now?"

"Well me and my new guy were getting it on when his girlfriend came home. She was supposed to be spending the night at her sister's. I had to crawl out the window and down the side of the house. He opened the garage door so I could wait for him," Alexis explained.

"Wait, wait, wait! Why are you waiting for him in his garage?"

Brooklyn asked as she searched for paper and pen.

"I rode over with him. He texted me after I got out that he'd opened the garage door and to wait here till he could come take me home," Alexis whispered into the phone.

"Alexis how long have you been waiting?" Brooklyn inquired, knowing it had to be awhile if she was calling her.

"Just under an hour," Alexis answered.

Brooklyn slipped on her shoes. "Dammit, give me the address. I'm coming to get you." She wrote the address down while shaking her head, then grabbed her wallet, keys, and coat.

It wasn't until she was in her car heading to pick up Alexis that Brooklyn thought about the sedan following her. She tried to reach some of their other friends to see if they could pick up Alexis, but she couldn't get anyone. Although she didn't like the idea of being followed, she couldn't leave Alexis hiding in the garage. Thirty minutes later, Brooklyn pulled up to see her friend climbing out the window of a two story house, sliding down the slanted roof and shimmying down a pipe.

Alexis ran into the garage. She hung a pair of boxers onto a grey car, then shook the car until the alarm went off. She ran to Brooklyn's car, clothes torn, her shoes and coat in her hand. As Alexis hopped in the passenger seat, Brooklyn saw the light come on in the window her friend had left.

"Let's go," Alexis ordered, dropping the contents in her hands on the floor as she buckled up.

"Alexis, what was your crazy behind doing coming out the damn window again?" Brooklyn demanded to know as she pulled off.

"His punk ass wouldn't bring my keys to me so I went back in to get them. Damn the girlfriend. If he didn't want to come down to take me home, the least he could do is bring my keys down so I can go home." Alexis slipped on her shoes.

"Instead of sneaking out, you should have let him be caught by his girlfriend." Brooklyn glanced over at Alexis's torn dress. "What happened to your outfit?"

"I ripped it on the window on the way out. He's busted anyway because my keys weren't the only things I left when I rushed out." Alexis laughed hysterically before catching her and saying, "I left my panties."

"Alexis!" She shook her head. "What the hell were you thinking? If you walked in through the front door then you need to leave through the front door." Brooklyn looked back to make sure she didn't have an irate girlfriend tailing her. The only suspicious car she noticed hanging back was the black sedan from last night.

"I was thinking I was getting some good loving. We just got interrupted," she smirked. Brooklyn cut her eyes over at Alexis. "And you thought it was a good move to go out the window?"

"I'm very athletic." Alexis laughed.

"All right, Miss Smooth Criminal climbing back into the room you escaped from. You know you're stupid, right?" Brooklyn glanced in the rearview mirror again.

"Girl, I'm just mad we got interrupted." Alexis played with her keys and crossed her legs. "Mmmhmm, he was definitely worth climbing out the window for."

"You say that now. You're going to catch a bullet to the ass one of these days. Messing around with these women's men," Brooklyn fussed as she pulled in front of Alexis' building. She was a little leery dropping Alexis off at home but her building had around the clock security. With the number of units in it, it would be very difficult for them to track her down at least she hoped it would be.

"Hey, are you coming out with us next week?" Alexis asked as she unbuckled her seat belt.

"Yeah, as long as you stay out of trouble and I'm not getting one-in-the-morning calls from my crazy friends," Brooklyn teased as Alexis got out of the car.

"Whatever. Just be there ready to party. Chavell will be in town that weekend. It's been a while since we've all been together." Alexis leaned into the car, glancing up to make sure no cars were coming.

"Chavell? Hopefully he won't have us swinging from poles butt naked." Brooklyn laughed as Alexis frowned.

"Ha ha, very funny. You know that incident is never to be mentioned, even under duress." Alexis started smiling. "Just have your behind there, ready for whatever craziness ensues."

"As long as I don't have to work that weekend, I'm in," Brooklyn replied. Alexis walked around the car and toward her condo building, then turned around and knocked on Brooklyn's window.

Brooklyn rolled it down. "What? Did you forget something?"

"I just wanted to say thank you for the save tonight. Text me when you get back to your place. And don't you dare let work make you miss the get-together, otherwise we'll be bringing the party to you!" Alexis waved then moved briskly towards her door.

Brooklyn watched her until she entered the building, then she pulled off. She dialed Hunter as she drove, hoping that he'd hear his phone in the club. It went to voicemail.

"Come on, Hunter. Call me back." She was a little reluctant to go back to her apartment, not knowing if the people in the black sedan were just watching her to make sure she wasn't sharing proprietary information or if something more sinister was going on. As she debated what to do, her cell phone rang.

"Hey, Hunter!" Brooklyn bellowed, taking the long way home.

"I didn't expect to hear from you tonight." Hunter's surprise filled his voice.

"You wouldn't have if I hadn't answered an S.O.S. call from a friend." She turned down the music. "I left out to pick up a friend and drop her off at home."

Hunter stated, "Alexis is at it again."

"How did you know?" Brooklyn chuckled.

"While all of your friends are slightly crazy, Alexis is notorious for getting herself into the strangest predicaments." Hunter laughed then his tone became very serious. "Is the sedan still following you?"

Brooklyn glanced back. "Yes."

"How far are you away from your house?" he asked, concerned.

"About five minutes," Brooklyn answered as she turned the corner leading to the final stretch to her apartment.

"I'll stay on the phone until you're safely in your apartment."

Brooklyn looked nervously in the rearview mirror. "Maybe I should come to the club."

"You could, but I know you're tired. I won't wrap up here for another two hours." Hunter rustling papers had the call sounding like there was a bad connection. "Look, they just seem to be keeping an eye on you. They had an opportunity to approach you while you waited for me at the club. Although neither of us like the fact that they're following you, I think you're safe going back home."

"If you're wrong about this, Hunter, I'm suing you." Brooklyn chuckled, knowing Hunter was right. They'd had plenty opportunity to attack her if they'd wanted to.

"You could always go by your ex's. He'll welcome you with open arms," Hunter teased.

"Ha ha. Why don't you come with so we can all hang out?" She paused, waiting for his response but only heard cricket. "Earth to Hunter! Hunter, are you still there?"

"Yeah. Yeah. I'm sorry. I was thinking about something else," he explained. "Have you made it home?"

She lucked out and got her same spot. "I'm parking the car now," Brooklyn replied, realizing he either hadn't heard her comment or decided to ignore it.

She glanced over her shoulder as she got out. The black sedan rolled past her as she entered the building. Brooklyn had wanted a distraction from thinking about Dante, but someone following her wasn't what she had in mind. Brooklyn had never had any of her clients follow her before. She laughed, thinking, *Not that I would have known.* If it wasn't for Hunter pointing out the sedan and looking into it, she wouldn't have known this one was following her.

Once she was safely in her apartment, Brooklyn made sure she asked Hunter to hang out with her next Saturday before saying goodbye. She texted Alexis that she was home, turned on the television, then headed to the refrigerator to try out her dessert. She sat on her couch at almost three in the morning indulging in the delicious treat, her mind focused on Hunter. She thought once Sophia got her hooks in him, that was all she wrote. It wasn't until Brooklyn met Dante that she stopped thinking that maybe she and Hunter should explore the attraction that simmered between them. Brooklyn smiled to herself. *"What better way to get Dante Nines completely out of my system than to turn up the heat between me and Hunter?"* she thought between bites.

Her eyes were getting heavy by the time she finished her snack. She turned off the television and headed to bed, thinking how nice it had been to wake up snuggled against Hunter's well-cut back. Her thoughts switched from thinking about Hunter to remembering waking up wrapped up in Dante's arms with those grey eyes staring down at her. She sighed as she changed into her sleeping clothes. It was clear she needed to tread lightly with Hunter because she didn't want to hurt him. Brooklyn was willing to put her friendship with Hunter on the line to explore the possibility of it being more. She climbed into bed, debating the pros and cons of getting involved with Hunter while she was still ensnared by Dante.

Chapter Nine

Dante had to quickly make progress with finding Megan's boyfriend, Ryan. He spent the weekend following a few leads. But in the back of his mind, he kept the reminder that he would have to deal with the situation he had caused for Brooklyn. He didn't look forward to setting her off, but he knew it couldn't be helped.

Dante's gut told him that Ryan's roommate, Mark, knew more than he said he knew about Ryan's disappearance the last time they spoke. Dante decided to revisit him. As he approached the apartment building, he spotted Mark crossing the street, heading home with a bag of groceries.

Mark spotted Dante at the same time. His reaction wasn't what Dante expected. He dropped his groceries, turned, and ran.

Dante swore under his breath and took off after him. *What the hell is he hiding, and why the hell is he running from me?*

Mark was young and fast. Dante prided himself on staying in shape, but this kid was either a former track star or so scared that adrenaline was fueling his legs to go at lightning speed. Dante had to think fast. Mark was running towards the subway. Dante took a detour and was able to head him off just before he reached the Metro entrance. He tackled him to the ground.

"What are you trying to do, man? Get me killed?" Mark stammered, his eyes filled with fear. He struggled to get Dante off him.

Dante pulled him to his feet, but kept a good grip on him. "I just wanted to ask you some questions."

"Look, man, I don't know what Ryan was into or where he is. What I do know is that I don't want that goon that came by after you talked to me last time to come back."

"Goon? What goon?" Dante pulled him into a nearby restaurant. He sat him on the inside of a booth and sat beside him to keep him from running.

"I don't know who he was. Just some big, burly white dude that kept threatening to knock my teeth out if I didn't tell him where Ryan was. I told him like I told you—I don't know. He stated that if he found out that I told you or anybody anything different, or if he found out I was holding back anything, he would come back and my teeth would be the last thing I needed to worry about." Fear was etched into the young man's face. "Now you show up again and he's probably not too far behind you. If he sees me talking to you again, he may think I'm telling you something I didn't tell him."

"I know you're saying you don't know where Ryan is or what he's into, but I got a sense last time we talked that you know something. I'm getting that same sense now, and my senses are rarely wrong. Now, tell me whatever it is you know, no matter how big or small you think it is, and I promise not to bother you again."

He watched the young man's face as he tried to decide what to do. Finally he gulped then stated, "I don't know where Ryan is. The day he left, he must have left in a hurry. The place looked like he'd rushed to pack what he could." He pulled a key out of his jean pocket and slid it over to him. "While cleaning up, I found this locker key by the door. I think he might have dropped it while rushing. I didn't say anything 'cause I was hoping to figure out what locker it belonged to. I'm a little strapped, especially since he left without paying his half of the rent." He gave a sheepish look. "I thought I might find some cash or something I could convert to cash."

Dante took the key and slid it into his pocket. "Look, kid, I think you should lay low for a while. I don't know who the goon is, but if he sensed that you were lying too, he'll be back."

"You don't have to tell me twice. I'm going to stay with some friends until either Ryan is found or I can find a new place that's off the radar."

Dante stood and let him out the booth. The kid went to the door, but abruptly stopped, looking wildly at his surroundings. The blood had drained out of his face. He made a beeline to the rear exit. Dante walked to the front door and saw a large man watching the place from across the street. "Must be the goon," Dante mumbled under his breath. He turned and followed Mark's lead, leaving through the rear exit of the restaurant. The time to be confrontational was coming, but it wasn't today. From a safe distance, out of sight of the goon, Dante snapped a photo of him.

After he made sure he wasn't being followed, he made his way back to his car and called Liang to fill her in. "I caught up with the roommate," he told her. "That young thunder cat took off running when he saw me. Once I caught him, he handed over what looks like a gym locker key. Apparently, he was trying to figure out what the key was to and was hoping Ryan had stashed some cash."

"Do you want me to check out the key you got from him?" Liang asked.

"I'm heading to the health club listed in Ryan's file now. Truthfully, I don't expect to find anything. If Ryan is still alive, then he would have come back for the key if it was important. I just sent you a picture of a man who threatened Ryan's roommate and was waiting outside the restaurant. See if you can find out who he is and who sent him."

"All right. I'll get back to you as soon as I know something."

""Hey, is everything in place for me to hold that conversation with Brooklyn on Monday?" Dante inquired.

"Yeah. Last night, I cleaned offices for hours to maintain my cover, then I checked her office before I left with the rest of the cleaning staff. Someone had already wired her office for sound, so you can be sure they'll be listening in when you talk to your girl on Monday. But watch your back. There's definitely more to this case than we originally thought." Liang hung up.

Dante continued on to the health club. He planned to check out the key and then track down Ryan's business partner, Tuck, to see if he could get more information out of him. Now that he and Liang weren't working under the radar, they had to move fast if they wanted to find their client's daughter, and even faster if they wanted to find her alive. Add to that the fact that now TriVision Media was suspicious of Brooklyn's involvement, and you truly had a fiery mess that needed to be put out immediately before someone's life was incinerated.

As he suspected, the health club turned up nothing. After enduring a tour of the facilities, he found out it was one of their older keys. They had changed the locks on the few lockers they had a year ago, and the key was no longer in use.

He checked his watch. If he wanted to catch Tuck, he would have to move fast. Tuck was a creature of habit and he always closed their shipping office at three p.m. on Saturday.

Dante made it downtown with fifteen minutes to spare. He entered the small shipping office and found Tuck Holder, owner of Bevik Media, sitting behind one of the three desks in the front office. The last time Dante spoke to him, Tuck had answered his questions but didn't have any information on Ryan's whereabouts.

"Mr. Nines." Tuck stood and shook Dante's hand before motioning for him to have a seat in the guest chair in front of his desk. "Have you been able to locate Ryan?"

"No, not yet. I was hoping I could ask you some more questions. Maybe some useful information would turn up."

"Sure. Ask away." Tuck sat back in his seat, his demeanor calm and cool, just as it had been before.

"The last time we talked, you stated you hadn't heard from Ryan in days. I assume that's still true." Dante just wanted to read him as he answered. Tuck shifted in his seat, his eyes shifting from Dante's for a moment as if he was thinking of what to say.

"Correct. I've tried calling and reaching out to him, but I haven't been able to contact him."

Dante decided to change directions. "How long have you two been in business with TriVision Media?" He noted the slight flash in Tuck's eyes before the cool demeanor returned.

"About five years now. They handle their own shipping for the most part, but from time to time they use our services for shipping items they view as extremely proprietary and sensitive. Things they don't want leaked out to the public before they release it."

"And how long have you two known Megan Chambers?" Dante inquired, referring to his client's missing daughter.

"Megan? Megan?" Tuck asked, as if he was trying to place her. Dante looked at him strangely, wondering why he was suddenly struggling to remember Megan. "Oh you mean Meg," Tuck added. "She started working for us about two years ago. She quit about a week before Ryan disappeared."

"Any ideas why she quit?"

Tuck shook his head. "I just assumed she found something better."

"What was her and Ryan's relationship?" Dante was hoping for some indication that Ryan wouldn't hurt her if he was the one who took her.

"Platonic, employer-employee, as far as I could tell. They never hung out after work or anything like that," Tuck reported, glancing down at his watch. "Can we table this discussion?" He pointed to his watch. "It's three o'clock."

Dante stood. "Thanks for your time."

"Not a problem. Call me if you have any other questions. Ryan and I were like brothers. I'm really worried about him." Tuck handed Dante a business card, just like he had before. He was indeed a creature of habit.

Chapter Ten

The weekend flew by. The sounds of R&B filled the office as Brooklyn reviewed file after file. Dante and Hunter had her thoughts spinning all over the place. However, this was the wrong time to not bring her A-game. Not only were millions of dollars on the line with this acquisition, but also her promotion to assistant vice president. Brooklyn barely looked up when Denise entered, smiling from ear to ear. Denise slid into the chair in front of the desk.

"Well, well, well." Denise leaned forward with a devilish grin.

"Well, what?" Brooklyn stopped and looked up at Denise.

"You have a very handsome visitor waiting to speak to you." Denise leaned back in the chair, crossing her legs.

Brooklyn pulled up her calendar on the computer. "Is it a client?"

"No. I told him that you were quite busy today." She smiled. "But he said that he would wait all day if he had to."

"Do you know what he wants?" Brooklyn cleared her desk off, setting the files on the cabinet behind her.

"To speak to you." Denise stood. "I just want to remind you that I'm single again. If you want to hook me up with your visitor, I wouldn't be mad at all."

"I'll keep that in mind." Brooklyn smirked as Denise exited the office. Brooklyn took a quick look in the mirror and reapplied her lip gloss, expecting Hunter to walk through the door. She almost adjusted her blouse to show a little more cleavage, but decided against it. The handsome face that walked through the door wasn't the one she expected.

"By the look on your face, I'd guess that you're not happy to see me," Dante stated as he closed the door behind him.

"Why are you here?" Brooklyn asked as he walked over to her desk.

"To ask you some questions." He rounded the desk and leaned right next to her.

Brooklyn pushed her chair back. "You can leave now."

"How well do you know Hunter?"

She noticed him looking at the files on her cabinet as he spoke.

"No, let's talk about how well you know the young lady you wanted to have a threesome with." Brooklyn stood, crossing her arms and glaring at him.

"Brook, this conversation is about business, not our personal life. What do you know about Bevik Media?" Dante stared intensely at her.

"I'm not at liberty to say anything about Bevik Media to you. Why in the hell do you want to know about them anyway? And, what does that have to do with Hunter?" she questioned as she gathered the files she'd sat on the file cabinet and placed them inside it.

"My client believes an associate of Hunter's has stolen something of value from them, shipping it out as if it came from Bevik Media." Dante stopped leaning on the desk and walked over to her. He was so close she was forced to step back some.

"Your client?" Brooklyn asked, confused about why he would be looking into it instead of the police. As far as she knew, his job entailed coordinating security for conferences and seminars.

"I'm a private investigator." Dante looked as if was bracing himself for her coming wrath.

Brooklyn tilted her head as she crossed her arms. "Since when?"

"Since you've known me." Dante watched the anger grow in her eyes.

"What did you say?" Brooklyn dropped her arms, put her hands on her hips, and stepped away from him. "Did you say that you've been a private investigator from the moment we met?"

"Yes, but—"

She rounded the desk and leaned on one of the guest chairs. "Oh so you're saying that you just didn't want us to work?" Brooklyn stood, shaking her head.

"Brooklyn, would you knowing have made that much of a difference?" Dante walked over to her.

She fought hard to contain her anger. "Yes, Dante James Nines, it would have made a freaking difference on all those nights I waited for an email, a text, or a call." She jabbed her finger into his chest.

He grabbed her arm. "Why? Would knowing I was a P.I. have convinced you I was telling you the truth when I told you I wasn't with another woman?"

"Yes, it would have. It would have explained a lot of things that you wouldn't." Brooklyn snatched her arm away from him. "I find it very interesting that you're telling me this now that you want information from me."

"Brook, it's not like that."

"Oh, it isn't? I don't freaking believe you." She pushed him aside and headed to the door. He blocked her path.

He grabbed her by the upper arms to prevent her from going around him. "I ran into you at the club the other night because I went there to see if Hunter's friend might show up. You being there was a pleasant surprise."

"Dante, I'm so angry with you right now for so many reasons. I always felt you were keeping something from me, but you always made it seem like I was overreacting. I don't even know how to feel about you right now." Brooklyn could barely see past the tears welling up in her eyes.

"Look, I'm coming clean right now. I just …" Dante slid his hands down her arms and held her hands.

She pulled her hands back. "I need you to leave."

"I knew you would be upset, but …"

"I was in love with you. If I knew that you were a P.I., I would have understood your secrecy and not assumed you were with other women on these long, unexpected trips. I understand client confidentiality. What I didn't understand was why security detail for a three-day conference extended to two weeks. You had me thinking about white picket fences and children, and that's saying a lot when my number one priority for the last few years has been my career. For you, I was willing to take chances that weren't in my norm. Damn you."

Dante couldn't speak. He had prepared for angry, irate Brooklyn, but not this. "I'm sorry. I …"

"You, what? You knew that I loved you. You knew I wanted us to work. I kept trying to be patient and understanding of your schedule. Since we parted ways, with every man I've met I've been trying to recreate the feeling I had with you, that wonderful dynamic atmosphere of tough love. You knew when to handle me with kid gloves; you knew when to take them off. You made me better. Even when you pissed me off, you managed to make me smile. You did something for me that I can't even find adequate words to describe. Now you stand here telling me that you didn't want us to work. It's like all of it was a lie. I don't know what to do with that."

"That's not what I said."

"That's exactly what your black behind said when you chose not to tell me the reason that you were unavailable was not because you were working security for these conferences all over the world, but it was because you were working these P.I. cases." The tears begin streaming down her face.

"Damn, Brooklyn!" He pulled her into his arms. "I messed up. I stopped telling women I was a private investigator long ago, when I started taking on celebrity and high profile clients. After I had a few bad incidents with a woman I was dating, it was just better to say I was working security because the questions were different."

Brooklyn broke the embrace. "You know what? I have work to do. You can understand that. You made it a point to say you had to make a living when you ended things between us. I don't have time for this bull. If you have a question about Hunter, you know where to find him.

Ask him your damn self. And Mr. P.I., the same goes for Bevik Media. Whatever it is you want to know, you need to contact them." Brooklyn wiped the tears from her cheek.

"You're right. I should have never put you in the middle when I saw you with Hunter. Then, when I found out your company was handling the possible acquisition of Bevik Media, I thought—"

"Stop talking and leave." Brooklyn walked over to the door, with Dante on her heels.

"The only way I'll agree to leave is if you agree to have dinner with me tonight." Dante put his hand on the door, preventing her from opening it. "This isn't about talking business or me using our personal relationship to see what you know. This is about us. About me explaining that assumption I made that led me to determine that it was best we go our separate ways."

"I'm working late. I'm not going to have time for dinner." Brooklyn leaned on the door, refusing to look in his eyes as she spoke.

"Brook, when I was working crazy hours, you would always squeeze time out to see me. Remember that time I flew back home for a couple hours and you met me at my house with pizza to spend a little time with me before I flew back out the next morning?" Dante turned her towards him. "Or when I had security meetings that lasted until one in the morning and you would be at my apartment waiting for me even though you knew I would be on the phone at least another hour making sure everything went off without a hitch? Do you remember that?"

"Yes." Brooklyn stepped back, crossed her arms, and looked down at the ground.

"Well, that's exactly what I'm prepared to do for you tonight." Dante took his finger and lifted up her chin so that she was looking directly into his eyes. "I know I messed up, but ..."

"Hey, there's nothing left to talk about. Call your playmate to talk. I have work I need to get back to." Brooklyn pushed him back and opened the door.

"I'll see you tonight." Dante stepped back towards her instead of walking to the door.

"No." Brooklyn put her hand on his chest as he leaned down to kiss her.

"Yes. I'm serious. The only way I'll agree to leave your office is if you agree to see me tonight whenever you stop working."

"Then I'll have security escort you out of here." Brooklyn strolled over to her desk and picked up the phone.

"Do that. I would love to talk to security to see if they only have cameras in the hallway, or if, back in the day, when your desk was seeing a little more action, they had hidden office cams in random locations." Dante smiled slyly as Brooklyn's fingers froze on the phone.

"Fine, I'll see you tonight." Brooklyn didn't think he'd do it, but today wouldn't be a good day to find out.

***

Liang looked up from the computer as Dante entered her office. "How did it go?"

"It didn't go exactly as expected. But I think it was enough to take her from under the magnifying glass." Dante took a seat on the couch, beneath a painting of a window.

"Then what's the issue?" Liang pulled some items off the printer and handed it to him.

"Let's just say having my ex involved is more of a challenge than I expected." Dante started looking over the printout.

"You need to keep your head in the game. Otherwise we all might end up six feet under, your ex included."

"Damn." Dante stopped when he saw the data on the third page. "This is not good." He looked up at Liang, then finished looking over the paperwork.

"The company has issued us an extended team. We need to find our client's daughter quickly and take our hands out of the pot."

"It's been a while since we had a case with this much heat."

"So much for me taking the downgraded case that had minimal risk of bringing trouble home to my door step." Liang felt the scar from the bullet she took in the gut when work followed her home. She had Dante to thank for being alive. It's too bad her husband wasn't so lucky. It happened years ago, but there were moments like these she felt the loss like it was yesterday.

Dante thought about what would have happened if he hadn't followed his instinct and followed Liang on that deadly night all those years ago. The image of her and her husband's bodies lying in a pool of blood in their kitchen was seared into his mind. It had been just three months shy of her downgrading to paper pusher so that she and her husband could start a family. In their line of work, making small mistakes and not having all the information were lethal.

"Yeah, this isn't the job where you want your work following you home." Dante reflected on the conversation he would have with Brooklyn tonight. He wondered how open and honest he was really willing to be with her. Dante had loved her enough to let her go to ensure her safety. Maybe it was time to love her enough to put aside his current occupation to make her picket fence dream a reality.

"Dante!" Liang waved her hand in front of his face. "Dante!" She snapped her fingers several times to catch his attention.

"Yes, what were you saying?" Dante put thoughts of Brooklyn to the side.

"What is our next move?" Liang grabbed her notebook off the desk. "Our team gets in tonight."

"They shouldn't bother. Split them up. Have two of them track down the goon and the other two follow Tuck. I need you back on the schedule tonight and tomorrow for the cleaning crew, to see if the plan worked or if Brooklyn is still on the radar. If there are no eyes and ears in Brooklyn's office, check her files on Bevik Media and TriVision Media. See if there are any names associated with either company that we weren't aware of."

"And what are you going to do?" Liang inquired as she slid her notebook into her messenger bag.

"I'm digging a little deeper into our clients' past to make sure it's truly their daughter that we're trying to track down. Once we check the parents out, then check the daughter out." Dante stood, shaking his head. Why was someone so deadly following Ryan's roommate? There was a big piece of the puzzle they were missing and if they didn't figure it out quickly, Liang would be right—they would all be in danger of ending up six feet under.

She shut down her computer and stood. "I'll check in with you in the morning."

"Liang, stay in one of the safe houses until this case is over." Dante folded the papers and tucked them into his inside jacket pocket.

"I hear you loud and clear. I don't think I'm the only one from the housekeeping company working another agenda. I checked Brooklyn's office early Friday night when I arrived. The bug wasn't there. By the time I left, it was. Saturday it was the same thing with her phones."

"Then be extremely careful. We don't want them to catch you going through Brooklyn's files. FYI, Brooklyn's working late."

Chapter Eleven

Brooklyn looked up at the clock. It was just after nine p.m. She wanted to stay until eleven, but she tried not to stay that late on days when the cleaning staff was working in the offices. She locked her files up in the cabinet, grabbed her things, and headed out. Her cell phone rang as she locked up her office. Her heart raced as she went digging in her purse. Brooklyn had been thinking about her conversation with Dante all day. She wasn't ready to have that real talk session with him tonight.

"I'll let it go to voicemail," she stated as she finally found her phone. But she knew Dante. He would be pounding on her door, making good on his promise. She smiled as Hunter's name was highlighted on her screen. "Hello, handsome."

"Hey, sexy! How was your day?" Hunter asked.

"Long. I'm just heading home now." She normally took the stairs when she was on the phone, but with everything that was going on, she decided it was best to take the elevator. "Hey I'm about to step into the elevator, so if we get cut off I'll call you back." The elevator door opened as soon as she hit the button. She stepped in, and as the doors closed, she caught a glimpse of the cleaning company coming out of the service elevators. *Was that Dante's little friend?* She reached to push the door open button but was too late.

"BK!" Hunter shouted into the phone.

"I'm sorry. One of the housekeeping employees looked very familiar." The call got choppy as the elevator headed to the lobby level.

"Someone from the club or someone you went to school with?" Hunter questioned.

"No. It's unimportant. Back to you, Mister Sexy. Are you going to be my date to hang out with the crew or what?" Brooklyn waved at security as she left the building.

"That's why I'm working tonight when the club is slow, to ensure my presence by your side Saturday night."

Brooklyn unlocked her car and slid in, tossing her bag onto the passenger seat. "Good. This is my hell week, so I'll be working late all week. Now that you agreed to be my date, I know what I'm wearing."

"What's that?" She imagined Hunter's mind flipping through his favorite Brooklyn outfits.

"I have this diva-on-fire dress I wanted to wear, but I definitely need a man on my arm when I'm rocking it." She pulled out of the lot and headed home.

"What does this diva on fire dress look like?" Hunter grilled Brooklyn.

"It's a red halter dress. The front is sheer except for the flames that look like they're leaping up from the skirt."

"Mmm, I'm going to have to bring a security detail with me," Hunter joked.

"You might have to, since I'll also have my glitterati heels on. I plan to have people thinking I have superstar status." Brooklyn laughed. She was looking forward to Saturday.

"What are glitterati heels?"

"High heels that glitter, sparkle and shine, just like the person that's wearing them," she explained.

"Well, well now. You need to try on that dress, take a picture, and send it to me as a sneak preview," Hunter pleaded.

"No."

"You know I already conjured up a picture of you in that dress," he announced.

"Well, I won't be spoiling the true reveal with a sneak preview picture," she replied.

Brooklyn and Hunter started talking and laughing about old times. Her voice trailed off in the middle of her story as she pulled onto her block and saw Dante leaning on his car.

"Is everything okay? Is the sedan following you?" Hunter quizzed her.

"Umm, no." She shook her head as she parked. "It followed me to work, but I haven't seen it since I left work, and I don't see it on the block."

"So you made it home?"

"Yeah. I guess I'll let you get to work. I'll check in on you tomorrow," she responded as she gathered her purse from the passenger seat.

"Cute. You're the one that needs checking on. Try not to get into any trouble tonight," Hunter teased.

"I'm going to try, but I'm not going to make any promises. Sometimes trouble is waiting patiently for me to arrive," Brooklyn stated as Dante approached. "Good night, Hunter."

"Good night, beautiful!"

Dante waited as Brooklyn opened the car door. "You didn't think I forgot, did you?"

"I knew you wouldn't forget. I just didn't expect you to be waiting for me when I got home. How long have you been out here?" Brooklyn locked the door and headed for her building.

"Not long. I remember your schedule. Monday, Wednesday, and Friday, the latest you usually work is nine or nine thirty in the evening unless you have a big meeting."

Brooklyn stopped and sat on the steps in front of her building. "Well, you have my attention." She placed her purse between her legs.

Dante leaned on the banister, looking down at her. "Really? You want to have this conversation outside on the porch?" He gave her a look as if to say, *Are you sure?*

"Yes. You can't come up. If you want to go grab a coffee somewhere, we can do that, but you can't come up to my apartment." Brooklyn knew how the night would end if she allowed that.

"Okay then I'll keep it brief. You know I love you, but I didn't think you could handle my lifestyle. Most women can't. I decided it was best for us to part ways." Dante sat down wide-legged on the step next to Brooklyn, his legs resting against hers. He leaned his arms onto his thigh.

Brooklyn shifted, turning to look at him. "First up, I'm not those women. I never have been and never will be. Second up, shouldn't it be my decision whether or not I could handle your lifestyle?"

"In all honesty, I was scared to trust it, to put myself out there, because of my history. I've missed you and what we had so much over this last year. You were my peace in a very chaotic world." Dante took her hand.

"Don't do this to me." Brooklyn stood, grabbing her purse and pulling her key out.

"Where are you going?" Dante asked as she entered the apartment building.

She faced him in the doorway. "You said what you needed to say."

When she turned and let the door close, he caught it before it could shut all the way, following her into the foyer. "No, I didn't. I didn't get a chance to tell you that I want another chance. After this case is over, we should see if we're 'picket fence' people."

"What are you asking me?" Brooklyn's heart raced. How long had she waited to hear him say these words to her? It seemed like forever.

"I'm asking you not to cross me off your list of possibilities quite yet." Dante stepped closer to her. "What we have is intense and powerful. It deserves to be explored."

"I'll think about it," Brooklyn hissed, putting her hand on his chest to prevent him from coming any closer.

He grabbed her arms and placed them around his waist. "Can I at least get a goodbye kiss?"

Brooklyn gave him a peck on the cheek. "Good night."

"That's not a goodnight kiss." He pulled her closer, kissing her passionately. Brooklyn's hands ran up and down his toned back. Dante pressed her against the mailboxes and continued to devour her like she was his last meal. The fact that they were standing in the foyer slipped her mind. Instinctively she locked her legs behind him as Dante lifted her up and moved them towards the stairs. Slowly he moved up the stairs. They made it to the door of her apartment.

Dante broke their embrace. "Keys, please."

He unlocked the door. Inside, he stood her against the wall near the door. Brooklyn's feet were on the floor but she felt like she was floating. Her purse hit the floor with a thump as he locked the door then proceeded to take her suit jacket off. She grinded her body against the bulge in his pants, wrapping one of her legs around his butt to pull him in closer. She started rubbing his head as his lips made a trail from her neck to her cleavage. Brooklyn tilted her head back, enjoying the fire that his touch had sparked.

"I want to show you how much I've been missing you." Dante's lips made their way back up to her neck as he unbuckled her belt.

"We shouldn't be doing this," she moaned as she pulled him close, pressing her lips against his.

'Oh, but we are," he breathed.

She fully explored his mouth, sucking his tongue briefly, knowing that turned him on. He ran his hand down her thighs. She kicked off her shoes as she started moving back toward the couch. Dante picked her up and carried her the rest of the way, then laid her down. She smiled as he placed kisses on her inner thigh while pulling off her slacks.

"What spell have you cast over me, Mr. Nines?" She felt her eyes glazing over with desire as he began to undo his shirt to reveal chiseled abs. Reaching up, she ran her fingers over his midsection.

Suspended over her lips, Dante stated, "I should ask you that question."

"Mmm, you're doing too much talking." She pulled his lips to hers. His fingers began unbuttoning her blouse as she wrapped one leg around his lower back, bringing him closer to her.

Dante suddenly broke the embrace and sat up. "You're right. We shouldn't be doing this."

Brooklyn popped up. "I'm right! Oh no you don't," she exclaimed as

Dante stood up, grabbing his shirt.

"You know I love you, but it's about more than sex with us." He placed one arm in the sleeve of his shirt. "I don't want you thinking, especially if things don't work like I hope, that I was just in it for another roll in the sack."

Brooklyn stood, grabbed him by his shirt again, and pulled him closer to her. "No sirree, that line of bull ain't going to work tonight." She refused to be teased and left frustrated just because he wanted to prove a point.

"Bull?" Dante looked at her as she wrapped her arms around his waist.

"Yes! I'm a grown woman. I can handle the consequences of my decisions, even if I don't like them. Stop making decisions for me." She slid her hands up his abs and to his shoulders, taking his shirt off. "Tonight I've decided I want you in my bed. I'll deal with the rest later. Can you handle that?" she asked as she began planting kisses down his chest.

"Oh, I can most definitely handle that," he replied as he lifted her up and carried her to the bed.

By the time he placed her on the bed, her blouse was gone and she was laying there in her peach lace bra-and-panty set.

"Why am I lying here half naked and you're in your slacks?" Brooklyn propped one leg up, giving him the 'come get it' look.

"They won't be on for long," he stated as he climbed into the bed. "I'm going to enjoy this." He was kissing her lips and slowly making his way down her body when his phone rang. He ignored it.

"Your phone is ringing." She moaned as her hand roamed the contours of his muscles.

He looked up from her navel, looping his fingers into the sides of her panties. "I'll call them back after I indulge in this wonderful dessert."

"Sounds good to me." Brooklyn inhaled in expectation of what was to come.

Dante's phone went from a normal ring to sounding like police sirens going off. He slid himself up Brooklyn's body then flipped onto his back, pulling her on top of him. Reaching in his pocket, he took out his phone. Brooklyn straddled him, sitting up and unclipping her bra.

"This had better be good," he barked into the phone as Brooklyn took her tongue and outlined his six pack. "I'm in the middle of something important."

"Alec McNier of Bevik Media and Alex Michaels of TriVision Media are the same person," Liang explained.

"What?" Dante exclaimed. Looking down at Brooklyn, he calmly stated, "I'll stop by the office in a couple of hours."

He turned the phone away from his mouth and pulled Brooklyn up to his face, kissing her as his hand roamed her backside.

"Sorry, but we need you here ASAP. We also found Ryan." Liang apologized.

"Damn!" Dante rolled Brooklyn onto her back, resting on one elbow with the phone in his other hand. "I'm on my way," he grunted into the phone. Dante kissed Brooklyn as he laid his phone on the bed next to her.

"I guess you have to go," Brooklyn sighed, seductively wrapping her legs around him and grinding her body into him.

"I need to, but I don't want to." His hands began caressing her curves. "You still keep condoms in your night stand?"

"Mmmhmm." Brooklyn opened the drawer, reached in, and handed him one.

The shrill police siren sound on Dante's phone sounded off again. "I guess this is just going to have to wait." He grabbed the phone off the bed. "What now? I said I'm on my way." Dante was upset already knowing this night wasn't going to end like he wanted it to.

"Ryan and one of the guys from our team have been shot," Liang explained. "The information is being sent over to your phone.'

"All right, I'll meet you there." Dante shook his head as he disconnected the call. He sat the condom on the nightstand then kissed Brooklyn on the forehead.

"The kiss of death," Brooklyn grumbled, disappointed as Dante stood.

"Sorry, you know I really wanted to finish what I started." Dante pulled her off the bed into an embrace.

"You'd better go before I flip you on the bed and have my way with you." Her arms circled his waist as his hands caressed her behind. He began nibbling her neck. "Go," she urged.

Exhaling, Dante took a step back. "I'll probably be out of town for the remainder of the week. Are you available on Saturday?"

Brooklyn grabbed a gown out of her dresser. "Nope, I have a date."

"A date?" He frowned, not happy with the idea.

She walked past him and into the living room to grab his shirt. "Yep," she stated as she handed it to him.

"Should I be worried?" Dante asked as he buttoned his shirt. He knew he should be moving faster to get to his destination, but the part of him that didn't want to go had him dragging his feet.

"Yes, very much." Brooklyn settled on the arm of her oversized chair, watching him put on his shirt.

Dante smiled. "I'm up for the challenge. Take care of yourself." He leaned down, kissing her. "Lock up after me."

When he exited her apartment, Brooklyn got up to bolt the door behind him. She made a mental note to make sure she had him turn off his ringer the next time they decided to take a stroll back down memory lane.

Chapter Twelve

Dante hopped out of the hired sedan before it came to a complete stop at the air strip, waving the driver off as he closed the door.

"He's here," Liang called back to the pilot in front of the airplane stairs and placed her Ruger .380 semi-automatic in her waistband.

"Sorry it took so long," Dante apologized as he walked towards her. "When I went home to grab my gear, I had a little company waiting for me that I didn't want to bring along."

"Our guy, George, didn't make it," Liang reported as they entered the private plane. "But Ryan is stable. The bullet passed through George as he was pushing Ryan down. It exited him and hit Ryan," Liang explained as they entered the private plane.

"Liang, we need to figure out what's really going on," Dante stated as they buckled up for take-off.

"I agree."

"I think this Alec McNier is the key to figuring it out." Dante made a mental note to dig deeper into his past.

Liang flipped her file open as the plane took off. "What's he shipping out that he doesn't want anyone to discover?" She looked over her information. "It can't be drugs or guns. They would never make it through most security check points."

"Megan was responsible for checking inventory and the manifest in Bevik Media's shipping department. Maybe she stumbled onto something she wasn't supposed to." Dante's thoughts flashed back to Brooklyn on the bed in her peach lace panty set. It was making it very difficult to focus on what Liang was saying.

"Then how does Ryan play into this?" Liang questioned, trying to figure out what they were missing.

"We've always assumed that he and Tuck were partners in all aspects of the business, but what if he wasn't? What if Ryan only was involved in the legitimate part of the business?"

"If Ryan and Megan were dating and not just employer-employee, then maybe she told him what she found out." Liang scrolled through her notes on her tablet.

"What else did you find out about Alec McNier?" Dante wondered if Brooklyn had gotten the quick message he'd texted her before he'd gotten to the air strip. He thought about how he'd left and shook his head. He'd better focus on this case right now. Otherwise, he might not be alive to pursue her.

"Alec McNier, aka Alex Michaels, has had his hand in quite a bit, but nothing that ever stuck. Word on the street is that he's a 'whatever you need' man." Liang gave Dante all the information she had on Alec.

"Okay, once we visit Ryan, we'll see what he has to say." Dante slipped off his jacket. "Then we can follow up on our theories and go from there. We need to get into the shipping office records. I think we should pay Tuck a visit. While I keep him occupied, you do your thing."

"Sounds good to me," she nodded then asked, "Do you know the layout of his office? Are they computerized, or am I looking through hard files?"

"Computerized, but they do have printouts. I doubt the stuff we're looking for will be in plain sight."

When they landed about an hour later at Philly's Airport, they went directly to see Ryan. He was asleep in a private hospital room when they arrived. Liang and Dante took shifts as they waited for him to wake up. According to their man, Stephen, he and George followed Tuck to

Ryan. After the two men exited the back of the building, Tuck went one way, Ryan the other. The team split up to follow them. Stephen trailed behind Tuck, and George stayed on Ryan's tail. Then Stephen heard gunfire coming from the direction his partner had run. Tuck jumped in his car and took off. Knowing he couldn't catch Tuck on foot, Stephen ran toward where the gunshot had came from. He found his partner and Ryan in the alley, both of them shot and bleeding George told him that he knocked Ryan out of the way when he saw someone come out of the other end of the alley and started firing a gun. Both men should have survived, but there was an unexpected complication in surgery and George didn't make it.

* * *

Three days passed before Ryan started staying awake for longer stints and was finally coherent enough to speak. Stephen had stayed there by Dante's request to explain to Ryan who they were and why they were there during the moments he was awake. Dante hoped he wouldn't have to call Stephen in as he leaned forward, asking a single question. "Where is Megan?"

"I wish I knew." Ryan shifted in the hospital bed.

"Why were you and Tuck meeting?" Liang leaned on the wall.

"Megan convinced me that Tuck was into something illegal and dangerous." Ryan shook his head. "Let me correct that, the goon I found going through my office convinced me that Megan may be right."

"Did she have evidence that Tuck was doing something illegal?" Dante inquired, cutting his eyes at Liang.

Ryan moved to the edge of the bed to sit himself upright. "She claimed she did."

"Why do you say claimed?" Liang inquired.

"I was making arrangements to lie low after someone ransacked Megan's apartment, but I happened to come back to our temporary spot early. We came here because I was supposed to meet a friend in Times Square in a couple of days. But I wanted to be within a three-hour drive of D.C., in case I needed to go back." Ryan took a long breath.

"I take it you saw or overheard something that made you think that maybe she could have done it," Dante prompted.

Ryan took a sip of water. "I heard her on the phone telling someone 'everything is going as planned'."

"You didn't know what she was referring to?" Dante inquired.

"We had agreed not to contact anyone until we figured out what was going on and what to do." Ryan shifted the pillows behind him.

Circling to the other side of the bed, Liang asked, "Why did Tuck come see you?"

"I asked him to. I needed to ask him a few questions." Ryan glanced at the door.

"You're safe," Dante stated.

"Am I?" Ryan questioned.

"We'll do our best to keep you that way," Dante replied, nodding to Liang to check the hallway. He didn't know if Ryan saw someone that made him ask that question or if he was just nervous from being shot.

"What did you want to ask Tuck?" Dante asked as Liang exited the room.

Ryan's eyes stayed focused on the hospital door. "I decided not to tell him about Megan's accusation, but I was going to warn him that he could be in danger and see if he knew why someone was going through our office."

Dante shifted his chair to better watch the door. "What did he say?"

"He said no, but I knew better. We've been friends a long time. He's an excellent liar, but something has him spooked. Tuck isn't an easy man to scare."

Dante started firing off the list of questions in his head. "How long has Megan been working with you?"

"About two years."

"How long have you been dating?" Dante didn't like the fact that Liang hadn't returned to the room.

"About a year." Ryan kept glancing at the door.

Dante stood, walking to the hospital door. "Did you know her history from before she came to work for you?"

"Not much. I know her work history. She avoided talking about her personal history too much. I didn't question it at the time because most of our activities didn't require much conversation," he explained as Dante stood watching him with one hand on the door knob.

Dante could tell by the awkward smile on Ryan's face they probably just recently upgrade from sex buddies to dating. He peeked into the hallway and knew something was definitely wrong. Dante slid his jacket back and placed his hand on his 9mm Beretta. He glanced back at Ryan and asked, "Do you think Megan is somehow involved in what's going on?"

"Prior to overhearing her conversation, my answer would have been no. After hearing her on the phone, I'm not so sure, especially since when I went back a couple hours later, she was nowhere to be found and her stuff was gone. She didn't answer my calls. And since we weren't scheduled to leave town until tomorrow …"

"You're not so sure," Dante finished his sentence as he watched Liang at the nurse's station. "Why did Tuck drive to met you?"

"He stated that it was best." Ryan took another sip of his water.

Dante watched Liang drop two fingers down towards the ground, and he knew Ryan wasn't being paranoid. He turned back to Ryan and inquired, "How are you feeling?"

Ryan gave him a puzzled looked. "Like a man that's been shot."

"Well, it looks like you may be right about this not being the safest place for you. Are you up to being relocated?" From past experience, Dante knew that it didn't matter what the doctors said in a situation like this. What did matter was what the patient thought about being moved. Attempting to move unwilling patients was risky for all involved. He had a scar on his leg to attest to that. Liang returned several minutes later and motioned Dante into the hallway.

"I'm stepping outside the room for a moment so that we can arrange a safe transport out of here for you." Dante made sure his jacket was covering his gun before opening the door.

"I'd appreciated that." Ryan reclined in the bed and started flipping through channels.

When Dante stepped into the hallway, he saw one of his men following the goon at the end of the hall. He knew they needed to get out of there immediately. Liang waited until the staff walking in the hallway was a reasonable distance away before she spoke.

"It's truly not safe for him to be here. I made arrangements to have him moved. However, I think we're going to have to do the old bait and switch to get him out of here safely."

Dante stood guard outside Ryan's room while Liang finished arranging the decoy's transfer to another hospital. He felt sorry for the man that got stuck playing decoy while they snuck Ryan out to one of their facilities. Getting assigned to decoy duty increased a man's chances of not making it home that evening. Hopefully, the bad guys would just attempt to snatch him at the next hospital and not ambush the ambulance in the middle of the street.

Liang returned to the room a couple of hours later with the transport plan completely in place. Dante shook his head. This was supposed to be a missing person case that was only a little complicated. But this situation didn't qualify as little. The fact that Alec McNier's name was on the radar concerned them. Whatever Megan had gotten herself mixed up in, it was not good.

He debated whether or not it was the best move to be trying to rekindle what he had with Brooklyn in the middle of this case. After Liang's shooting, the court proceeding, and the client's threat, Brooklyn's safety became his greatest concern. That was the reason why he had ended things with her in the first place. That case proved that what a client doesn't tell you or doesn't know could be lethal to their health. Liang had no idea that the high profile client that had requested that they save his foster sister years ago was certifiable. Now Dante was feeling the same way about this case. He couldn't wait to get Ryan somewhere safe so they could finish questioning him. He hoped that Ryan would tell them something that could at least help them find the key piece of information that they were missing.

Chapter Thirteen

The work week had been long and grueling but it was finally the weekend. Brooklyn smiled as she finished applying her makeup. She checked the time then slipped on her glittery red, orange, and black heels that complimented her dress. She stood, looking in the full-length mirror. She angled her body to show most of the front of her dress and just enough of the side to show off how it dipped low in the back as she snapped several pictures. A sly grin crossed her face as she texted the pictures to Dante.

Her apartment buzzer rang and she quickly buzzed Hunter in. Grabbing her purse, she made sure she had her flats and other essentials in there. Hunter knocked twice on the door.

"Hey, handsome," she beamed as she let him in.

"Hey, sexy. Are you ready?" Hunter leaned in, kissing her on the cheek.

"Yeah, I just need to grab a jacket." Brooklyn turned around, heading to the closet.

"Girl, you don't need a bodyguard. You need a damn booty guard in that dress." Hunter stared at the red material tightly wrapped around her behind.

"I told you I'd be a diva on fire," she teased as she pretended to drop her jacket then bent over inappropriately to get it.

"BK, you keep playing like that and your sexy behind won't be going anywhere but to your bedroom."

Brooklyn stood. "Hunter, I don't know what you're talking about. Besides, Chavell, Alexis, and the crew would come find us, demanding to know why we didn't show up." She opened the door and pushed Hunter out of it.

After Brooklyn locked up, Hunter walked her to a red sports car and opened the passenger door. "For the diva on fire." He smiled as she slid into the car, giving him a clear view down her dress. "I am definitely on bodyguard duty tonight," he murmured and chuckled as he walked around to get in the car.

Brooklyn had brought her jacket with her to cover her legs when she was sitting but she decided to lay it on the back seat. Crossing her legs, she shifted in her seat and buckled up.

"Sweetie, I'm going to need you to uncross your legs," Hunter insisted. "Otherwise, I'm guaranteed to crash the car because I'll be watching to see how far up your skirt will go." Hunter glanced over at her well-oiled, shapely legs then pulled out of the parking spot.

"Why are you acting brand new?" Brooklyn laughed, pulling down her skirt. "It's not like you haven't seen me in outfits like this before."

"We were both coupled up and unavailable to play at those times. I don't have to be on my best behavior now." He looked over at her and licked his lips.

* * *

Back in the DC area, Liang and Dante sat at a table reviewing files. They had been there for hours, analyzing information they'd gotten while interviewing Ryan and while searching Tuck's office. Dante's phone buzzed on the table. He grabbed it and nearly dropped it when the picture of Brooklyn in the red dress came through.

Liang looked up from her paperwork. "You okay over there?"

"Yeah," he replied, shifting in his seat.

Liang shook her head at him. He attempted to go back to reviewing the files, but his mind was somewhere else. When he realized that he had been staring at one page for over ten minutes without reading a single word, he knew that it was time to go. Dante closed the file in front of him, standing.

"I've put most of my notes in." Dante handed Liang the files while heading to the door. "Let's go over what Ryan told us and what we learned from Tuck's office on Monday. I want to work on the connection the goon had to this case. Is it Tuck or Alec? Or are we still missing a player?"

"We also need to figure out why TriVision has been monitoring your activities," Liang reminded him.

Dante paused at the door. "You know what? You have a point. They didn't follow me from Hunter's club. They were waiting for me at home. I'm sure there was nobody following me from the airport. How did they know where I lived? That address shouldn't have popped up when they looked me up."

"I'll look into it. Maybe that's the piece of the puzzle we're missing." Liang sounded like she had a bad feeling about it.

"Find out who referred the client to us. It could be something or it could be nothing, but we need to check everything out. Something is fishy about this case, and we need to put a finger on it so we can get a handle on things." Dante looked at his watch, wondering where Brooklyn was headed in that fiery outfit.

"I'm on it," Liang responded as she stood.

"Don't stay here much longer. And keep your eyes wide open." His eyes widened to emphasize his point.

"And you stay out of Hunter's club because evidentially your phone doesn't work too well in there. I would hate to do a repeat incident of last time," Liang teased, though he knew she was serious. Dante smiled and waved goodbye.

* * *

Hunter pulled up to the valet. Brooklyn grabbed her coat off the back seat as the attendant opened the door and extended his hand to her. She swung both legs out, stood, and adjusted her skirt just as Hunter rounded the car. Hunter placed his arm around her waist as the valet slid behind the wheel. "Whose idea was it to come to this place, Alexis or Chavell?" he asked.

"Alexis." Brooklyn laughed as they bypassed the line.

The bouncer removed the rope. "Hey, it's been a while since you rolled through. Good to see you."

"Is Anton in tonight?" Hunter asked as he shook the bouncer's hand and patted his arm.

"Yeah, I'll let him know you're here."

The club was already crowded. There were several girls dancing in cages around the room. Brooklyn scanned the people, looking for familiar faces. They had only been standing there a few minutes before a tall, skinny guy wearing a grey suit with an afro approached them.

"Hunter Torres, what brings you to my humble establishment?" He grabbed Hunter's hand and pulled him into a man hug.

"Partying with my girl and her friends." Hunter stepped back, pulling Brooklyn closer to him. "Brooklyn, Anton. Anton, Brooklyn."

Brooklyn smiled, shaking Anton's hand. "Hunter, I'll be right back. I think I see Alexis."

"Damn, you're a lucky man," Anton stated as they watched her stroll over to Alexis. "I'm hoping she's Sophia's replacement."

"I'm trying to make that a reality, but the way she's working that dress, I'm going to have my work cut out for me tonight." Hunter smiled as the group started heading his way.

Anton chuckled. "You're right, because she almost made me forget that I had a girl. Follow me. You and your friends are my VIP guests."

"I don't know if you want to do that. They're a wild bunch," Hunter joked.

"Drinks on me. I just need you to find out which of those lovely ladies are single. My brother and his friends are rolling through a little later."

"I think I can handle that." Hunter nodded for Brooklyn to follow him.

Brooklyn walked up to Hunter. "VIP again?"

"What can I say except that I know people who know people." He laughed as they entered the roped-off area.

* * *

Brooklyn was having a blast. Chavell kept them laughing. The drinks were flowing. The music was on point. She was enjoying her dance partner. On the crowded dance floor, Hunter was sandwiched in between her and another friend, with his back to Brooklyn. She had to grab Hunter by the waist when the person behind her bumped her. Her hand slid across his well-cut abs as he turned to face her. It was almost her undoing. Hunter motioned for them to take a break and he escorted her off the dance floor.

"Where are Alexis and the girls?" Brooklyn questioned when they returned to the VIP section.

Brooklyn's friend, LaShawn, explained, "Chavell has persuaded two of them to enter the Wet T-shirt and Thong Contest. However, Alexis is without thong today and someone is donating to the cause."

"That's just nasty." Brooklyn walked over to the table and poured herself a drink.

Hunter walked over, leaning on the banister. He turned around to Brooklyn and her friends. "It looks like the show is about to get started."

Brooklyn slid behind him, holding him around the waist as she looked over his shoulder. "I can't believe these fools are doing this!" LaShawn came up standing next to her and gave her the 'girl you know they are crazy' look.

"Oh believe it," Chavell exclaimed, squeezing between Brooklyn and LaShawn. "And I will have it on video." Brooklyn had to steady herself on Hunter to keep Chavell from knocking her over.

"Can you see, Miss Tippy Toe?" Hunter asked, noticing Brooklyn's height kept changing.

"Sometimes." She laughed.

Hunter shifted her in front of him. "Is that better?" he asked as he placed both hands on the banister on either side of her.

"Much," Brooklyn replied, soaking in his scent. She knew she shouldn't, but she leaned back into him.

"BK, you're making it hard for a brother to be on his best behavior. The way you were moving on the dance floor damn near had me wishing

I had a real back seat in my car." He tilted towards her. "Now this? You're playing with fire."

She started swaying to the music, then turned around and put her breasts on his chest as she wrapped her arms around his waist. "Is that a bad thing?" Brooklyn looked at him with slanted eyes full of desire.

"Only if I'm going home alone tonight." Hunter leaned down and kissed her.

"Hey, you two need to get a room if you're going to be doing all that," Chavell shouted over his shoulder. "Brooklyn you should have been in the contest. Once your t-shirt got wet, hell you wouldn't even have to turn around and hit them with the derriere to bring them to their knees."

She popped Chavell as she turned around. "Whatever."

"Hey, keep them things off me," he teased as he bumped her breasts with his elbow.

"You're stupid, you know that, don't you?" Brooklyn continued watching the contest, shaking her head as Alexis clowned on stage. Alexis did a move that had the crowd roaring. Brooklyn knew in that moment that Alexis was taking the prize home.

"Your girl's got moves." Hunter chuckled.

"Evidently." Brooklyn covered her eyes with her hands, then opened up two fingers to peek through.

Anton strolled into the VIP section with several guys in tow. "Hunter, you remember my brother, Ed. These are his friends."

"Hey." Hunter shook Ed's hand and nodded to the rest.

"Where are the rest of the girls?" Anton inquired.

"Two are on stage. The others are near the stage for moral support."

Anton smiled wickedly at his brother and his friends. "Have fun."

"It seems we will." Ed tapped his brother on the shoulder as he exited the VIP section.

"I'll make introductions once the girls get back," Hunter stated as the contest ended and the crowd went back to partying. "These three tables are ours. Your brother has provided drinks and snacks, so you go make yourself comfortable. This is a real friendly bunch."

Chapter Fourteen

Dante watched Brooklyn from across the room. The pictures had not done the outfit justice. He only felt slightly guilty for using her phone to track her down. Watching her and Hunter together, he knew she wasn't joking when she stated he should be worried. He'd almost texted Brooklyn when she was kissing Hunter. Before he could, her friend interrupted them. Dante pondered ways to keep Brooklyn out of Hunter's bed. She was drinking, and he recognized that look in her eye. Brooklyn was trying to get some tonight. Dante was going through ways to make sure that he was the one that was fulfilling any needs she had. The incident with Liang had put him at a disadvantage. If she slept with Hunter, he knew it would greatly reduce his chances with her. He texted her: *I'm still speechless from the pictures. Hopefully, I get to see you in that dress in person. Call me when you get in.*

Dante stood. It wouldn't work in his favor to be caught in the club. He watched her smile as she read his text. His phone vibrated as her text came through with the words, *Maybe, we'll see.*

He cut through the crowd and headed to the door. *At least put me on the schedule for brunch tomorrow*, he texted back. Taking one final look at her, he exited the club. Dante smiled when she texted back, *Done*. Shortly after, Liang texted that Ryan's story had checked out.

* * *

Brooklyn looked over at Hunter as she slid her phone back into her purse. He was right, she'd better stop playing with fire. Otherwise she would end up ruining their friendship.

"You okay?" Hunter noticed her mood had changed after checking her phone.

"Yeah." Brooklyn debated what to say. "It was Dante inviting me out to brunch tomorrow."

Before Hunter could respond, Alexis came and grabbed them, pulling them over to the area in their VIP section that they'd designated a 'dance floor' since the club was so crowded. Brooklyn was glad for the save.

"Only my friends make their own dance floor," Brooklyn shook her head walking towards the table where their drinks were being delivered.

"Let's get this party started," Alexis shouted, dancing with Ed.

Hunter grabbed a beer off of the table and handed Brooklyn her martini. She knew she would have to schedule some time to talk with Hunter. She smiled, putting the glass to her lips.

Hunter watched; she could tell that he was wondering what it would take to win first place in her heart.

Brooklyn drew Hunter's attention to her friend, who was now dancing on the table. "Look at Alexis' crazy behind."

"Take it to the cage," Chavell shouted.

Alexis used Ed's shoulder to get off the table and followed the other girls to the cages. Brooklyn laughed as the girls tried to outdo each other for male attention.

"Hey, Brooklyn and LaShawn, y'all up next," Chavell called as he filmed their friends dancing in the cages.

"Only if you get in first, Chavell," LaShawn insisted. "You're good for egging people to do something crazy and that is it."

Hunter played with the back of Brooklyn's dress. "I brought singles for you, and you don't even have to strip."

"Dude, forget singles. I need you to be tucking hundred-dollar bills in my waistband, Boo." Brooklyn laughed, finishing her martini.

"I got those too," Hunter teased.

"You'd better be glad Chavell is taping. Otherwise I'd take your money." Brooklyn hollered for Alexis to work it. When she turned to say something to Hunter, her mouth hung open as a young woman pushed a guy up against the wall. But that wasn't what made her mouth drop open. It was when the girl did a handstand that placed her crotch right in the guy's face. The guy's eyes began rolling in the back of his head.

Hunter turned and looked at the spectacle.

Brooklyn finally stopped staring as Hunter turned back towards her. "Wow! That's all I can say," she exclaimed.

"It looks like Alexis ain't the only one in here with skills." Hunter glanced back at the gymnast as she did tricks that brought more people over to watch her in action.

"Clearly there are some moves that I need to add to my repertoire," Brooklyn stated sarcastically, thinking that some moves really need to be reserved for the bedroom.

"If you want to practice that move on me, I'm more than willing to be your guinea pig." Hunter snickered as Brooklyn hit him. "I guess that's a no."

Later, when things were slowing down and a few of her friends had left, Brooklyn was cuddling next to Hunter with her jacket over her legs, sipping on a French Kiss Martini. She looked out over the thinning crowd when she heard Chavell say, "LaShawn, no! Somebody grab her." Chavell and Alexis exited the VIP section, hurrying towards LaShawn.

LaShawn had vaulted off the banister and onto the main floor, and was marching toward the other end of the dance floor.

"Hunter," Brooklyn warned, "you need to get someone to stop her. If she makes it over to where that couple is snuggled up, she'll set it off up in this place."

"I'll take care of it," Hunter replied.

Brooklyn grabbed his arm. "Be careful. She has a hell of a right hook. Don't let her size fool you. She's a beast."

Hunter exited the VIP section just as Chavell and Alexis caught up with LaShawn. She pushed past them, heading towards her boyfriend. Brooklyn shook her head at LaShawn's boyfriend, wondering why he'd come here with someone else. He knew how his girlfriend was. Brooklyn decided she'd better go over and assist, as security followed Hunter through the crowd. By the time Brooklyn reached them, Chavell and Alexis were trying to hold LaShawn. The other woman stepped forward, put her finger in LaShawn's face, and screeched, "Stay away from my man!"

"First up, heifer," LaShawn answered, struggling to break free from her friends' grip. "This ain't got nothing to do with you. I'm talking to that chump behind you."

"Don't be calling my man no chump." The girl stepped between Chavell and Alexis, pushing LaShawn. LaShawn's boyfriend tried to grab the girl, but he wasn't quick enough. Chavell and Alexis looked at each other and let her go. LaShawn punched the girl, sending her falling back into her boyfriend. Pushing the girl out of the way, she grabbed her boyfriend by the collar. The girl pushed again, only to receive LaShawn's fist slamming into her gut.

When the security guards finally stopped watching LaShawn whip her boyfriend's and his other woman's behinds, they had a hard time getting her off of her boyfriend. As security dragged her across the floor, she screamed, "You bet' not come home tonight. I hope that heifer cat has somewhere for your 'always between jobs' behind to sleep permanently."

Hunter gave Brooklyn the side eye as they followed security across the room. LaShawn finally stopped hollering and struggling when the security guy sat her down near the door.

"I'm good. I'm good." LaShawn adjusted her clothes.

Chavell ran into the VIP section, and grabbed his and LaShawn's things. He came back over to the group as Hunter and one of the guys from security stepped to the side. "LaShawn, I can't take you anywhere, can I?" he teased, pursing his lips like a parent chastising an unruly child.

"Whatever, Vell. Whatever." LaShawn took her purse from him.

"You okay?" Brooklyn asked.

"What is wrong with that fool? If he wanted to break up, he should have just said so instead of bringing that chick to a club he knew for a fact I would be at." She watched as the other security guy talked to her boyfriend and his other woman near the end of the bar. Moments later, a heated argument arose between LaShawn's boyfriend and his date.

Hunter walked over to the group. "Well, LaShawn, your imitation of a prize fighter won't be getting you arrested tonight. However, the party ends for you now. No more vaulting over banisters and beating boyfriend down tonight, at least not in this club." He scoffed as LaShawn smiled.

"All right, peeps! It was a fabulous, fun, and crazy time as always." LaShawn hugged everyone. "Love you. We'll go out next week to celebrate my return to singleness."

"Just let me know the time and the date," Brooklyn spoke as they walked to the door. She doubted that LaShawn would actually leave her boyfriend, as she had been saying the same thing for years. It would shock her if LaShawn stuck with her decision beyond two weeks.

Brooklyn hugged Chavell. "I guess I'll see you next time you're in town, troublemaker."

"Troublemaker? I wasn't the one pretending to be a track star and boxer tonight," he teased, receiving a friendly pop on the arm and a push out the door. Chavell waved at the group as the door shut.

The crowd of onlookers returned to the dance floor and to the bar as Brooklyn and Hunter returned to the VIP section. They laughed and talked about the incident for a while before they went back to drinking and dancing. Brooklyn glanced at her watch. *I guess we are shutting down the club tonight,* she thought as she shook her head at her crazy friends.

Hunter leaned near Brooklyn's ear. "Your friends do realize this isn't a strip club, don't they?"

Brooklyn glanced over to see Alexis giving Ed a lap dance. "Well Alexis can't blame that on Chavell since LaShawn is dropping him back at the hotel." She looked back at Hunter. "Don't be getting any ideas."

"I already have ideas. They started the moment you opened your door tonight."

Brooklyn's hand rested on his thigh as she took a sip of martini.

"I'm surprised they are still on," Hunter remarked.

"What?" Brooklyn asked, looking at him strangely until she noticed him looking down at her shoes. "Oh, I was planning to persuade a very handsome gentleman to give me a foot massage when we return to my place. I hear he has wonderful hands. I thought it would be easier to convince him if I had heels on instead of flats."

"You know all you had to do was ask. I'd give you a full body massage if you'd let me." Hunter gave her a sexy smile. She turned, wrapping her arms around his waist.

"Hunter, I would like that. While you know I'm very attracted to you, I need to figure out this thing with my ex. I honestly don't want to hurt you while I figure it out." Brooklyn glanced up at him, apologizing with her eyes.

"BK, it's not the most ideal situation, but I'm willing to put it all on the line—my heart, our friendship—for a chance to see if we have what it takes." Hunter's lips slowly descended, kissing hers.

"Umm, I guess you two won't be hanging out with us at Ed's for the after party," Alexis stated as she approached with the rest of the gang only steps behind her.

Brooklyn broke the embrace. "You're correct." She laughed, grabbing her jacket off the booth as Hunter walked over to talk to Anton. "Text me whenever you get home."

"If I get a response, you've done something seriously wrong." Alexis nodded her head towards Hunter, who was heading back their way.

* * *

It was almost three in the morning when Hunter parked on Brooklyn's block. Her shoes were killing her, but she refused to take them off. Every time Hunter looked at her with a mixture of appreciation and lust, it sent a tingle up her spine. She unlocked her door, stepped in, then held the door for Hunter to follow. He stepped in and planted a kiss on her cheek.

"Thank you for a wonderful and eventful evening!" he whispered as he stepped back out of the door.

"You aren't coming in?" That tingly feeling she had was now laced with disappointment.

"It's been a long evening." Hunter stuck his hands in his pockets, ignoring Brooklyn's pouting.

"You do know I have a second bedroom, right?" Brooklyn leaned on the door with her hands behind her back. "Besides, you promised me a foot massage."

"I'll have to give you a rain check on the foot massage. If I sit down anywhere besides behind the wheel, it's a wrap for me." Hunter grabbed his keys out of his pocket and turned to walk away.

Brooklyn quickly grabbed his arm. "Come on, Hunter. Stay awhile. We've barely had any alone time."

"BK." He inhaled, looking as if he already knew he would give in to her.

"Look, you can even take a power nap before you head home." She turned him towards the door and began pushing him through it.

"It's seems like you're giving me no choice." He laughed as he put his keys back into his pocket.

Brooklyn kicked off her shoes as she closed and locked the door. Hunter headed for the couch. She grabbed a blanket out of the ottoman and started pushing the ottoman closer to the couch.

"You need some help?" Hunter asked.

"Nope, just kick off your shoes and get comfortable. Do you want anything to drink?" Brooklyn inquired, shifting the coffee table over to make room for the ottoman.

"I'm good," Hunter replied as he sat at the end of the couch.

Brooklyn put Hunter's feet on the ottoman then grabbed the remote off the table. Before Hunter knew it, Brooklyn was putting her feet on the ottoman and throwing the blanket over them. She turned on the television as she cuddled next to him.

"Hunter, I'm very glad you were my date tonight. It was definitely a good time. I enjoy spending time with you." She wrapped her arm around his waist, looking up at him.

"So when are you going to allow me to take you on a real date, just the two of us?" Hunter questioned as she threw one leg over his legs.

"Soon," Brooklyn responded as he caressed her bare back. She had never been one to bed hop. Brooklyn was always intimate with one guy at a time, but as she laid in Hunter's arms, she knew she was in danger of breaking her own rule.

Brooklyn sat up, straddled Hunter, and began kissing him. Hunter's hands caressed her behind as he inhaled Brooklyn's essences. He laid her down gently on the couch, pushing the edge of her skirt up as his hand slid under the material. Brooklyn unhooked the clasps on her halter.

"BK, are you sure about this?" Hunter tried to focus on her eyes instead of her barely covered breast. "Because there's no going back if we do this."

Brooklyn paused, looked down then back up. "I'm sure."

Hunter sat up, pulling her up. "I'm not sure you're sure. So let's take a rain check on this too. Where's that second bedroom of yours? I think it's time for my power nap and for you to go to bed."

"Hunter." Brooklyn paused, frustrated that she wanted him, but knowing he was right. It wasn't the best time to explore this. It was only last week that she and Dante almost revisited their sexual escapades. "It's this way."

She held the top of her dress up as she led him to the second bedroom. "Thanks, I'll set my alarm for an hour, then be out of your hair." Hunter set his alarm on his phone.

"Let me go grab that blanket. For some reason this room gets really cold." Brooklyn went into the living room and when she returned with the blanket, Hunter was asleep on top of the covers. Brooklyn slid into the bed next to him and pulled the comforter over them, making herself quite comfortable on his chest. Hunter's hand slid around her waist and the evening of dancing and fun claimed its second victim.

Chapter Fifteen

It took everything within Dante to not go sit outside Brooklyn's apartment building to make sure the only thing Hunter did was drop her off. Glancing at the clock, he'd thought she would have called or texted him by now, but she hadn't. He hoped that she was just so tired from partying that she'd crashed and burned. Dante decided his efforts to wrap up this case and find a new career would work more in his favor as far as getting Brooklyn back in his life for the long haul.

He jotted notes on a pad, things like who was Megan talking to on the call Ryan overheard? He still hadn't figured out the connection to the goon and this case, besides the obvious fact that he's keeping an eye on Ryan's associates. As another hour passed, Dante sat his notes to the side, pulling out his phone. He texted Brooklyn that he'd be by her place by one p.m. to get her for brunch. She texted back okay. He decided to work another hour and call it a night. Wondering what Hunter and Brooklyn were doing made it impossible to stay focused on work.

Dante texted Brooklyn the next morning that he was on the way. He didn't get a reply back, but that wasn't unusual. As he parked the car, he wondered if she would be in her 'I partied all night' jogging suit or full makeup and sexy throw-on dress to hide the fact that she had partied too hard. After seeing her in that red dress, he was wishing for the latter. A resident was coming out when he was getting ready to ring the bell, so he just went in. He knocked on her door several times and waited. There was no response. He pulled out his phone and called her cell but no answer. He wished he hadn't erased her home number out of his phone.

"Hey, Brooklyn, are you in there?" He knocked louder, wondering if something had happened.

* * *

Brooklyn and Hunter popped up, hearts racing at the pounding on the door. Brooklyn looked at Hunter. "What time is it?"

He picked up his phone. "I don't know. My phone's dead." Hunter looked at the alarm clock on the nightstand and cursed. "I'm going to be late."

Brooklyn scooted across the bed, trying to fix her halter. "Only me," she exclaimed as she adjusted her dress. "Dante, hold on I'm coming."

"Brooklyn, I'm running late for an appointment. While I hate to put you in an awkward position, I really have to get going." Hunter looked apologetic, but Brooklyn also saw a little mischief in his eyes.

"That's fine. Just grab your stuff while I let Dante in." Brooklyn turned quickly and made her way to the front door.

Dante knew something was up the minute she opened the door. She was still in the red dress. Her hair and outfit were both disheveled. "You did remember our date?"

"Of course. Come in." She grabbed him by the hand and pulled him in. He walked in and came face-to-face with an equally disheveled Hunter. There was an awkward moment of silence until Hunter spoke, "Well, I need to get going. See you later, BK." He gave her a quick peck on the lips then patted Dante on the shoulder as a greeting and taunt on his way out of the door. "I'll call you later," he added as he walked away.

Brooklyn closed the door and looked at if she was daring Dante to say something. "It's not like you explained who the beauty was that occupied your bed the other night." She smiled at him. "It could be worse. I could have returned your threesome offer," she told him and nearly choked with laughter at the look on his face. "I'm just kidding. Come on, have a seat. I need a few minutes to shower and get dressed."

Dante muttered under his breath, "What the hell?"

When he heard the shower running, he decided to do a quick peek into Brooklyn's bedroom. He knew immediately she hadn't slept in her bed. He looked the couch over on his way to the guest bedroom, but it didn't show any telltale signs of a wild romp. In the guest bedroom, he noticed the tossed-aside blanket and the fact that the bed covers weren't pulled back. He decided that both Hunter and Brooklyn had slept in the bed. The fact that the bed covers weren't too askew led him to believe that all they had done was sleep. He knew from experience that they would have been in disarray if Brooklyn had had sex on them. He smiled to himself as he made his way back to the living room.

Thirty minutes later, Brooklyn appeared in her 'partied all night' jogging suit. *Damn*, Dante thought to himself.

"What? You don't like what I'm wearing?" Brooklyn questioned, looking at the disappointed look on his face.

"No, you look nice. But for the next date, we're definitely doing something that warrants you wearing a dress like you had on earlier." Dante stood. "Are you ready?"

"I am," Brooklyn replied, grabbing her purse.

Just as Dante helped Brooklyn into his car, his cell phone started ringing. He pulled it out. It was Liang. He held up his finger to let Brooklyn know that he needed a minute to take the call. She nodded, leaned her head back on the head rest, and closed her eyes. Dante stepped away from the car so that Brooklyn couldn't overhear the conversation.

"Hey, Liang, what you got?" Dante asked.

"It struck me that our guy was shot and killed, and Ryan was shot and laid-up in the hospital for days. But not one cop came to investigate. When I called the hospital to see if anyone had reported it to the police, they claimed there was no record of our guy or Ryan being admitted.

I tracked down and called the staff that was on duty that night. Each one claimed that no gunshot victims were admitted while they were on duty. And let me tell you I could feel the fear resonating off of them. Now George's body is missing and all records of him being there have vanished into the wind. We have to figure this out soon, Dante. The scope on this thing is getting wider and wider. Whoever is behind this has to be powerful."

Dante cursed under his breath. How had he let that slip past him? No cops showing up at the hospital should have been an immediate red flag. Where was his head? He turned towards the car, looked at the sleeping Brooklyn, and immediately knew the answer. Should he pull back from her until he figured this out? Would pulling back open the door wider for Hunter to come sweeping in?

"I think we need to regroup. I'm going to have to wrap things up with Brooklyn quickly. I'll call you when I'm done."

"All right. In the meantime, I'm keeping an eye on Tuck. My gut tells me that he's a key player here."

"Just be careful," Dante told Liang before hanging up.

* * *

Liang sat in a coffee shop across the street from Tuck's office. She thought about the events that had happened up until now. It was apparent that Tuck, who had at the very least heard the shots fired at Ryan, didn't feel frightened for his life. He had returned to work the next day and hadn't been scared into running or hiding. Had he been the one who had set the ambush up? It seemed likely. Her earlier search of the office hadn't turned up anything that would blow the case open.

Drumming her fingers on the coffee table, it occurred to her that sitting outside waiting for Tuck to do something unusual wasn't the best use of her time. He had shown himself to be a creature of habit. Maybe it was time to go search his place. Unless he finally broke his routine, she had at least two-to-three hours before he left work. She knew his home address from her earlier search of the office.

She was about to stand up to leave when the receptionist exited the building, holding a package with the business logo. Why was Tuck sending the receptionist out to deliver a package? Liang watched as the woman climbed into her car and pulled off. Tuck was now alone in the office.

Five minutes later, the goon from the picture Dante had taken pulled up in front of Tuck's office building and got out of his car. "What the hell is going on?" Liang whispered under her breath. She watched as the goon entered the building. She quickly wrote down the goon's license plate number. Liang sent a quick text to Dante. *Goon has arrived at Tuck's office.* Twenty minutes went by and Liang became nervous. Was Tuck in trouble?

As soon as she stood and grabbed her bag, the goon rushed out. He swiftly made his way to his car, got in, and drove off. Something was definitely up. Liang was about to exit the coffee shop to rush across the street when everything around her shook and the windows of Tuck's office blew out. The force of it almost knocked Liang down. People came rushing out of nearby businesses. Tuck's office was engulfed in flames.

* * *

Brooklyn was tired, but not so tired that she missed the fact that Dante was preoccupied. When the first text came in, his preoccupation became something more. "Brooklyn, I hate to do this, but I just got a lead on a case that I have to follow up on immediately. Do you mind if we wrap things up early? I promise I'll make it up to you."

"Uh, sure. I'm tired anyway."

Dante quickly waved their waiter over and handed him a large bill. "This should cover the check plus tip, right?" The waiter gave a pleased look and Dante grabbed Brooklyn's hand. "Come on. I'll have to drop you off quickly."

They were fifteen minutes away from her place when a second text came in. Dante read it and cursed. He made a sudden u-turn in the middle of the street, startling Brooklyn. "I'm sorry, something major's come up. I need to drop you at the bus stop."

"The hell you will. You'll have to take me with you and drop me off later."

"But, Brooklyn, I don't want you in any danger."

"Then don't drop me off at the damn bus stop," she demanded with a serious attitude.

Though it was against Dante's better judgment, Brooklyn would just have to come with him. He picked up his cell and called Liang.

"Are you sure you're okay?" He didn't bother with hello.

"I'm fine. I'm definitely doing a whole lot better than Tuck."

Liang stood behind the police tape with the crowd, watching as the firefighters battled the flames. She had parked a few blocks down and had walked to the coffee shop. She hadn't wanted to draw attention to herself by rushing back to her car, so as people spilled out of the buildings, she mingled with them. The firemen had arrived on the scene first, then the cops. It was the arrival of the cops that delayed her departure, "Dante, you aren't going to believe this. The goon is back on the scene. He's a cop."

* * *

One thing Ryan had to learn rapidly was to follow his instincts when they claimed he was in danger. He immediately sensed it when an unexpected knock resounded on the door of the apartment Dante's men had him holed up in. He wasn't the only one who sensed trouble.

"Just a minute," Jason, the larger of his two body guards, called. He gestured to his partner, Paul, to take Ryan and go. Not needing any prompting, Paul took Ryan by the arm and made for the back bedroom. Taking an escape route that they had already mapped out, they climbed out on the fire escape. But instead of going down, they went up to the roof. As they reached the roof, they heard the sound of gunfire coming from the apartment. They picked up their pace and crossed over to the next building via a large board they had placed there days ago for such a moment as this. The bodyguard pulled the board across once they reached the other building. They heard more gunshots.

"Come on," Paul whispered. They moved under the cover of night. Still carrying the board, he led Ryan to the other side of the building and strategically placed it so that the chimney would block any followers' view of them as they crossed over to the next building. When they made it to the adjacent roof, he pulled the board across so that it no longer connected the two buildings, then left it laying on the roof. Crouching, they made their way to the purposefully-broken roof door of the abandoned building they were now on. Once inside, they moved quickly down the three flights of stairs.

Ryan crouched down by his protector when he positioned himself under a window in the kitchen at the back of the first floor apartment. From there they had a clear view of the alley. No one was there. He signaled for Ryan to follow his lead. Ryan stood and a sharp pain from his wound shot through his body. He bit his lip to keep from crying out, ignoring the pain as they ran quickly out the back of the building. Paul pulled a black tarp off a motorcycle hidden behind a gate covered with overgrown weeds. "Get on," he told Ryan as he climbed on. Ryan was on in an instant and had just taken hold when the bike shot out into the night. He held on for dear life, fully expecting bullets to fly by or even slam into his back. It was ten minutes into the ride before he finally let himself feel some relief.

The relief was short lived. They pulled into an abandoned lot. Paul climbed off the bike, then pulled Ryan off and threw him to the ground. He pulled out his gun and pointed it at Ryan. Taking a step towards the scrambling Ryan, he demanded, "Who the hell did you contact?"

"What do you mean? I didn't contact anybody." Sharp pains shot through Ryan's wound again as he tried to reverse crab-walk out of the way of the gun.

"You're a damn liar, and if you don't start talking soon, I'm gonna blow your lying head off. My partner is most likely dead because you couldn't lay low without calling somebody. Now who the hell did you call?" He aimed the gun at Ryan's head.

"All right, don't shoot. I lifted your partner's cell phone earlier and tried to call Megan. I had to find out how she was mixed up in this. I couldn't believe she had played me."

"And what did she say?"

"She didn't answer, so I slipped the phone back when your partner wasn't looking. I didn't think they could find me from that."

"Now you know." Paul cursed under his breath and lowered the gun. He looked at his watch and cursed again. "Come on. We have to get out of here." They were walking back to the bike when Paul's phone rang. He looked at it and answered fast. "You got out?" He listened.

Ryan looked down as Paul grunted and he seemed to repeat Jason's answer. "Barely."

"Meet us at the Pivot," Paul told Jason, giving him the code name of their meeting location. "And do me a favor; get rid of your cell phone. It's been compromised." He gave Ryan a searing look before hanging up and climbing on the motorcycle.

"Get on," he commanded gruffly. Ryan did so without hesitating.

Chapter Sixteen

Liang decided it was time to make her exit. The cops would scour the crowd for suspects, and she didn't want to be seen. She walked closely behind a group of patron from the coffee shop returning to their cars after viewing the exciting events. When they broke off from the larger crowd to head back to work, Liang pretended to walk with them.

When she reached her car, she climbed in and tried to start it. It wouldn't start. "This day just gets better and better," she barked as she hit the steering wheel. She called Dante and provided him instructions on where to meet her. He pulled up within twenty minutes.

Though she was surprised to see Brooklyn in the passenger seat, she didn't show it. She climbed into the back seat and instructed, "Let's get out of here. I'll have to get my car later."

"Are you okay?" Dante asked as he pulled off. Liang noticed he was trying to ignore the deadly look Brooklyn was shooting his way. It was apparent she remembered Liang from the night of the offered threesome.

"Like I said, I'm fine."

"Good. Uh, Brooklyn, this is Liang, my partner. Liang, Brooklyn."

"Hey," they both stated, neither happy to see the other, but Liang suspected it was for two entirely different reasons.

"What's going on with all the fire trucks and cops?" Brooklyn asked with a frown.

"Are we going to drop her off so we can talk?" Liang asked, not trying to be rude, but anxious to talk to Dante.

"No," Brooklyn challenged. "Maybe you should be the one we drop off. After all, you interrupted us.'

"Dante, we don't have time for the jealous girl bull," Liang snapped. "We need to work fast to figure this out before someone else gets killed."

At the mention of someone getting killed, Brooklyn changed directions. "What the hell is going on? Who got killed and why?"

"Brooklyn, it's a case Liang and I are working on. I don't want to drag you into it. Look, Liang is right. I need to drop you off and spend some serious time figuring this thing out. I know I'm in a race with Hunter, so I'm going to ask you to hold off with him a minute while I work through this case."

"That's a lot of damn nerve. I'm supposed to sit around while you and Liang Liang go traipsing around for who knows how long? She may be your 'partner,' but she was also comfortable enough to climb into your bed."

"We really don't have time for this." Liang was worried that they would let precious time slip away by trying to coddle Brooklyn and explain things to her. "Look, I did that because I was trying to get rid of you that night. Dante and I have never crossed that line. This case that we're working on is serious and people have died. While I would love to leave you with a warm fuzzy feeling about you and Dante's relationship, I can't. We have a widow who can't bury her husband because his body is missing. We have a rogue cop who's apparently killing people, a missing girl who is either in over her head or playing a supporting role in all of this, and a client who most likely has ulterior motives. So if you can get over yourself for a minute, we just need a little time to sort this out. Then you and Dante are free to skip down lover's lane for all I care."

Dante had parked in front of Brooklyn's place during Liang's tirade. He caught Brooklyn and pulled her out of the car just as she was about to go over the seat and tear into Liang.

"Let go of me, Dante. I'm tired and I don't need any of this." She pulled away from him and turned back to the car, pointing at Liang in the back seat. "You're lucky he stopped me because I would have torn that smart ass tongue right out of your mouth."

Liang chuckled.

"Go solve your case, Dante, and leave me alone. My life has finally settled into a sweet spot and I don't need you and all your P.I. drama to go f'ing it up."

* * *

The sound of the bedroom door bursting open startled a sleeping Megan awake. "We have to go," her partner, Aaron, told her, grabbing her arm and pulling her out of the house. She had never seen him frightened and that fact alone had her terrified.

Megan trotted behind him. "What's going on?"

"I'm not sure. Tuck's dead. I would have been too if I hadn't got caught by that damn train," he stated, heading to the car.

"What happened?" Megan asked as she fastened her seatbelt.

"The office blew up. I don't understand what's going on. Tuck just wanted me to get you away from Ryan and safely to your husband now that he's back in the States." He drove quickly away from the area.

"Where are we going?" Megan questioned as she dug around in her purse, pulled her gun out, and sat it on her lap under her purse.

"Somewhere safe. Tuck set up this housing arrangement." He continued to look in his rearview mirror. "If they came after him, they might know where we are. I don't want to stick around to find out."

Megan continued digging in her purse until she found her phone and sent a text. "Did Tuck tell you where to find my husband?"

"No, that's why I was supposed to be meeting him, so he could tell me where to take you." He was continuously looking in the mirrors.

Megan slid her gun back into the recesses of her purse. "Look, I don't know what's going on with Tuck, but that had nothing to do with me. How about we go get a room in one of the hotels up the road?"

"Megan, I don't know. Tuck told me I needed to keep you safe until I took you to your husband." His hands were shaking. He rolled down his window to let in fresh air.

"Aaron, you did. You got me away from Ryan without any confrontation and you've been making sure he doesn't show up." Megan touched his arm. "That was all Tuck wanted. Whatever else Tuck has gotten himself mixed up in has nothing to do with this."

"I hope you're right," he responded.

"Look. We'll get some sleep. I'll contact my husband's aunt. He normally always goes to her house to retrieve his things once he gets back in the States." Megan smiled as Aaron visibly relaxed.

"It would be no problem dropping you off at his aunt's place. That was probably the address that Tuck was going to give me before the accident occurred," he spoke, sounding like he was trying to reassure himself.

She pointed to a motel up the road. "Hey, why don't you see if they have two rooms for the night?"

He pulled in the parking lot and Megan handed him some money. As soon as he exited the car, she pulled out her vibrating cell.

"Did you take him out?" the man on the other end asked without saying hello.

"There's no need. Tuck told him nothing." Megan kept a watch on the motel door.

"Are you sure?" he questioned.

"Positive. What happened to Ryan?" Megan's purse fell from her lap and onto the floor.

"I'm taking care of it. But you need to take care of your watcher. We can't afford for anyone to find out our plan before we're ready to reveal ourselves." His voice seethed with anger.

"You're right. We can't have him going back speaking to anyone that could help him piece things together." Megan reached down to retrieve the contents of her purse. "I'll take care of him in the morning. You take care of Ryan and I'll meet you at the spot."

* * *

Aaron paid for the room, got the key, then headed back to the car. His movement suddenly halted near the car and he stood there, momentarily frozen in place and listened through the open driver's side window before slowly walking back to the front end of the car. When he tapped on the hood, Megan's head popped up and he heard her mutter, "We're good to go."

He waved the key at her, then motioned for her to come on. "We lucked out. They had two rooms, but one is upstairs and one is downstairs."

"Aren't you going to grab your stuff and lock up?" Megan shouted out the window.

He walked up to the window. "Yeah. Yeah." He laughed awkwardly then opened his door and rolled up the window. "Let's get the bags and I'll take you to your husband's aunt's house in the morning."

She picked up her purse as he grabbed the back pack he'd tossed on the back seat in his haste to get out of the house. "That sounds like a plan." Megan took hold of her bag, smiling as she followed him to the hotel, muttering, "He won't even see me coming."

* * *

Gus, the goon, sat in front of Alec McNier, the man who was holding his life hostage. It was odd for him to not be the one striking fear into a person's heart. But the guy pulling his strings had no heart to strike fear into. Alec just sat there behind his computer, saying nothing for a while. The goon wasn't going to enjoy telling him this.

"Gus, did you retrieve the file from Tuck?" Alec stared intensely at Gus.

"No." Gus inhaled deeply.

"Well, I guess that explains the fireworks." He leaned back in the chair, smiling wickedly. "At least the file was destroyed."

"Maybe not." Gus braced himself for the reaction.

Alec quickly sat forward. "What?"

"As I was leaving the office after arming the bomb, Tuck snickered and stated that the files weren't there. We wouldn't know where they were until they innocently popped up." Gus studied Alec as he stared, lost in thought, saying nothing for a long time. There was no way Gus would have had time to disarm the bomb or untie Tuck. He wasn't a bomb expert. He was just following instructions. If Tuck didn't give up the file, he and the office were to go up in smoke.

"The file has to be in the acquisition paperwork." Alec stood, walking over to the bookshelves and staring at the photos. "We can't have Brooklyn coming across it, especially with her relationship with Dante. That would be a huge problem."

"What do you want me to do?" Gus stood, thinking this thing wasn't going to end well for him. If it was only his life on the line, he would throw in the towel because, at the end of the day, he would be the only one paying the cost for his mistake.

"Hit Brooklyn's office tonight and retrieve the file. It has to be there." He turned away from the pictures.

Gus grabbed his jacket off the chair. "How will I know it's the right file?"

"If you find a picture of me in it, then it's the file that I'm looking for." Alec returned to his chair as Gus exited the room.

Chapter Seventeen

Dante stared at Liang as they arrived at the office. The car ride over was unexpectedly silent. He replayed the interaction between Brooklyn and Liang, shaking his head. Dante said nothing until they entered her office and closed the door.

"Liang, what in the hell has gotten into you? I know I threw you for a loop by bringing Brooklyn, but your reaction was out of line and unprofessional. Yes, you should have thrown me the 'what the hell' look, but—"

"Dante, I'm sorry." Liang shoved her hands in her back pockets as she rested against the wall.

"Brooklyn should not have been privy to any of that information, especially considering what she does. If she sees the news and connects her acquisition case to our incident today, we may have a bigger problem on our hands." Dante paced the office. He stopped in front of Liang. "If you can't handle this case, I need to know now."

"This case has me on edge." Liang took her hands out of her pocket, pushed herself away from the wall, and walked over to the file cabinet.

Dante crossed his arms, watching her as she searched through the files. "Yeah, but an outburst like the one you had with Brooklyn will get us killed. You told her a rogue cop is apparently killing people. You told her about our client's daughter. Come on! If you need my head in the game, I need yours in the game too."

"You're right. Let's break this case down because we need to figure out if Megan in fact needs saving." Liang pulled out a stack of files.

"Or is she part of the problem?" He grabbed some of the files from her and sat at the desk. She followed suit. They were in for a long day.

* * *

Brooklyn was fuming. She didn't know why she let Liang Liang get under her skin. Dante wasn't officially her man, so why was she tripping? It wasn't like Hunter wasn't at her place when Dante picked her up. She had a big meeting tomorrow morning to review the acquisition. Her boss was notorious for moving meetings up. Brooklyn figured she'd put a few hours of work in before heading to Tyson Corners to meet the girls at the mall. Maybe it would help her take her mind off of Dante and Liang.

She decided to review the last few files that she had recently received from Bevik. She hadn't had a chance to look at them because she accidentally left them locked up at home. Brooklyn grabbed her specialty console table and pulled it away from the wall. It was designed to become her desk and safely house her work files. She unlocked her file cabinet and pulled out her laptop and files.

After working a couple of hours, she decided it was a wrap. She put her laptop and files in her workbag, never noticing that she had left one file in her desk. She locked up the cabinet, slid the console table back against the wall, and rolled the chair back into her room.

Her cell phone rang and she grabbed it off the console table. She smiled when she saw Hunter's name on the screen. "Hey, sexy. What took you so long to call me?"

Hunter laughed. "I thought you were all caught up in your ex."

"Mmm, sometimes a person needs to accept that there's a reason things didn't work out the first time," Brooklyn stated as she locked her workbag in the storage closet in the back room. It was a habit she started when the super let a plumber in to fix her sink while she was out. She had found that files she'd left in her work bag were on her coffee table. Gratefully, her laptop wasn't stolen. Brooklyn made it a point to lock up her workbag any time she wasn't using it. It had been embarrassing to send her privacy team the email that confidential documents may have been exposed to the public.

"What's the rest of your day looking like?" Hunter asked.

"I think I'm going to hit the mall, then maybe catch a movie. It has to be an early night. I'm back to the grind tomorrow." She sat on the couch and put on the gym shoes she'd taken off earlier.

"How about when you're done with your shopping, I meet you for movies and dinner?" Hunter inquired.

Brooklyn grabbed her purse and keys. "I would love to …"

"But …" Hunter supplied the lingering word.

"But, I'm meeting Alexis and LaShawn. I don't know if you're up for an evening of dinner and a movie with them." Brooklyn laughed, imagining the foolery that having Hunter with her at the movie would bring on.

"Is going to the movies with them worse than partying with them?" Hunter asked in a tone that sounded as if he was wondering if the 'no' had more to do with her ex than her friends.

"Hopefully not! Hey, I'm heading to the mall now. If I don't get a text or a call to confirm that they're going, I'll call you for dinner and a movie." Brooklyn walked down the stairs, not noticing the guy across the street staring at her intensely.

"Sure," Hunter responded. "Well, I've arrived at my destination. I'll holler at you later."

Brooklyn slid into her car and switched to her hands-free set. "Umm, where are you going that you can't talk to me till I get to the mall?"

"I'm grocery shopping for the week." Hunter ignored her laughter saying, "BK, I do keep my place full of food."

"I'm sorry, Mister Always Eating Out." She continued laughing.

"Ha, I keep trying to eat out, but you keep denying me." Hunter chuckled.

"Behave, Hunter. Behave." Brooklyn smiled, enjoying the banter. He continued to keep her entertained with colorful conversation on her drive until her other line beeped. "Hey, Alexis is on my other line. If they flake on me, expect a call back."

"Okay, but don't let them get you into too much trouble," Hunter stated before Brooklyn clicked over.

Brooklyn was kind of hoping that Alexis and LaShawn would cancel so she could hang out with Hunter. He brightened her day and kept her smiling long after they parted ways. She hated that Dante still had his hooks in her heart.

"Brooklyn, if you're busy, call me back," Alexis stated as if she didn't think Brooklyn was listening.

"No, I'm almost at the mall. I just got distracted by a pocket of traffic." Brooklyn maneuvered through the traffic into the lane to that lead to the mall parking lot. "Sorry," she apologized and focused on the conversation.

"I was just saying that we'll meet you by our favorite store in about thirty. We're running late."

"Well, I'm here already." She stated as she put on her blink to grab the spot of the car just pulling out. "I'll walk around till you guys get here. Text me when you park so I know to go to the meeting spot." Brooklyn parked her car.

As she strolled around the mall, she didn't know if it was her incident in the car earlier with Dante and his partner that had her nervous, but she could have sworn someone was following her. She had been going into coed stores. So she went into a couple of women's stores. If he didn't come in, he might still be somewhere lingering outside when she exited the store. She wondered if it was Dante's doing. He claimed he didn't want to put her in danger, but she was being difficult. She should have caught the damn bus home or called Hunter to come get her.

She nearly jumped out of her skin when someone touched her on her shoulder.

"Brooklyn, are you okay?" Alexis moved her hand.

"Alexis! Girl, you can't be rolling up on me like that." Brooklyn had been so busy watching for the guy that she hadn't noticed them come up. "I thought you were supposed to text me."

"We did," LaShawn interjected. "Where's your phone, Missy?"

Brooklyn reached into her purse, pulled out her phone, and saw the text.

"I guess it's a good thing we saw you. I'm looking forward to discussing who's got you all distracted." Alexis smiled, wrapping her arm around Brooklyn as they began walking. Brooklyn glanced out the corner of her eye to see if her shadow was moving with them.

* * *

Megan packed everything in her back pack. She looked at the gun in her purse. The fact that she didn't have anything to silence the shot made things complicated. Now she wished they had gotten one room so she could have at least tried to muffle the shot with a pillow, shooting Aaron while he was asleep. Her mind couldn't conceive of a way to enter his room, get a pillow, and shoot him. Every scenario that ran through her mind did not play out well for her. Megan decided she would kill him at one of the secluded rest stops along the way. She went down the stairs and knocked on Aaron's door, but got no answer. Glancing around the parking lot, she didn't see the car. Megan went into the office in search of the clerk.

She walked to the counter and smiled. "Hey, I wanted to know if the guy in room twelve checked out."

"He must have because the key is back. Hold on. I just got here. Let me find out from Fred when he checked out." He looked her up and down before heading to the back.

Megan didn't have a good feeling about this. Normally Aaron would text her if he was making a run or was going to be out for a while. She checked her phone again. There was no text and no missed call.

The clerk called from the back. "Miss, what is your room number?"

"Twenty-four." She impatiently tapped on the counter. She heard an okay, then silence.

A few minutes later he reentered the room. "He only had one room. Fred stated he left last night shortly after getting his lady friend settled in. He did mention that you would be checking out this morning. Are you checking out now or later?"

Megan played with the key to the room. "No. I'll be checking out in about thirty minutes."

She exited the office calmly, but as soon as she was out of sight of the office she did a quick trot up to her room. She threw her bag on the bed, quickly unzipped it and pulled out her laptop. She flipped it open and turned it on, then called her husband while it powered up.

"We have a problem," Megan stated as she sat on the bed logging into the computer.

"What happened?" he asked.

"He's in the wind," she replied, pulling up the information she was looking for.

"Did you track him?"

"I'm trying to now, but so far it's a no-go." Megan continued to peck away at the laptop keys.

"Look, get out of there. We have to accelerate our plan, but I don't want the big reveal to happen until we hit our target date. Now that the file is in the wind as well as Tuck's little errand boy, it's imperative. Especially since Ryan is still off the radar."

"They didn't find the file in Brooklyn's office?" Megan continued to pull up various programs, attempting to track Aaron.

"No, but they say she tends to bring files home. We're going to attempt to check the files that she took home later."

She began closing out her programs. "Well, let me know if I should stick around to help."

"Let's keep you out of their way for now. If we need to send you in, we will. Just get to the meet-up point."

Megan was so frustrated that things were starting to fall apart when they had just begun to come together so beautifully. "Are you sure you don't want me to reconnect with Ryan and find the location of the vault?"

"No. Go to the meeting place. Once we hit our target date and this situation is behind us, we can find Tuck's partner in crime and find the location. And once we do, we can be together without worry that someone will rip our life apart."

"Okay. I love the sound of that. It's going to take me a little longer to make it there, but I'm on my way." Megan shook her head as she slammed the laptop closed. Finding a motel without surveillance cameras was supposed to have worked in her favor not against her. Now she didn't know exactly what time Aaron left or which way he was heading. *Damn,* she thought to herself. *Clearly he saw this coming, but I didn't.*

Chapter Eighteen

Alec put the construction plans away that he had been reviewing when Megan called. He logged into his computer, sending an email to get an update on the progress of the construction project. Tuck had made a mistake digging into Alec's past and threatening to expose him. Alec had waited too long to get this plan in place to allow some greedy lowlife to ruin it. Dante and Liang would pay for what they'd done to him too. Once he executed his plan, not only would he get his revenge, but he could stop living his life in the shadows and be with the woman he loved.

* * *

Brooklyn grabbed her work bag and headed out to her favorite morning coffee shop before work. She mentally replayed her weekend. Dante hadn't called her since he dropped her off after their aborted brunch, and that thought bothered her. She texted him as she waited for her coffee. He was a grown man that could take care of himself, but she couldn't help it. She always worried about him when he was traveling. Now that she knew exactly what he did for a living, it was worse. Brooklyn took her coffee and headed back to her car. She noticed a familiar black sedan. She wondered if it was Hunter that made her paranoid or Dante.

When she arrived at work, the energy in the building was different, but she couldn't put her finger on what it was. She slid her badge through the turnstile to get to the area with the elevators. Lifting her cup of coffee, she said hi to security as she entered the crowded elevator bank and started planning her day as she waited. When it came, she got in and was sandwiched behind a heavyset man burdened with two boxes of donuts, a briefcase, and a rolling suitcase. As she reached around him to punch the button for her floor, she caught a glimpse of a man that reminded her of the guy in the mall. She couldn't be sure because the door closed too quickly.

Her cell phone beeped as a text came through. She adjusted her bag to grab her phone. Across the screen came, *Sorry beautiful for not getting back to you sooner. I'm fine. I'm glad to see you're still talking to me.* Brooklyn replied, *Not really, just wanted to make sure you were still in the land of the living.* She squeezed past people, careful not to spill her coffee as she exited the elevator.

The receptionist was on the phone when Brooklyn entered the office. Brooklyn waved hello and walked past her, hearing her ask the person on the phone to hold.

"Brooklyn, wait!"

When Brooklyn turned around, the receptionist was standing and motioning her back to the desk. "Mr. Haskins would like to see you in his office. There's been an incident."

"Should I be worried?" Brooklyn walked back to the desk.

"Mr. Haskins will have to explain." The receptionist glanced down at her phone. "He's off the line. You can go in."

"Thanks." Brooklyn tossed the remainder of her coffee in the trash bin at the end of the desk then silenced her phone before placing it in her purse. She gave a slight knock before entering the office. Mr. Haskins looked up.

"Brooklyn, glad you made it in." He stood, motioning to the guest chair as he went to close the door. "All your meetings for today have been cancelled."

"Is there a problem I should be aware of?" Brooklyn felt dread filling her chest as he returned to his seat. She sat her bag down next to her chair.

He leaned forward on his forearms, looking at her intensely. "There was a break-in last night. Several offices have been hit, yours being one of them. We're assuming they were looking for files. I need you to spend the morning listing the files that you were working on. We need a clear idea of what client's information has been compromised."

"We don't need to cancel any meetings for that. I keep a detailed log of all my projects and tasks in my laptop to make sure I don't drop the ball. All I need to do is log in and print the information out for you." Brooklyn grabbed her work bag, sitting it on her lap. She fought not to smile as relief permeated her being. She was glad that she wasn't being reprimanded or fired.

"Well, the police report has been filed. However, I still need you to work in one of the remote offices today. Protocol requires that our own security do an investigation." He stood and Brooklyn followed suit.

"Not a problem." She put her work bag on her shoulder.

He glanced down at her bag. "I'm very relieved that you took the laptop home. Your office was hit the worst. It looked like a tornado went through there."

"So I'm not allowed to grab anything out of there?" Brooklyn walked with him to the door.

"Probably not until this afternoon, which is why we'll keep your day clear. I don't know how the lack of access to your office will affect you." He opened the door.

"Okay, I'll head to the remote office to print that list for you and figure out how to proceed with my day." Brooklyn exited his office and headed straight to the receptionist desk to find out what other offices had been broken into. From what the receptionist knew, it was Brooklyn's office and the offices on either side of it. After finding out which remote office was available, she strolled past her office on the way there.

It was crazy. The two offices next to hers had a few papers and files on the floor, but the back cabinets were intact. Her office, on the other hand, was completely ransacked. Every file cabinet was open. All her file boxes were open, the files scattered on the floor. She shook her head and continued to her temporary spot.

Despite not having access to certain files, Brooklyn's morning flew by. It wasn't until she heard a knock on the door that she realized it was lunch time.

Denise peeked in. "Are you working through lunch again?"

Brooklyn glanced at the time on her computer. "No, I'm planning to run out in about five and grab something."

"Cool. Are you going to your favorite spot?" Denise asked as she stepped into the office.

"Yep." Brooklyn started logging out of her computer.

"Could you pick me up a number eight? I took an early lunch to go to an appointment. I just got back, and I didn't have time to grab anything to eat while I was out. It's been a crazy day." Denise pulled out money and sat it on the desk.

"No problem." Brooklyn locked down the laptop and grabbed her purse. "I shouldn't be too long. I'm trying to make it an early night because I have dinner plans." She smiled as they walked out of the room.

***

Brooklyn sat in the seated area of the Gallery Place enjoying her lunch, then grabbed a frozen yogurt before ordering Denise's food. She took the shortcut between the buildings to grab Denise's food on G and 7th. The walk never bothered her before, but today was different. She heard footsteps behind her. She glanced back to make sure it wasn't the guy from the mall. A few homeless people gathered on the walkway. If it wasn't for the fact that the brick driveway was for the cars using the garage she would have walked on it, instead of the slender walkway. Before she could get a good look at him, the man that seemed to be tailing her stopped, pulled out a cigarette and leaned on the wall a few feet from the homeless people. Brooklyn put some pep in her step to catch up with a group of ladies walking ahead, until she made it out to the street. Once Brooklyn grabbed Denise's food, she decided to take the long way back. Heading towards the corner, she noticed the guy that stopped for a smoke had moved. She told herself she was just being paranoid—until she noticed that he was behind her as she made her way towards G and 9th. It suddenly dawned on her that maybe Dante was behind her shadow. She pulled out the phone and called Dante.

"What's up, Brook?" Dante asked, his voice registering surprise.

"Is it necessary to have me followed?" Brooklyn glanced back to see if the guy was still trailing her.

"Followed?"

"Don't pretend that you aren't having me followed. I get the point. Next time you say a situation is dangerous, I'll believe you." She noticed that her shadow was on the move.

"Brooklyn, sweetie, I'm not having you followed. When did you notice someone following you?" His voice was filled with concern.

Brooklyn explained everything that happened, from the mall to the office to just now. "Maybe I'm just being paranoid after all that has happened." She informed him about the break-in at work.

"Look, if you're wrong, we can laugh about it later. But if you're right, you have a serious situation on your hands. Can you describe him?"

Brooklyn leaned on the outside of the building right next to her building, watching her shadow pass her and cross the street. "I'm just being a bit of a drama queen. He kept walking."

"If you think you're being followed, don't go home," Dante cautioned. "Call me and I'll meet you some—"

Brooklyn cut him off. "Don't worry about that. I have dinner plans. If I'm followed to the restaurant, then I'll be in good hands." She stood and headed towards her office building.

"Text me after your date with Hunter and let me know you made it home without any incidents." Dante's voice became increasingly stern, with a slight hint of jealousy as he spoke.

"I will. I'm back at work. I've got to go," she replied as she reentered her building.

"Seriously, Brooklyn. Text me, or better yet, call me. Otherwise I'll be banging on your door starting at ten p.m.," Dante stated in a voice that conveyed how serious he was.

"I'll text you. I promise. Bye, Dante." She hung up.

As people milled about her, Brooklyn kept looking to see the face that had been following her. She relaxed when she didn't see any familiar faces besides the ones she was accustomed to seeing every day.

* * *

The man following Brooklyn stood, leaving the newspaper behind on the bench as she entered the building. Walking across the street from the building, he headed for his car. Once in the car, he made a call. He continued to watch the people entering and exiting the building.

When the call connected, he stated, "I think she knows I'm following her."

"That's fine,' Gus replied. "Did she come in with anything other than her purse?"

"Yes, coffee and a computer bag." He pulled out another cigarette and lit it up.

"Tell your replacement to discreetly steal the files out of her bag. If he can't do that, just snatch the whole damn thing."

Chapter Nineteen

Dante waited for Liang in one of their Virginia safe houses. He did not like the idea of Brooklyn being followed again. He hated she'd met Liang, otherwise he could send her to follow Brooklyn. He looked at the clock, wondering what was taking Liang so long. She was just supposed to be doing some digging on Megan. An hour later, he heard a knock on the door and keys jingling in the hallway.

"About time," he huffed as Liang let herself in.

"Dante, Dante, Dante. Miss Megan is something else. This former honor roll student has been arrested for aggravated assault, drugs, and other things. However, it's her talent for hacking computer systems that almost got her put away for a long time." Liang pulled out the notepad and file from her bag and sat next to Dante.

Dante could tell by the way her eyes sparkled that she had found something big. She flipped open the file and slid it in front of him. "Miss Megan is actually Mrs. Megan. This chick had been married for at least a year prior to showing up to work at Bevik Media."

"What? Married to whom?" Dante scanned the file in front of him for information. "You're kidding me, right?"

"Nope, she's married to Alex Michaels." Liang just looked at him.

"What?" He hadn't expected her to be married to TriVision's owner. That would explain why TriVision was able to find his home residence. After Liang's incident, he put his personal residence under an LLC. With Megan's skill set, Dante could only assume that she was able to dig beyond the layers. He made a mental note to have that and other information encrypted so it could no longer be easily found.

"My question is why was she really working for Bevik?" She started jotting in her notebook.

Dante shook his head. "Why did she start dating Ryan if she was married?" It felt like the more they found out, the more questions it produced.

"Don't know. I called her parents to update them on our progress. They were clueless to the fact that their daughter is married." Liang flipped through her notebook. "Now if we find out how she met her husband, maybe we'll understand this mess we're tangled in."

"Hey, I'll go to the parents' this evening. I want to find out who referred them to us." He glanced at the list of questions that they hadn't answered.

"Okay, I'll attempt to find out more on Alex Michaels/Alec McNier and how he met Megan."

"Oh, we may have another problem. Brooklyn thinks she's being followed," Dante reported, debating how much they should tell Megan's parents about their suspicions. It may prevent them from cooperating with them in the future if they had further questions.

"Followed by who?" Liang questioned. "We got TriVision off her."

Dante stood. "She thought it was me trying to teach her a lesson so that she'd listen when I tell her a situation was dangerous."

"Clearly it's not you. Maybe you bringing her with you freaked her out a little." Liang shook her head.

"Probably, but someone breaking into her office this weekend didn't help any." Dante walked into the kitchen, grabbing a soft drink.

"What did they take?"

"From the sounds of it, they ransacked it while looking for a file." Dante reached back into the refrigerator, grabbing Liang's favorite fruit drink.

"They must be looking for something important," she stated as Dante walked over and handed her the drink.

"Yes and that something must be big if it makes someone blow up Tuck's office and break into Brooklyn's office all in one day," Dante spoke as he sat back down.

Liang smiled, opening the drink. "It looks like you got what you wanted."

Dante stared at her, confused. "And what's that?"

"More time with Brooklyn." She shrugged her shoulders and took a sip of her drink.

"How do I get more time with Brooklyn?"

"If she has information, we need it, especially if they're going after it like that." Liang explained then unapologetically added, "I want this case over and if it means you spend time with your ex to accomplish it, then it is game on."

Dante thought about it for a moment. Finding Megan was the best and most efficient way to keep Brooklyn safe. Even if it doesn't put her out of the line of fire, it freed him up to focus on watching over her. "Look, while I am up for spending time with Brooklyn, we need to find out who's behind sending our client to us and why. We also need to find out how Megan met her husband. So …"

"So Brooklyn is not at the top of the list?" Liang raised an eyebrow at him.

"For all we know, they've found what they were looking for. If she has another incident or says she thinks someone is still following her again, we'll reassess things." Dante looked at the scowl on Liang's face. "Look, if I put a male to follow her, it will be hard to tell if she's still being followed or if it's our people. All the other females I trust to watch over her have other obligations right now but will be free to help me out in a couple of days. If she has another incident before that happens, then I will put someone on her immediately."

Liang gave him a very stern, motherly look. "I think if it was any other person besides Brooklyn, you would have put someone on her."

"Our concentration should be on doing what we were hired to do, which was to find Megan."

"You're right. Hopefully, finding Megan will help Brooklyn out as well. Nevertheless, if something happens to Brooklyn because you didn't want to spy on her—" she tilted her drink towards him— "You will never forgive yourself. Think about it."

"I will."

Liang sat her drink down on the table. "And, when you do spend time with her, we need you to be a nosy investigator, not an ex-lover."

"I'm hoping that we'll resolve our case without me having to play P.I. with my ex." Dante drank his soft drink.

Liang grabbed her stuff and headed for the door. "All right, I'll meet you tomorrow around this time for the update."

"Be safe," Dante instructed as he threw out the trash and began gathering his stuff.

He knew why Liang was so sensitive. The traumatic assignment that led to her husband's death had a similar feel to this. Like now, the information they had before them wasn't quite what they thought. They'd known they were going into a precarious situation in an attempt to save their client's sister. They'd found his sister and found out that she was not in danger; but she'd gone into hiding from her foster brother. They'd informed him that they were not able to find her, returning most of his money, minus the nonrefundable deposit and expenses.

After they had wrapped things up with the client, Liang had rushed home for her belated anniversary. Dante had gotten a gut feeling that something wasn't right and decided to follow her out. When she had pulled out, he noticed the client's car trailing her. He had rushed to his car. He just wished she had picked up the phone when he got caught by a train. It may have saved both her and her husband's lives. That's why they'd created two emergency numbers. The first one rings police sirens for very important things. The second ring was a shrieking alarm for things that escalated to extremely dangerous.

To this day, Dante couldn't believe that that client had murdered Liang's husband and almost killed her to get the whereabouts of his sister out of Liang. For six months, Liang was out of work. It was years before Liang stopped doing support and recon and took an occasional case. Now this case turned out to be more complicated and deadly than expected. They needed to wrap it up. The longer they worked the case, the more jittery Liang became, and that was alarming and potentially deadly for him and everyone involved. It didn't help that he was thrown off of his game by having Brooklyn involved. With neither him nor Liang on top of their games, it was in their best interest to solve the case quickly, even if it meant going against some company policies.

* * *

Hunter sat in his office, placing orders for the club to make sure he would be available to enjoy dinner with Brooklyn without interruption. It was a pleasant surprise when she called after the movies to say she decided she would not work late on Monday if he was up to going out for dinner. Normally he didn't work Mondays, but switched his off days. He had come in to meet with some clients to discuss their upcoming VIP event at his club. Hunter rechecked his order against the client's request to make sure he hadn't missed anything, then he hit submit. He was wrapping up the last of his to-do list when his cell phone rang. Levi's cell number hadn't graced his screen in years.

"Man, what's up?" Hunter swiveled his chair to stick the file he had been working with in his follow-up bin on the counter behind his desk. "I haven't heard from you in a minute."

"Yeah, I'm trying to fly under the radar these days. Contacting old friends sometimes brings up old memories, and I find myself falling into old ways," Levi answered.

"So why call now? I'm assuming you got that urge to go back to your old ways under control." Hunter checked his clock and began shutting down his computer.

"It was necessary. Have you heard from Ryan?" Levi asked.

He grabbed his car keys out of his top drawer. "Not in a couple of weeks. I thought he was clean and staying out of trouble. He's part owner of some media company, mainly handling their shipping division."

"I thought that too. That is, until this weekend when his partner died in a suspicious explosion." Levi sighed. "I hope Ryan isn't in trouble but I can't shake the feeling that something's wrong."

"When was the last time you spoke with him?" Hunter grabbed his jacket off the back of the chair.

Levi answered with his voice full of concern, "A couple of months ago, but that's not unusual. We tend to play phone tag, but at least he usually returns my texts."

"Have you spoken to Vince?" Hunter inquired as he locked up and headed to his ride.

"You know me and Vince fell out." Levi's voice trailed off.

"You want me to contact him?" Hunter inquired as he got into his truck. He didn't know all the specifics. All he knew was Levi had used information provided by Vince to blackmail someone.

"If you could, I would appreciate it. If Ryan's in trouble, Vince will find out. I don't think he'd hold what I did against Ryan." Levi sounded as if he was trying to convince himself.

He sat waiting on the garage door to open. "I'll get Vince on it, and I'll check in with you later."

"Thanks. Hopefully my old lifestyle has me thinking the worst, and my baby brother is just distracted by living his own life." Levi muttered goodbye then disconnected.

Hunter switched to hands-free before pulling out, then called to confirm with Brooklyn that she was still meeting him for dinner. They agreed to eat at a restaurant near her job. He was curious about the incident that happened that pushed back their dinner plans for two hours, but she said she'd tell him once they met at the restaurant. Hunter made a quick call to Vince before he forgot. He was at the light at the end of her block when he noticed Brooklyn heading out of the building. Hunter went to call her but before he could dial the number, he saw the danger she was about to step into, and the light couldn't change fast enough.

Chapter Twenty

Brooklyn slung her computer bag onto her shoulder as she headed to her car. She was a little leery of leaving her bag in the car after the break-in at the office. However, she didn't feel that taking it to the restaurant was the best plan either. After pushing her dinner plans with Hunter back two hours, she didn't want to have him wait longer while she dropped the computer off at home. Brooklyn glanced around to see if the guy from earlier was still lingering around, but she saw no one. She was almost at her car when she felt the strap being yanked from her shoulder, which caused her to completely lose grip on the bag. Brooklyn turned quickly, grabbing the bag straps. She and the would be thief struggled for control of the bag. He released the bag like he was going to let her have it, and that sent her and her bag tumbling to the ground. He grabbed the bag and took off running. Brooklyn took off after him, jumping on his back and putting her arms around his neck.

"I'm not going to make it that easy for you!" She started tightening her grip on his neck. He tried to jab her with his elbow, then he spun around, trying to get her off his back. To her surprise, he dropped the bag as he took his hand and pushed both of her legs back. Before she knew it, she could feel his body pitch forward. She locked her knees into his back to prevent him from throwing her forward. He then shifted his weight backwards. Brooklyn groaned as his body smashed her into the pavement. He stood, grabbing the bag and running away.

Hunter ran over to her. "You okay?"

"Don't let him get away." She pointed at the guy running down the street with her bag.

Hunter ran after him.

When he looked back and saw that Hunter was behind him, he cut between two cars. Hunter followed him and almost tripped over Brooklyn's computer bag. He bent down, then stood back up.

"Why did you stop chasing him?" Brooklyn came up from behind Hunter, hitting him on his back.

He held the bag up so she could see it. "'Cause I thought it was the bag that you wanted." Hunter handed her the bag then picked up the files that were scattered on the ground.

"Sheesh, what is really going on? First my office, then this." Brooklyn threw the files into the bag.

"Do you want to file a police report?" Hunter inquired as she looked through her bag.

"I don't think so. The computer is here. It seems like all the files are here. I'll double check later." Brooklyn hoped she didn't regret that decision.

"How about this, we either go to your place or mine and order food in." Hunter grabbed her laptop bag from her as they walked to her car.

"Let's do my place. How about you order it, pick it up, and meet me at my place?" Brooklyn pulled out her car keys.

"How about this? I'll order the food and have it delivered to your place. No way after this incident am I going to let you go home alone." Hunter grabbed her keys out of her hands, glancing at his truck parked in a no parking zone.

Brooklyn slid into her car, grabbing her keys and bag from him. "Well I want orange shrimp and egg rolls."

"I got you." Hunter closed her door, quickly trotting across the street before he got towed.

* * *

Once in his truck, Hunter put his hazard lights on until Brooklyn pulled out. He dialed and ordered their food. He shook his head, picturing Brooklyn jumping on the guy's back. Following her car, he kept checking the rearview mirror to make sure they were not being followed. His cell phone rang.

"Hey, Vince. Thanks for getting back to me so quickly." Hunter sat behind Brooklyn at the light as it started to lightly drizzle.

"You were right. Ryan is in trouble. From what I hear, he's had a few run-ins and is in hiding. Give me a few days, and I'll find out the whole story."

He flicked on his windshield wipers as he pulled off. "Thanks."

"Hunter, don't let Ryan and Levi pull you into any craziness," Vince reminded him.

"Hey, isn't that what I have you for, to make sure I keep my hands clean while I continue to watch my boys' backs?"

"Yeah, we've been boys for a long time, but you need to cut the cord on some friendships." Vince's voice indicated that he was serious.

"Look, I know you and Levi fell out," Hunter began. "But—"

Vince immediately cut him off. "Levi has some heat on him that you don't need in your life. If you allow him…"

"Hey, I know," Hunter stated, defending his actions. "Up until Ryan pulled a disappearing act, I hadn't heard from him. So I don't think he wants to catch up over drinks. He just wants to make sure his brother is all right"

"Fine." Vince huffed. "I'm just warning you to keep your conversation with Levi short and only about his brother. Don't go back down memory lane."

"I get the message loud and clear," Hunter told Vince.

"Good. Is Brooklyn being followed again?" Vince asked.

"I didn't think so, but someone attempted to snatch her bag tonight." Hunter watched as Brooklyn pulled into a parking spot in front of her building. He checked the cars on the street and there were no cars that stood out.

"I'll dig into that further for you. Something about this is bothering me. Since Brooklyn's up to be my next play sister, I got to make sure everything is all right."

"Bye, Vince." Hunter shook his head, smiling.

Laughter filled Hunter's ear. "Oh you don't want to talk about your new love interest?"

"I'd rather spend time with her than talking about her." Hunter parked the truck while keeping an eye on Brooklyn the best he could.

"I'll let you have that. Bye." Vince ended the call.

Hunter got out of the truck and ran up the street to catch up with Brooklyn. He grabbed her computer bag, monitoring the street for trouble.

"Is the food on its way?" Brooklyn questioned as they headed to the door.

"Yes, it's on the way. I can follow instructions, Miss Thing," Hunter said sarcastically as she opened the common door.

She jogged up the stairs to her apartment. "This has been a crazy day."

"It seems like it."

"Now I'm wondering if I should have filled out a police report," she spoke as they entered her apartment. "I got the laptop back but …" She locked the door then pointed to where Hunter should sit the bag down.

"What about the files?" Hunter asked as he grabbed a seat on the couch.

"Well, I didn't bring any business files home. They were personal files. One was full of my personal goals and projects for the next five years. The other was my research on houses, neighborhoods, and statistics." Brooklyn kicked her shoes off near the door then pulled off her suit jacket and laid it over the chair. "With the redoing the waterfront, I would really like to purchase something in Southwest."

"Every time I come into Southwest, it feels like a new building is popping up. In a couple of years this area will be the place to be." Hunter picked up the remote.

"I know, right?" Brooklyn exclaimed as she picked up her computer bag.

"Maybe you should call the police station," Hunter insisted, noticing Brooklyn staring at the bag for a moment before locking it up. "See if they say you should file a report. If they say yes, then we'll ride down and get it done. If they say no ..." Hunter shrugged his shoulders as Brooklyn walked past him, pulling her shirt out of her pants.

"I'm about to change into some chill wear. I'll be right back." She smiled, cutting her eyes back at him.

"You can change right here. I don't mind the show." Hunter gave her a sly grin before flipping through the TV channels.

"Funny. I'll keep that in mind for a later date when we won't be interrupted by our food being delivered." She smiled seductively as she unbuttoned a few buttons on her shirt before heading to her room.

She emerged twenty minutes later barefoot and wearing brown fitted jogging pants with a light tan tank top that had the words *brown sugar* written on the front. Hunter looked up from the television and shook his head.

"I was expecting something different since it took so long for you to come out." Hunter laughed to himself thinking, *I am definitely up for a taste of her brown sugar.*

"I decided to call the police station." Brooklyn sat on the couch then kicked her legs over Hunter's thigh.

"So what did they say?" Hunter shifted her legs slightly so he was angled to look at her.

"Since nothing was taken, they stated I can let it go, but if it happens again, I definitely need to make sure I fill out a report." Brooklyn frowned. "I don't know if I should believe the officer. He didn't seem to want to be bothered with me."

"You sure TriVision Media is above board? I can't recall you having issues like this before." Hunter's hand glided up and down Brooklyn's leg as he spoke.

With a wickedly seductive glint to his eyes, Hunter's hands moved to her upper thigh. He could tell by the way Brooklyn responded they were about to be in trouble.

"Mmm, I guess we can get something to drink while we wait for the food." She quickly swung her legs off his lap and stood. "What do we have, thirty-to-forty-five minutes before it comes?" She took a deep breath and tried to stop thinking too much about the decision she would eventually have to make between Dante and Hunter.

"It shouldn't be that long." Hunter watched as Brooklyn just stood there staring at him.

"When I call before I leave work, it comes at least forty-five minutes to an hour after I get home." Brooklyn looked at her watch as if she was mentally recalculating the estimated delivery time.

"Trust me, it won't take that long. Back to TriVision, they were following you before. Do you think they're behind the break-in and the attempted snatching of your bag?"

"Haven't a clue," Brooklyn replied as she headed into the kitchen. "What are you drinking tonight, wine, beer, or soda?"

"I'd better stick to the soda since you plan to kick me out early tonight." He noticed that she was lost in thought for a moment and attributed it to all that happened at work earlier.

"Who said I was kicking you out early?" Brooklyn grabbed two glasses from the cabinet, rinsing them before filling them with ice.

"BK, I believe your exact words to me were 'dinner, no dessert. We can't stay out late.'" Hunter smiled as his phone rang. "It looks like the food's here."

"What? They've never delivered so quickly." Brooklyn checked her watch.

Hunter held up his finger. "Hey, where are you?" He lifted the phone, speaking to Brooklyn. "Buzz him in."

A minute later there was a knock on the door. He walked over to the door and looked in the peep hole before opening it.

"Thanks for the quick service," Hunter said as he pulled out his wallet.

"For you, anything." He handed him the bag. "You know there's no charge for this."

Hunter passed some money to him. "Just accept this as an appreciation of your time and fast service." Hunter put his wallet back into his pocket.

"Will I see you this Friday?" the delivery guy asked as he slid the money into his pocket.

"Most definitely. Take care." Hunter closed and locked the door, then turned to see Brooklyn standing with her hand on her hips and head cocked to the side. "BK, you should know the service is always better when you're with me." He laughed and headed to the dining room table.

"You're spoiling my behind, making it hard for all the average brothers that come after you." She came over and sat the two glasses down.

"I'm working hard to convince you that you can't do better than me." Hunter pulled the food out of the bag.

"Whatever, Hunter. You're spoiling me now, but when you find your new Sophia, you're going to drop me like a hotcake," Brooklyn teased as she went back into the kitchen for plates and silverware.

"Yeah right, BK. You want to put it on me because you don't want to be the heartbreaker in this scenario," Hunter responded as Brooklyn reentered the dining area.

"Me the heartbreaker? Never." Brooklyn looked at him, smiling devilishly as she sat down.

Hunter raised his eyebrows as he piled food on his plate. "So you never told me how brunch with your ex went." When she didn't answer, he said, "Well tell me about your day then. Clearly it had a lot going on."

Brooklyn poured sweet and sour sauce over her egg rolls then told him all about the break-in at work and her call to Dante because she thought he was having her followed to prove a point.

"Since it wasn't your ex, do you think it's TriVision following you again?" Hunter asked between bites.

"I guess maybe I need to do a little more research on the client. Most of my research is usually focused on the company the client is trying to acquire." Brooklyn responded sounded as if she didn't want to say too much. "Can I have some of your egg foo young? Since ordering Chinese is a treat for me, I usually always stick to my favorite."

"Help yourself." Hunter slid the boxes near her. "There's also crab Rangoon and pot stickers."

"I've never seen pot stickers on their menu." Brooklyn reached in, grabbing one.

"At one point they were, but when they reduced the menu it was taken off. They still make them for me." Hunter smiled and waited to see if she was going to make a smart comment.

"Mmmmm, so how was your day?" Brooklyn asked, thoroughly enjoying the food.

"Not as exciting as yours, just pushing papers today." Hunter thought back to his conversations with Levi and Vince. He decided not to mention it to Brooklyn.

They talked about the latest news and celebrities, laughing about the most embarrassing moments in their past. Hunter helped Brooklyn clean up and they returned to the living room. It was midnight before they knew it. Even though Brooklyn had to work in the morning, she didn't want the night to end. Brooklyn teased him about keeping her up late anyway. He laughed, pulling her into his arms. She resisted the urge to give him a reason to stay. Hunter gave her a quick kiss on the cheek and told her to be safe, then exited.

* * *

Brooklyn locked up behind him, grinning from ear to ear. Something about being with Hunter was good for her soul. All the stress and pressure of the workday just dissipated. The atmosphere he created was becoming addictive. While she loved Dante and was extremely comfortable with him, he never made her feel this sense of peace and feeling of home. She had yet to confirm whether the rumors and accusations of illegal dealings were correct.

Chapter Twenty-One

Dante hated that his visit with Megan's parents only produced more questions. They received several calls from Megan's friends when she first went missing, and one of them suggested they get in touch with Dante's company. They gave Dante the friend's contact information. Liang ran the name against all their cases, current and past. She came up with nothing, and Dante came up with exactly the same thing when he searched for the infamous friend.

Pulling his car into a driveway, Dante honked twice and waited. A few minutes later Liang walked out with a large duffle bag. She threw the bag in the back and slid into the passenger side without a word. Dante pulled off, heading to see Ryan.

"Do you really think Ryan can shed any light on this situation?" Dante questioned.

Liang stopped staring in the side view mirror and looked at Dante. "He and Megan were together for over a year. Is it really possible that Megan could completely stay away from her husband for that long?"

"The question I keep asking myself is why this friend of Megan specifically told her parents to ask for us?" Dante continuously glanced in the rearview mirror. He couldn't wait until they made it to the point where they could discretely switch out the car.

"If the deranged doctor wasn't dead, I'd think it was him." Liang stared out the window.

Dante tried to reassure Liang. "While he did threaten to destroy us and everything we loved, he's not here to make good on that threat."

"I know this sounds crazy, but it's possible that before he got killed in prison he paid someone to execute his plan. He was serving an extremely long sentence," Liang stated with unease in her voice.

"Hey, considering who we're talking about, it's not unreasonable to think that. When we get back from speaking with Ryan, we'll get one of our people to look into who the insane doctor was contacting in his last days. Maybe then we can cross off the possibility that he sent someone after us."

"I hate being so paranoid, but the fear in the pit of my stomach won't go away," Liang declared as they turned onto the road that led to a garage next to an office building.

"Maybe we should give this case to someone else," Dante questioned as he pulled his card off the visor and swiped into the garage. He pulled in and stayed there a moment by the door as it came back down. He drove through the aisle of cars in the blue section until he entered the red zone, then began looking for a space.

"I think that'll work. If this is really about us and not about finding Megan, then the mystery friend will have the parents demand to put us back on the case," Liang stated as he parked.

"Yeah, but the one hole in our theory is that if the contact information the parents gave is not working, how will he find out we are no longer on the case?" Dante turned off the car, pulling out the key and handing it to Liang.

They grabbed their bags, heading for the black truck in the green zone. "We've got to move quickly," Dante stated. "Whatever they're up to must be going down soon if they're breaking into Brooklyn's office." He lifted the hatch on the truck and threw the bags in.

Liang got in and buckled up as Dante did his normal check of the vehicle. He started the truck, exiting the garage through a tunnel that led to an access road about a mile away from the facility. Once they made it to the access road, it was another two-mile drive to get to a main road.

"Dante, I still believe the information we're looking for has unknowingly landed in Brooklyn's hands. Maybe we should focus our energy on finding out what exactly she has that they want back."

"Liang, I know. That's why I plan to spend some more time with her. It's clear that they didn't find what they were looking for, since they tried to snatch her bag."

Liang looked over at him, surprised. "You didn't tell me that."

"I just found out this morning. I called to check in on her when I was getting ready to head out and pick you up." Dante slowed as they made it to the end of the tunnel that led out to the access road. He swiped his card so the gate would lift. "She said she hadn't thought about the incident until I asked her about the break-in at the office." He moved the truck forward and waited for the gate to close before driving away.

"Did they get anything when they snatched her bag?" She pulled out the GPS from the glove compartment and typed in the address.

"I don't think so. I was debating whether I needed to actually have her followed. Brooklyn may not realize how dangerous a situation this is." Dante blocked the negative scenarios out of his mind.

"I thought you stated if she had another incident that you'd put someone on her immediately."

"When we ..."

"With her being on guard, it's going to be hard." Liang continued talking as if Dante wasn't trying to speak. "However, I suggest you stop treating her like the ex that you're trying to get back with and start treating her like an innocent caught in the crossfire. You'll never forgive yourself if something happens to her because you were trying to handle her with kid gloves. Trust me on this," Liang insisted.

"When we come back on the grid, I'll put a call in to have eyes on her full-time. I have a female friend whose assignment ends Friday. She will keep an eye on her starting Friday when Brooklyn is scheduled to get off work until we get back on Saturday."

Liang looked over as if to say 'do you really want to wait?' However, he had no choice. He tried the entire drive to arrange for someone to watch over Brooklyn. The one person he thought would be free to watch her immediately, didn't return his call before he had to go dark.

Dante looked at his phone in the cup holder, wishing he could turn it on and check on Brooklyn. To make that call now would put all of their lives at risk. He couldn't risk having a device active that could allow Megan to hack and track their location.

* * *

The work week flew by for Brooklyn. Since the start to her work week had already been thrown off, this was a late Thursday night for her. She wanted to call Hunter, but his sleep/errand schedule was different on the days he was at the club all night. Anyway she already had plans to hang out with him Friday and Dante on Sunday, once he got back in town.

Luckily she didn't see anyone following her at any point during the day, and that made her relax just a bit. She decided it was best to leave her computer at work since she was leaving so late. The death of Tuck, one of Bevik Media's owners, complicated the acquisition she was working on. Now she had to wait for her company's legal department to get back with her so she would know how to proceed. It made her wonder how Dante's case was wrapped up in Bevik. Brooklyn decided that with what had happened to Tuck, it was best she minded her own business.

Coming home late usually meant that finding a parking spot would be an issue. When she made it home, it looked like she would have to park on the next block, but luckily a car pulled out just ahead of her. All she could think of as she walked to her apartment was that she could not shower and change into her sleeping clothes fast enough. When she opened the door to her place, her mouth dropped. The apartment looked like total chaos. Brooklyn wanted to go in and assess the damage, but after the earlier incident, she thought better of it. She went downstairs, called the police, and waited for them near the entrance.

The rest of the night was a blur. Brooklyn was not comfortable staying in her apartment until she figured out how to handle this situation. Her first instinct was to call Hunter, but he was at the club tonight. It felt wrong to interrupt his evening as if he was her man. She would stay at Alexis' tonight and talk to Hunter tomorrow night over dinner. Considering what Dante did for a living, he might be best suited to help, but she knew he would be out of town until Sunday. Not being able to reach him when she needed him had always been a point of contention between the two of them. Police stood guard while she packed a duffle bag so she could spend the night with Alexis.

***

The doorman at Alexis' building greeted Brooklyn. She signed in with security then headed up to Alexis' condo.

Alexis smiled as she let Brooklyn in. She poured them both a glass of wine while Brooklyn explained what happened. She handed Brooklyn a glass, taking a seat next to her on the couch.

"Well, let me lighten your mood by telling you what happened to me." Alexis shifted on the couch so she was facing Brooklyn.

"Ooh no, what did you do?" Brooklyn asked, looking over her glass of wine before taking a sip.

"Well, I met this older gentleman who has an art studio. We got to talking about art and I told him that I was considering making my hobby my career."

"Your artwork," Brooklyn spoke, slightly surprised but not shocked. "Nothing's strange about that."

Alexis cut her eyes at her as if to say just wait. "You know strange things always happen to me. So I was a little apprehensive since he was kind of flirting, but LaShawn convinced me that this could be a great opportunity." Alexis finished her glass of wine and got up to pour herself another.

Brooklyn chuckled. "You … apprehensive?"

"Yes, it does happen." Alexis responded with an attitude.

"You're right. I'm being judgmental." Brooklyn apologized. "What happened?"

Alexis returned with the entire bottle of wine. "This supposedly well-to-do man took me to a little hole in the wall restaurant—I will save that story for later—then we went over to his art studio." Alexis poured a little more wine into Brooklyn's glass.

"Was he all over you?"

"I've done some crazy things in my life, but he wasn't going to be one of them. So I played along and let him get his feel on while I thought about how to get out of the situation." Alexis looked as if she was trying not to picture the scene in her head.

Brooklyn had never known Alexis to allow anyone to touch her that she didn't want touching her.

Alexis poured more wine into her glass. "Don't give me that same speech that LaShawn did about I would have knocked his behind out. If the cops were called, who would they believe? The older, established man or the woman that is forty years younger than him?"

"What? You didn't want to come across as the gold digger going after the old man's money?" Brooklyn laughed, finishing off her drink.

"Hell naw. I'm not trying to land my behind in jail. I could see me knocking him out, then him bringing me up on assault charges. To boot, he was my ride home," she replied, staring over the wine glass at Brooklyn.

"So how in the hell did you get out of it without giving up the cookies?" Brooklyn put her hand over the top of her glass so Alexis wouldn't pour her any more wine.

"Well, I thought I had convinced him that a free feel was as good as it got. But when he dropped his pants and started talking about giving me a happy ending, I knew I was in trouble. So I sent an S.O.S call to LaShawn on the sly." Alexis smiled, shaking her head at herself. "I had to dial LaShawn then hang up so that she would call me back."

Brooklyn laughed. "Too funny. Only you."

"Not that damn funny. I finally got him to take me home, but not until after watching him give himself a pleasurable ending. Oh he promised that next time we'll have to make time to thoroughly enjoy each other." Alexis rolled her eyes.

"You're lying." Brooklyn laughed harder, imaging the scenario.

"I'm giving you the edited version, but trust and believe that this incident goes on the wall of shame, right beside the pole incident." Alexis stood, grabbing the empty bottle of wine and heading into the kitchen.

"Oh lawd," Brooklyn cried out, trying to contain her laughter.

"Oh lawd is right. I'm all about getting mine, but I've got to be attracted to it. I damn near gagged when he kissed me." Alexis made a face.

"I'm really surprised that you didn't go all crazy on him." Brooklyn had seen that happen before. It wasn't a pretty sight.

"Look, I'm serious about the career change. I can survive this incident and still possibly not have trouble down the road if my path crosses his. I just hope there were no cameras present." Her eyes widened as she looked at Brooklyn. "I never want to see the playback on that mess."

"Hey, I'm just glad things didn't get ugly."

Alexis went into the linen closet and pulled out some towels. "Yeah his old butt was six feet six, thick, and muscular. He looked like if he hit me once I would shatter like broken glass. Just picturing him actually hitting me makes me shudder." Alexis hugged the towels, shaking her body to emphasize her point. Handing the towels to Brooklyn, she declared, "I know I'm a mess. But me and Ed got a good thing and I'm content with that right now." Alexis smiled.

"You don't say. Wow! Alexis is settling down." Brooklyn laughed, having a hard time picturing that happening.

"Whatever! Have you gotten some from Hunter yet?" Alexis tilted her head as she waited for a response.

"Damn, where did that come from? We were talking about you." Brooklyn started messing with her bag.

"I was just wondering. Girl, if he's half as good as his cousin, you better get you some of that." Alexis' sly grin revealed that she was using the subject of Hunter to get the conversation off of her settling down with one man.

"You are silly." Brooklyn pulled her sleeping clothes out of her bag.

"I'm serious." A huge smile crossed her face.

"Hunter told me you wore him down and he agreed to go out with you. But catching you with his cousin getting it on in his private bathroom put a stop to the date." Brooklyn watched as Alexis avoided making eye contact for a moment. "So thanks for not being able to keep your hands off his cousin."

"While I indulged in the appetizer instead of devouring the main course, the appetizer had me so delighted that I have not had a single regret about it," Alexis stated smugly. "So I'm going to tell you again, you better get you some from Hunter. I heard some of the rumors about Hunter's talent in the bedroom. If they are true, they put his cousin's skills to shame."

"I'll keep that in mind." Brooklyn didn't want to get into the Hunter/ Dante conversation with Alexis. Alexis wasn't the friend that she had those types of discussions with.

"You do that, but since both of us have to work in the morning, I'll see you in a couple of hours. You know where everything is." Alexis headed to her room.

Brooklyn looked at her phone, tempted to text Hunter, but decided just to tell him when he called to confirm the dinner date. She grabbed the towels, her sleeping clothes, her overnight bag, and headed to Alexis' guest room. Sleep was essential to functioning properly and with all that was going on, that is exactly what she needed to do.

Chapter Twenty-Two

The club was finally quiet and the last employee had left for the night. Hunter made sure everything was locked up before heading to the office. Since he knew he wouldn't be in tomorrow night, he double checked to make sure everything was in order for the next night. The last thing he wanted was for his date with Brooklyn to be interrupted by business. He knew her ex had lost brownie points for allowing business to interrupt their dates. On the other hand, Hunter knew he was at a disadvantage because her ex had a foothold on her heart. However, he thought he and Brooklyn had something special that he was willing to fight for. He would never admit it to her, but she had him truly thinking things that he had never thought before. Hunter laughed, imagining himself switching his work schedule to days to be able to spend more time with her and maybe ultimately settle down. The idea of coming home to her every night excited him. He never thought of marriage as an option, but because of Brooklyn, it was now in the forefront of his thoughts. His cell phone ringing stopped his daydreaming.

He answered quickly when he saw who it was. "Hey, Vince. What did you find out?"

"That Ryan has landed in major trouble. It's like finding a penny buried under ten feet of rubble. It's an extremely complicated situation. Ryan is fine for now. Your new girlfriend's ex's crew is keeping him safe." Vince spoke clearly, but swiftly.

"What? Evidently not that safe if you were able to find out about it." Hunter did not like that fact that Brooklyn's ex was wrapped up in this.

"It's only because Ryan had his nose wide open and almost got himself killed over a girl. I'm continuously pulling back the layers to get to the root of what's really going on. Until I figure it out, keep an eye out on Brooklyn." Vince replied, sounding like he didn't think wise to go into all the details with Hunter.

"Vince, you need to be honest with me and tell me what's going on." Hunter needed to know what type of situation he was getting into. Was it something he could handle on his own or did he need some help?

"Bruh, I'm trying to find out. Right now the only thing I know for sure is that Bevik Media and TriVision Media are not what they seem."

"I figured that out when they started following Brooklyn," Hunter huffed, frustrated that he hadn't dug deeper into the company in the beginning.

"Yeah, but from what I hear, they were originally keeping an eye on her ex's place. When she showed up there, someone recognized her," Vince explained.

"Why were they watching her ex's place?" Hunter asked, sounding as if he was blaming himself.

"Hunter, did you not hear me when I said this is a complicated situation? Look, the only reason I'm contacting you now is because Brooklyn's name keeps coming up." Vince knew how much Hunter cared for Brooklyn.

"How worried should I be?" He held his breath as he waited for Vince to answer.

"Very. From what I hear, Ryan's partner, Tuck, was attempting to blackmail someone, and as you know from Levi, that didn't turn out so well. Two more of Tuck's associates are missing. Plus Tuck's wife seems to be in hiding and the information that was to be used to do the blackmailing is rumored to be in Brooklyn's possession."

Hunter could tell Vince didn't want to say too much more than that until he figured out what was really going on. "I don't think she has it. They broke into her office and also tried to snatch her bag but—"

"Listen," Vince interrupted. "They broke into her apartment tonight."

"What? She didn't call me." Hunter started shutting down his computer.

"I sent someone over to check on her. She must be staying with a friend because her car isn't there." Vince tried to offer Hunter some comfort.

"Well that's good," Hunter replied, although he would have preferred for Brooklyn to come to him.

"Hunter, go home, get some rest, and come up with every excuse to spend time with her until I get more information. Can you handle that?" Vince quieted, waiting a little before a reply came.

Hunter finally answered. "I can handle that. Thanks, man."

"You might need to knock the rust off of those old school habits that you developed when we used to hang out all the time." Vince hinted at the seriousness of the situation.

"Basically, you're saying that anything might jump off at any time." Hunter's life had finally gotten to the point where he rarely had to look over his shoulder and he didn't have to always be on guard. It had a lot to do with the fact that he didn't constantly hang out with his old crew like he did in his younger years. Vince was the only one that he talked to on a regular basis. Everybody else just checked in every once in a while. They got together occasionally for drinks or dinner, but nothing like how they used to kick it.

"Man, whoever is orchestrating this is good." Vince paused then reluctantly admitted, "It's been a long time since I've had this much trouble getting to the bottom of something."

"Yes, and that's what has me concerned," Hunter confessed as he tried not to run scenarios through his mind.

"Stay alert and I'll work on getting you answers." Vince hung up without an official goodbye.

Hunter opened his safe, debating whether he needed to start carrying his gun again. He closed the safe without grabbing his Glock. When he headed to his car, he hoped he didn't come to regret leaving the gun. History had taught him that things could quickly go wrong when guns were involved. The last thing he needed to do was make the situation worse.

* * *

Dante and Liang came through the back door of the little brick house. As they headed to the living room, they nodded their heads at the guys sitting in the kitchen. The two guys guarding Ryan left out of the living room when the pair entered. Ryan sat up and turned off the television. Liang stood near the bulletproof window. Dante sat in the chair near Ryan. The tension in the air was undeniable as he began asking Ryan some of the same questions they asked before, along with some new ones. Ryan reiterated what they already knew. Dante started to think this trip was a waste of time. Shockingly, it was not. It provided them with something new to work with. Liang looked over at Dante as Ryan stated, "I still can't believe Tuck is dead. I should have listened to him when he told me that I needed to stay away from Megan, that she was trouble that I didn't need." Ryan kept rubbing his head and his neck like a nervous tick.

"When did this happen?" Dante leaned forward in his seat.

"The last time I saw Tuck, he told me that Megan wasn't what she seemed and that I needed to get away from her and lay low for a while. He offered to help me out." Ryan stood and started pacing back and forth.

"Did he say why?" Liang asked as she glanced out the window.

"No, he just stated that the story that she was feeding me wasn't exactly true." Ryan sat back down.

"What story was that?" Dante questioned.

"She claims that she came across an extra shipment of specialty DVDs that wasn't on the docket. When she opened one and played it, it contained data and information on people and organizations. Megan thought Tuck was doing something illegal, and she panicked." Ryan reached for the drink he left on the coffee table.

"Is that when you two took off?" Dante inquired.

"Yeah, which is why when Tuck caught up with me, I thought he was lying. Until …"

"Until what?" Liang looked at him intensely as she typed notes into her tablet.

"Until I tried to contact Megan and they tracked me to the safe house. I just couldn't believe Megan was a master hacker and could track me. Tuck was right when he told me not to use electronic devices. Once they tracked me to the safe house, I knew." Ryan looked as if he was trying to recall his conversation with Megan.

"What do you know about Megan prior to her coming to Bevik?" Dante asked as he scrolled through his tablet checking off questions.

"Like me, she had some previous run-ins with the law. This job was her attempt to clean up her act. Her parents threatened if she got in trouble again, they were cutting her off. So her friend called Tuck and got her the job." Ryan shrugged his shoulders. "Nothing stood out as strange to me about that at the time. Now I wished I'd bothered to ask what type of trouble she had gotten herself into."

Dante and Liang looked at each other. Pieces of the puzzle were finally starting to make sense. Megan went to work in Bevik Media's shipping department in hopes of finding something that she was planning to use Ryan's skill to procure. They continued questioning Ryan for about another hour, then left to see if they could track down the infamous Megan.

When they arrived at another one of their rural Maryland safe houses, Liang pulled out her laptop. "Megan's our missing piece. The question is, what was she hacking when she left Bevik?"

"Better question, who got her the job and was Tuck using her special talent?" Dante paced the room as he contemplated the case.

"I still can't figure out what they are looking for in Brooklyn's file. We looked through her apartment and her office after that weekend you bumped into her at Hunter's club. Neither of us saw anything that was unusual." Liang exhaled heavily as she set up her work station at the table.

"Yeah, but maybe the files were in the office when we checked her home or vice versa." He knew Brooklyn was good for working from home. "Or maybe there was a new batch of files sent to her office."

"Okay, as far as we know, TriVision was above board and Bevik Media is rumored to be shipping stuff other than movie DVDs." Liang tapped her fingers on the table and waited for her laptop to come to life.

"Yes, but the intel on what they were shipping out other than DVDs has been inconsistent, so we can't trust it." He stopped pacing and sat down next to Liang at the table.

"Maybe it is accurate. Maybe what Tuck shipped out depended on his client." Liang grabbed her notebook and a pen. "Think about what Megan told Ryan that she found a DVD with data on people and organizations."

"You maybe right, especially since taking on Bevik in my opinion would do little to improve TriVision's status." Dante looked over the breakdown of the two businesses.

"What does Bevik Media really have that TriVision is willing to pay millions of dollars to acquire?" Liang flipped through her notebook, writing something down before returning to pecking on the keys of the laptop.

"Is the friend that referred Megan's parents to us the same person that got Megan into Bevik Media? Better question is why did Tuck let her in?" Dante was formulating a theory, but he wasn't ready to tell Liang yet.

"Okay, let's review what we've got. Master hacker Megan is sent into the shipping department of Bevik to access something for TriVision." Liang paused, writing in her notebook. "After two years, she clearly didn't find what she was looking for so TriVision tries to buy out Bevik. Why did Tuck and Ryan agree?"

"Look, I'm going to run back out to see Ryan and ask him about the business side of Bevik." Dante stood, grabbing his tablet and truck keys.

"Ryan clearly wasn't a part of the illegal side of the business," Liang interjected as she reviewed the information.

"You may be right. If we understand the dynamics of Bevik, maybe it will help us make sense of this." Dante wondered if this tied into the sudden influx of clients asking to work with him and Liang. The clients rarely hired them specifically. Over the last few years, there had been several requests for them. It was because Liang wasn't taking cases at the time that it didn't raise any red flags. Dante was wondering if Megan was using Bevik Media to search for Liang. If Megan figured out who Tuck's associate that was rumored to acquire all of Tuck's special client's hard-to-find information, she possibly could have wanted to use him to track down Liang.

Dante peered out the window into darkness. "Tuck didn't know Ryan and Megan were an item. Why didn't Megan want Tuck to know she was dating Ryan?"

Liang stood, stretching a bit before heading into the kitchen. "Yes, and did Megan specifically target Ryan? If so, why?"

"It must have to do with the trouble that Ryan has been trying to stay out of. Pull up his info again. Let's see what Megan was trying to pull him back into." Dante grabbed his jacket.

"I'm on it." She grabbed a bottle of water out the refrigerator then headed back to her work station.

"You know what? We'll talk to Ryan in the morning. I'll dig into Ryan's information, you dig into Megan's, then we'll go from there." Dante set his jacket down. If it was Liang they were after, it wasn't smart to leave her alone to go ask Ryan questions. At least this way, he could pull the records of the cases over the years where clients specifically requested them and see if the date that the requests stopped correlated with when Megan started at Bevik Media. He also needed to see if the requests restarted after TriVision threatened to take over.

Liang's shoulders visibly dropped in relief as Dante announced that he was staying. As he sat back down at the table, she stated, "Good thinking. We can ask him all the questions in one more visit."

"Did you bring the file on Tuck?" Dante asked, noticing that Liang had started staring off into space.

"Yeah." She reached in her bag and handed him a flash drive.

Dante got up, grabbing a few things out of the refrigerator before sitting back down. "We also need to check to see what other Bevik personnel have gone missing."

"I'm on it." Liang's fingers started moving quickly over her keyboard. "Whoever is missing is involved in the illegal part of the business."

"Exactly, which means they could have the answers that we're searching for." Dante smiled as he started researching information.

They worked well into the morning before shutting down their laptops and calling it a night. Dante felt a sense of relief, like they finally had a handle on this case. Seven years ago, Dante and Liang's lives went from both of them talking about settling down to both of them scrambling to survive. When Liang got shot, he and Brooklyn were discussing making their unique relationship official. He maintained their relationship for as long as he could. But when the deranged doctor threatened in court to get revenge, the image of Liang's husband popped into his head. He couldn't imagine having to find Brooklyn like that. Looking back, he should have taken the route Liang had taken and accepted a position that didn't require him to be in the field. Now he wished they hadn't talked Liang back into taking cases.

Chapter Twenty-Three

After debating the pros and cons of her current situation, Brooklyn decided she needed Dante's help. She was a little nervous about going to work as she left Alexis' place. It was a great relief when Hunter called to reconfirm their dinner plans. They talked during her entire ride in. After she parked in front of the building, Brooklyn looked around to see if there were any familiar faces. She rushed to her office to call Dante, but in the middle of dialing, she decided it was best to make the call in the conference room. She was paranoid that there were cameras or listening devices in her office. Keeping her game face on, she moved through the halls, speaking to co-workers.

Upon entering the conference room, she closed the door and pulled out her cell phone. "Hey, Dante, I know you're out of town and out of touch until Sunday morning, but the moment you get this message, call me. My apartment was broken into last night. I think I need your skills to figure out what's going on without costing me my job. So please call me. Love ya. Bye."

Brooklyn leaned on the door and exhaled. Now she understood that he wasn't lying when he said he loved her but his job would put an unfair strain on their relationship. *Is Dante really willing to give up his career for me?* Brooklyn wondered. *Would he come to resent me and I lose the man I love anyway?* Brooklyn glanced down at her phone. *One issue at a time.* She shook her head, slid her cell into her suit pocket, and then exited the conference room, almost jumping out of her skin when Denise ran into her.

"Brooklyn, you okay?" Denise touched her shoulder. "I didn't know anyone was in there."

Putting her hand over her heart, Brooklyn answered, "Girl, I almost screamed."

"Sorry about that," Denise offered. "I was coming to your office to tell you that your four o'clock meeting was cancelled. Legal stated they would get back with us on the Bevik Media/TriVision Media situation. According to what I heard, the big guys are having trouble getting someone from TriVision Media to get back in touch with them."

"Well that's great. I would love to get out of here early. It's been a hell of a week." Brooklyn and Denise walked and talked as they headed back towards her office.

As they entered Brooklyn's office, Denise asked, "Do you plan to see Hunter and Dante both this weekend?"

"Yeah, having dinner with Hunter tonight and most likely hanging with him Saturday. Dante returns Sunday, so I'll be hanging out with him then." Brooklyn smiled, shaking her head.

"Player, player." Denise teased. "Can you be my mentor?"

Brooklyn closed the door. "As your mentor, I advise against putting yourself in this predicament."

"What's going on?" Denise inquired in a serious tone.

"I …" She exhaled, trying to find the words to express herself. "I had a friend who turned up pregnant, not knowing who the father was because she was hopping between two guys' beds. She miscarried and was left grieving alone for the child."

Denise scrunched up her nose in confusion as she took a seat. "What does that have to do with Dante and Hunter? You haven't slept with either of them since you started dating them both."

"That's the problem. When I'm with one of them, it feels like he's the only one in my life. It's like I forget about the other one until something happens to remind me that I'm not just dating one man." Brooklyn plopped down in her office chair with a huff. "I could never see how my friend had gotten herself in that situation until now. Here I am putting myself at risk of being in the same predicament."

Denise slanted her body forward, giving a maternal look. "Hey, you'll just have to roll the dice and pick who you want to be with."

"That won't be an easy choice." Brooklyn cut her eyes over at Denise and sighed.

"Continuing to date them both will only make that decision harder. And this isn't one of those situations where you avoid making a decision to see how things play out."

"Ugh! Dammit, I don't want to lose either one of them. But you're right. This month will be the last of me having two men," Brooklyn declared as she gathered the paperwork she had been working on. "I guess I'd better get to work."

"Well if your schedule allows, how about we do lunch? We can finish this conversation then." Denise stood, turned to walk out, then circled back. "Oh, do you have a minute to talk about the other project we're working on?" She grabbed a seat when Brooklyn nodded.

For the time being, Brooklyn put all thoughts of Hunter, Dante, and the break-in aside.

* * *

Hunter knew he had to wrap up what he was doing at the club so he could make it to the restaurant on time to meet Brooklyn. He frowned when his cell rang, until he saw who it was. Using his shoulder to hold the phone to his ear, he answered, "Hey, Vince, I didn't expect to hear from you so soon."

"Well, I didn't expect to contact you this soon but I found the man I was looking for—kind of sort of."

Hunter knew how Vince operated, but he didn't want to be shielded from the entire truth in this instance. "What do you mean kind of sort of?"

"I've been looking for Tuck's other partner, Alec McNier," Vince explained.

Hunter got up, made sure his office door was locked, and returned to his desk. "I take it he's Tuck's partner on the other side of the business."

"Yes. Look, I need to get through a lot of information quickly, but while I'm doing it, I need you to stop what you're doing and get to your girl," Vince conveyed calmly.

"Well, get to it," Hunter said as he closed out the files on his computer, shut it down, then grabbed his work bag.

"Alec McNier referred some woman named Megan to Tuck. Tuck is in the business of shipping digital payments and information. However, it slipped past him that his new partner/money man was not who he said he was. Tuck took on a new partner because he was trying to expand his business. I had to do some more digging to find out who he thought he was aligning himself to." Vince's voice was one level above a whisper.

"What happened?" Hunter asked as he did a quick sweep of the office to make sure he hadn't forgotten anything. He exited and headed towards the car. Stopping, he turned around and headed to his safe.

"Tuck caught Megan snooping and shut her out of the special shipments."

"Why didn't he fire her?" Hunter inquired as he grabbed his gun and locked the safe back up. He hoped that he didn't have to use it.

"Long story short, we believe Tuck found out Megan's connection to TriVision. He wanted to know what she and Alec McNier were really after, which is how he found out that the guy that vouched for McNier as being legit was blackmailed. According to Bobbie, Tuck's second in command, Tuck recently started putting the pieces together when he was asked about Ryan and Megan dating."

Hunter shook his head, knowing Ryan's special skill set. "Megan wants Ryan's skills for breaking into highly secured places." He wished Ryan was a better people reader.

"Exactly," Vince exclaimed. "She was secretly dating him because Alec had told Tuck that Megan's husband was doing time."

"What does all of this have to do with Brooklyn?" Hunter made it to his car in the garage and peeled out into the parking lot, hitting the remote to close the door then he pulled into the street.

"Tuck found something to back TriVision off him, or so he thought," Vince stated.

Hunter's Bluetooth took over. "Don't tell me Brooklyn has it."

"According to Bobbie, Tuck sent it to her office because he thought it was the safest place."

"Dammit." Hunter glanced at the clock as Vince muttered curses. "What?"

"Ummm." Vince stuttered as if he was thinking of a way to avoid answering the question. "Oh, sorry. I was getting a message about something else. Anyway, Bobbie's trying to locate Tuck's go-to guy, Aaron. Tuck used him to get Megan away from Ryan."

Hunter weaved through the rush hour street traffic. "And that didn't alert her that Tuck was onto her and McNier's agenda?"

"Bobbie said Tuck gave her the impression that she was meeting someone that would give her the information she'd been looking for. Aaron's a little slow, so Tuck and Bobbie always gave him a cover story. Megan knew that Aaron wasn't there to get her away from Ryan and played along with it." Vince's voice conveyed that he wouldn't go into details on how Tuck really convinced Megan to agree to it.

"Wait, I have to interrupt. Does Tuck have a secure facility that Megan wants Ryan to break into? If so, why didn't he take the information there?" Hunter didn't like the idea of Brooklyn holding the smoking gun.

"His every move has been monitored over the last few months. Tuck didn't want to risk it. There were only a select few who knew the location of the facility." Vince paused. "I'm not trying to get into how the business works. You don't need to know all that."

Hunter knew he had to deal with the situation at hand and not speculate. "Vince, I don't like this."

"You shouldn't. Look, Bobbie has a meeting with the data specialist, who works in their remote office, to find out what information he gave Tuck. He's still tracking Aaron down. So I won't have any more information until Bobbie does his thing."

Hunter kept an eye out for cops as he sped through the streets. "I know you didn't want to tell me so much."

Vince stated, "You needed to have some sort of idea what you're dealing with."

"Thanks, Vince." Hunter knew he'd be hitting traffic soon. He hoped it wasn't terrible.

"Hunter, get Brooklyn somewhere safe and let me do the rest. You've managed to keep your hands clean. The one thing I know is that situations like this can change your life in an instant and things happen that you can't take back," Vince stated as if he hoped Hunter heeded his warning.

"Hopefully it won't come down to that." Hunter slowed some, thinking it wouldn't be a good idea to get pulled over.

The sound of someone knocking on Vince's car window could be heard as he told Hunter, "Text me when you and Brooklyn are somewhere safe."

Hunter was not happy about the update Vince had given him. He had just disconnected with Vince when Brooklyn called. "Hey, beautiful, I was just about to call you. I was going to suggest that I pick you up from work."

"Well I was calling to let you know I got off work early. I'm heading over to the restaurant now. I should be there soon." Brooklyn sounded excited to get her weekend started.

Hunter took the first opportunity to start heading towards Shirlington. "I should be there a few minutes after you."

"Well, I'll grab a table while I wait and you can save your Mister Big Shot card for another time." She laughed.

"Funny." Hunter's mind raced, trying to figure out the best way to handle this without freaking her out. "BK, maybe we should skip the restaurant and you meet me at my place. Let me cook for you."

"While I'm eager to have you cook for me, my mouth has been watering all day for an everything-but-the-kitchen-sink pizza, extra sauce, no anchovies, on a wheat crust." She smacked her lips as if she was eating. "So unless you know how to make one of those, I'll take a rain check for another day."

Hunter insisted, "I can order and have it delivered."

"What's going on, Hunter?" Brooklyn asked, sounding as if she did not like the tone of his voice.

"Hey, after what you told me about your apartment being broken into, I just started to think maybe it's best for us not to be out at a restaurant." Hunter checked the clock on the dashboard, wondering how close she was to their destination.

"I'm more than willing to relocate dinner to your place tonight, but I need a drink."

"Baby girl, let me order the pizza and I can mix up whatever you want to drink." His home bar always stayed fully stocked.

"Okay."

Given how stubborn and independent she could be, Hunter was shocked but relieved when she gave in to his request. That feeling lasted all of two seconds, then he heard her car door slam, followed by the sound of her car alarm beeping and her heels clicking on pavement. "What are you doing?" he just about screamed into the phone.

"Look, I'm not even three steps from the grocery store." He could imagine her putting her hand on her hip. "I'm just going to pick up my prescription and grab some cash so I can get a shake at the Shake Shack on the way to your house."

"I'm less than a minute away from you." Hunter sped through the yellow light. "Do you really need that prescription today because I'll give you the cash." He hadn't figured out how to express how serious the situation was without telling her all the details. "Would you trust me when I say we need to head straight for my place? I'll explain all the whys when we get there."

"But I'm in the store already." Brooklyn paused. "I'll call you when I get back to the car."

"Brooklyn!" Hunter shouted to the silence on the other end. "Dammit!"

He was at the end of the block that she was on, but the thick traffic was moving in spurts. He had only made it to the middle of the block by the time Brooklyn exited the store. With all the traffic, she didn't notice him as she strutted to the parking lot. Hunter's heart stopped when he saw a white van pull alongside her and the side door open. It felt like déjà vu as he watched things unfold, feeling much more helpless than during the previous incident. He started leaning on his horn, trying to get the car in front of him to move out of his way, but the driver was doing a slow motion parallel park. Hunter threw his car into reverse, but couldn't go anywhere for the line of cars behind him. And even though there was no oncoming traffic at the moment, the tall median dividing the two sides of the street kept him from jumping in those lanes to get to Brooklyn.

A guy in black jumped out of the van and grabbed Brooklyn. She elbowed him in the face and started running back towards the store.

Hunter put the car in drive again and tried to edge around the guy who was still trying to park, but there wasn't enough room. *If this fool can't get that little raggedy car in the space an SUV came out of, he shouldn't be driving!* He leaned on his horn again. He debated jumping out the car, but it wouldn't do Brooklyn any good if they got her in the van before he made it to her. Hunter watched helplessly as Brooklyn fought the guy who grabbed her again. Another guy jumped out of the van and grabbed her feet. Brooklyn's body was bucking until the guy held a cloth over her mouth.

The car in front of Hunter finally moved enough for him to maneuver around. The two men threw Brooklyn into the van and closed the door just as he reached the driveway leading to the parking lot. He sped up, using his car to block the van's path. The van went into reverse, hitting a car coming out of a parking space. Swerving around that car, the van did a fast backward turn then headed for the other exit. Hunter followed, passing the hit car as the driver jumped out and began yelling at the van. Never taking his eyes off of the van, Hunter called the police and told them what was happening. He pursued the van down the street speeding through a light to stay on its tail. When the van hit a main street, it begin weaving in and out of traffic. Hunter stayed on them, jumping lanes whenever they did.

The van hopped on 395 North into slow-moving traffic then merged to get off at Glebe Road West. After getting through the congested off-ramp, Hunter used the long stretch to cut the distance between them down to one car. The van veered to the right as if it was going to turn onto Jeffery Davis Highway. Hunter did the same, giving the emergency operator the direction the van was headed and ignored the repeated instructions not to pursue the vehicle.

"Don't do it!" Hunter screamed as the van started cutting across lanes of traffic to make a left turn onto Jeffery Davis Highway. He held his breath, watching the van execute this dangerous maneuver in an attempt to shake him off their tail.

He exhaled when they made it. The traffic wouldn't allow him to pull that maneuver safely, so he took the right. At the first opportunity, he did a u-turn. Hunter was not feeling very confident as he sped through the street, turning onto the block where he'd lost the van. It was nowhere in sight. He informed that emergency operator where he lost them and disconnected the call. The fact that he didn't hear or see any flashing lights didn't comfort him. He drove a couple more blocks before he hit the steering wheel in frustration.

"Dammit!" He started driving to the police station. "Call Vince," he commanded and waited as his phone dialed up Vince.

"They got her." He sighed as soon as Vince answered.

"I'll get the boys on it. You know the protocol," Vince replied.

"Yes, heading there now." Hunter stopped at the red light. He grabbed his Glock from between the seats and placed it in the glove compartment.

"My associate had been in the middle of something and couldn't get me the information on the plans to snatch Brooklyn earlier. Otherwise, this would have never happened." Vince apologized. "I will check in with you later."

"Later."

Hunter questioned every move that he'd made from the moment Brooklyn called. Now he wished he had just told her straight up that he thought she was in danger. Hell, he wished he would have rammed the car that was trying to park and just gotten to her. While it would have been risky, he wished he would have rolled down his window and shot the tires out on the van. It was all water under the bridge. Brooklyn was gone. Hunter parked his car and took a deep breath before heading into the police station.

Chapter Twenty-Four

"I think she's coming to," Brooklyn heard a husky male voice say. She tried to open her eyes, but realized they were covered and her hands were tied. In an instant, it all came back to her. She had been kidnapped. *All because I didn't pay attention to the urgency in Hunter's voice.* Now more than anything she wished she had listened to him.

"What do you want from me?" she asked, hoping that because they blindfolded her they were planning to let her go.

"We don't want anything from you, little lady. So sit back and enjoy the ride. You can ask our client what he wants with you once we drop you off."

"But—"

"Not another word or I'll have to gag you." The tone of voice let Brooklyn know he was serious. She was smart enough to keep quiet. Her mind on the other hand was busy trying to figure out what was going on. Why had she been grabbed now? Did they think she had something they needed? Is that why they'd broken into her office and her place? She was certain that the men that grabbed her didn't have current plans to harm her, but she wasn't certain of their client's plans. That unknown element made her feel sick to her stomach. What the hell was all this about?

They drove about an hour longer before they turned off the smooth highway and onto a bumpy, uneven road. The longer they drove on the road, the less Brooklyn heard the sounds of other cars. It felt like another twenty minutes or so before the van finally came to a halt. Brooklyn jumped as someone opened the side door. "Come on, little lady. Your host awaits." Someone grabbed her by the arm and pulled her out the van. She tried to pull away, but she was held firm.

Brooklyn was led up some uneven stairs and into a dank smelling place. "Here's the package." She was pushed slightly ahead of her captors. "Now if you'll give us our payment, we'll be on our way."

"Not a problem." A new masculine voice sneered then two shots fired and Brooklyn heard two bodies hit the floor.

* * *

Hunter left the police station and called Vince. "Any news?" He hated feeling helpless.

"We're on the trail, but give me a little time," Vince stated. "I already have a good lead, but don't want to say any more until I'm sure it'll pan out."

"Vince, you have to give me something," Hunter begged, hopping into his car.

"You could help me out by contacting Brooklyn's ex and seeing if he can pick up any leads." Hunter could tell that Vince was trying to give him something to do that was productive but that would also keep him out the way. "Maybe work with him and keep me posted. That way, we have more irons in the fire and can move faster."

"I would, but I don't have Dante's number." Hunter hissed through gritted teeth.

Vince asked, "You have a pen?"

Hunter dug through his glove box and pulled out pen and paper. Vince gave him Dante's number, promised to keep in contact, and then hung up. He didn't even want to know why Vince had Dante's number on hand.

Hunter dialed Dante's number. To his annoyance, it immediately went to voicemail. *Dammit, Dante, now is not the time to be hard to reach,* he thought as he began to leave a message. "This is Hunter. Brooklyn's in trouble, call me back ASAP." He hung up and dialed again. He was going to keep calling until Dante answered.

He was fuming by the time he reached his place. He had continued to call Dante every five to ten minutes and still hadn't gotten him. He grabbed his gun out of the glove compartment, tucking it in the waistband of his pants. Speed walking, he headed to the stairs and took them two at a time until he made it to his floor. Inside his home, he went in search of his old phone book that had Brooklyn's friends' numbers. Some of the info had probably changed over the years, but he was counting on someone's being the same. Hunter dialed Dante a few more times as he looked for the book. When he found it, the first number he searched for was LaShawn's. She was most likely the one that Brooklyn gave her extra key to. He wanted to search Brooklyn's place for the file. Before dialing LaShawn, he called Dante again.

"This had better be an emergency, with the way you're ringing my phone," Dante answered, annoyed.

"Hell, man, how could it not be?" Hunter yelled, then took a breath to calm down. "This is Hunter. Brooklyn has been taken and we need to find her. Where can we meet?"

Dante dropped the f-bomb then stated, "I'm two hours outside of town. Tell me what happened."

Hunter quickly filled him in. "We have to find her soon. I don't think the cops are going to move fast enough."

"I'm certain they won't," Dante roared. "Look, take down this address and meet me and my partner, Liang, there in thirty minutes."

"I thought you said you were hours away," Hunter questioned.

"I'm calling in a favor. Now will you be there or not?" Dante asked. "We're going to need a ride."

"I'll be there," Hunter replied and hung up, grabbing his Escalade's keys then heading to the garage.

Thirty minutes later Hunter waited impatiently by a large, rickety shed next to a huge open field. He had checked the address four times because this wasn't what he was expecting to find. A sound off in the distance caught his attention. He stepped out of his vehicle and looked up in the sky. Sure enough, a helicopter was fast approaching. Minutes later it landed, and Dante and a female quickly exited and ran his way.

"Let's go," Dante commanded, pushing past Hunter and climbing in the driver's seat of the Escalade. Liang climbed into the back seat.

"What the hell?" Hunter asked, then decided now wasn't the time for fighting. He ran over and climbed into the passenger seat.

As Dante pulled off, Hunter's phone rang. "What do you have?"

"Did you get a hold of Dante?" Vince asked.

Hunter bellowed, "Yeah, I just picked him up."

"Good, good, look we think we got a lock on the location of the van." For the second time that day Hunter found himself jotting down an address.

Skeptically Dante asked, "How reliable is your source?"

"Very," Hunter retorted, giving him the address.

On the drive there, Dante grilled Hunter about everything he saw and everything that happened. Hunter ignored Dante's look that conveyed, "Why didn't you save her?" He was already beating himself up over it.

They found the van on a remote road in front of the dilapidated cottage bearing the address they had been given. "Come on, Liang," Dante ordered pulling out his gun. "You stay here," he told Hunter.

"Not on your life," Hunter replied, pulling his Glock out of the glove box.

* * *

They approached the van cautiously, all the while keeping an eye on the cottage. The van was empty. Carefully they made their way to the cottage. Dante signaled Liang and Hunter to go around the back. He climbed the stairs and waited a minute to give Liang and Hunter time to get in place. He peeked into the window beside the door and darkness looked back at him. Gingerly, he reached out and slowly turned the door knob, which opened without much effort. He pushed the door in, careful to keep himself out of the line of fire. Silence, instead of gunfire, filled the cottage. With his Beretta leading the way, he stepped in carefully. Immediately the two bodies in the middle of the floor caught his attention.

Liang and Hunter entered the room from the rear of the house. "It's clear," Liang yelled, holstering her gun. She looked down at the bodies and asked Hunter, "Are these the guys that took her?"

Hunter's stomach dropped. "Yes," he grunted.

"Liang we have to move quickly," Dante instructed. Liang pulled out equipment from her side bag to scan the dead men's fingerprints and took their pictures. She sent her findings off to their resources, asking that they try to identify the victims as soon as possible.

"Can you send those to me as well? I'd like to have my resource look into them," Hunter requested of Liang, who looked over at Dante for approval.

"Maybe you should tell us who this resource is. How exactly was he able to track down the van so fast?" Dante asked Hunter.

Hunter stood his ground. "Not going to happen. My resource is working the streets while you're working through red tape protocols. The streets work much faster. We need to work all the angles if we want to get BK back soon."

Dante gave Liang the go ahead nod and she forwarded the information electronically to Hunter, who quickly sent it off to someone else.

With worry etched in his face, Dante said, "We need to get out of here. We can notify local authorities after we get a jump start. We don't want to be slowed down with their questions."

As they carefully made their exit, Hunter asked, "What's next?"

"Dante, I think we should head to Brooklyn's place," Liang suggested as they jogged back to the truck, constantly surveilling their surroundings. "Since they grabbed her, they must not have been able to find what they were looking for at her place. If we find whatever it is they were looking for, it'll let us know what our next step should be."

"I'm with you," Hunter weighed in. "We need to find whatever it is that made them desperate enough to grab her."

Dante's gut instinct had told him this as soon as he saw the two dead men in the cottage. If they didn't figure this thing out sooner rather than later, Brooklyn would be added to the body count.

Chapter Twenty-Five

Brooklyn was using everything within her power to not lose her mind. After the gunfire and hearing the bodies hit the floor, she was taken on another long drive. Whoever had her now hadn't said a word to her. Something told her that whoever it was wasn't to be messed with. She kept her mouth shut.

She had been brought to another location. Now she sat, still blindfolded and with her hands tied together, waiting for whatever was to happen next. She prayed the next step wasn't her getting harmed. The sound of a door opening caused her to jump. She listened to the footsteps entering the room. They approached her and did a slow circle around her.

"Let me cut straight to the chase," a female voice whispered. "You have something my husband wants. You are going to tell me where to find it."

"Since I have no idea what you're talking about, please enlighten me." Brooklyn tried her best not to sound glib. "Trust me when I tell you, I'll gladly hand whatever it is over if it means you're letting me go."

"Smart girl," a male voice slightly familiar to Brooklyn spoke. Her mind started trying to place it.

The female voice asked, "Where do you keep your work files?"

"Work files?" Brooklyn asked. "Which work files?"

"Do you want to ask questions and possibly have to be put down for knowing too much?" The female voice sounded impatient. "Or do you want to tell us where you keep your client files for work?"

Brooklyn bit back the smart response that tried to flip off her lips. "Various places. I keep files at work, some files are in my briefcase, and some at home in my desk."

"Desk, what desk?" The male voice questioned and again Brooklyn couldn't shake the familiarity of it.

"My desk at home. Well right now it's acting as my console table. It converts into my desk when I work from home. I keep some files in there. You have to pull it away from the wall to see that it has a place for files." She barely finished her sentence when the footsteps all hurried out of the door. The door slammed shut and once again she was left waiting.

* * *

Liang picked the lock to Brooklyn's place while Dante and Hunter kept watch. They entered and started to look around. Twenty minutes later they hadn't turned up anything. The console caught Dante's attention. It wasn't the one she used to have when they dated, but he wondered if it was the same type. He pulled it away from the wall, and sure enough it was Brooklyn's convertible desk. He tried to open a drawer but it was locked. Liang was quicker at picking locks than he was, so he waved her over and she picked it within seconds. She pulled out the files and they started going through them.

Hunter's phone began to ring. It was Vince. He stepped into Brooklyn's bedroom to take the call. "Hey, man, what do you have?"

"I tracked down some partners of the two gentlemen you sent photos of earlier. They were just a couple of hired hoods. They weren't prone to violence, just guys looking for quick, easy money," Vince explained.

"Were you able to find out who was their last client?"

"It's rumored that they followed the guy that hired them after their meeting and devised a plan to blackmail him and extract more money. If it's true, that's most likely what got them killed."

"So what's the name of the person who hired them?" Hunter looked out to see Liang going through the files.

"Alex Michaels. Does that name sound familiar?"

"Not to me, but I'll run it by Dante and his associate," Hunter said and thanked Vince before hanging up.

Hunter stepped back into the living room. Liang was staring down at the files on Brooklyn's desk. "My source pulled up a name that I need to run by—"

All three of them snapped their attention towards the door as someone started rattling the handle. The rattling stopped once the person realized it wasn't open. Liang mouthed to Dante, "Someone is picking the locks." Dante and Liang pulled out their guns. Hunter hesitated before reaching for his, slipping the phone in his pocket. The door opened and two goons stood in the doorway. They quickly spotted the guns, turned tail, slammed the door, and took off running before anyone could fire a shot. Dante, Hunter, and Liang went into pursuit mode. The goons took the stairs and jumped down five stairs to the landing as they rushed toward the ground floor. Hunter and Dante followed suit, with Liang close behind. The goons rushed out of the building, each taking off in a different direction. Without thought, Hunter and Dante split, each following one of the goons.

* * *

Liang came outside last and was about to go after Dante and his goon when a third man caught her eye. He was standing at the end of the alley, watching and waiting. When he saw the action, he turned on his heels and started to walk off. Liang took off after him. She didn't realize she was in trouble until the black SUV pulled up beside her and someone dragged her in.

Liang immediately placed her Ruger in between her arm and her side and pulled the trigger. Her assailant's hand dropped away from the door handle. Pushing the door open, she jumped out of the SUV just as the driver turned, trying to use his right hand to grab her. With the passenger door opened, Liang quickly dropped to the ground on her back and fired into the vehicle. The truck door slammed closed as it peeled off. She could hear feet running toward her from behind. Rolling onto her stomach, she reloaded, preparing for round two. Relief filled her as she saw Dante running towards her.

Dante extended his hand to help her up. "You good?"

"I am now." Liang used his hand to pull herself up.

"We need to get out of here." He started jogging and Liang fell in line, both occasionally glancing back.

"Where's Hunter?"

"We went in opposite directions. I doubled back when I lost the guy when he crossed the street. I couldn't make it across traffic without getting hit. Once a van passed, I had no idea where he went."

When they rounded the corner, they found Hunter on the opposite end of the block with his knee in the neck of the guy he was chasing and his Glock pressed against the man's forehead. Dante and Liang picked up speed to get to him. Hunter was demanding to know where Brooklyn was. They could hear the sirens in the distance.

"Look, we need to take this interrogation somewhere else," Liang said, looking down the street to see if she saw the flashing lights of the police cars. They sounded as if they were getting closer, but they weren't within sight yet.

Hunter yanked the guy to his feet. "You take my truck and him. I'll go back to Brooklyn's to grab the files before the boys in blue get here."

"Don't you need a vehicle?" Dante asked as he grabbed the badly beaten guy from Hunter.

"Don't worry about me. Get this guy someone where you can beat Brooklyn's location out of him."

"Gentleman, we need to move," Liang urged.

"Call me if you find the file," Dante stated as they headed to Hunter's truck. "It didn't seem to be in the pile Liang was going through."

Liang glanced around. The flashing lights could be seen in the distance and curious people started peeking out windows. "Grab them anyway," she instructed. "We just skimmed through them; we could have missed something."

"Call me if he gives you anything," Hunter stated, taking off running back to Brooklyn's apartment.

* * *

Once in the apartment, Hunter was relieved to see that no one had doubled back. He looked again in the desk drawer to make sure Liang had grabbed all the files from the convertible desk. One file was wedged in the back. He pulled it out, then pushed the console table back in place and swiftly exited the premises. He took the back way out of the building that led to parking in the alley and did a brisk walk out of the there as he saw the cop cars pull up to the building. People were starting to gather in the street. Going the opposite way of the crowd, he called a friend to pick him up.

* * *

Brooklyn paced the room. While grateful she was no longer blindfolded and tied up, she was still terrified. She looked around to see if there was anything she could use to break the glass wall. There was only a bed, a remote, and a dresser. The television was just beyond the glass wall. The curtain was closed, which, she learned quickly, she preferred. When the curtains were drawn back, she felt like a lab rat with her masked assailant staring, taunting her. *What in the hell is going on?* she wondered, racking her brain to figure out who would want to do this and why. Nothing that made any sense came to mind.

She was extremely afraid this would not end well for her, especially since the guys that snatched her had been gunned down. She was hoping beyond hope that her usefulness would not expire before Hunter and the police tracked her down. She trusted that Hunter went to the police instead of putting this in the hands of the bad boys he was rumored to have grown up with and who he still saw occasionally. *Hunter's* businesses are legit. *He'll go to the cops and let them know I'm missing*, Brooklyn told herself as she fought her fears. She didn't have much faith in cops putting out any real effort for a black woman but she would take whatever she could get in the way of help at this point.

It was possible that Dante would come back earlier than expected and find out she was missing. She prayed he was good at his job and would find her quickly. Brooklyn jumped as the curtain was drawn back. He sat in a chair facing the glass. In spite of the mask that he wore, his eyes seemed to sear through her. It stopped her in her tracks.

"It seems we have a problem. Someone has the file, which means you won't like what happens next." He stood, walking towards the glass. "You are now bait in an accelerated plan. You can relax for a little while longer. Maybe." He laughed wickedly as he closed the curtain.

In that moment, Brooklyn decided that if she was going to die, she'd do it trying to escape. Every time the curtain opened, she'd pay attention to other things in the room. He always turned around a chair from the dining room table to sit and talk. It freaked her out a bit that the table was set like he was expecting someone for a romantic dinner. Brooklyn began mentally cataloging items in that setting that she could use as a weapon. She wondered if the dresser was nailed down. She examined it and found it was nailed in place. *Maybe the drawers come out and I can use one as a weapon*, she thought, tugging on the drawer. Seeing that it wouldn't come out made tears form in her eyes. She kept repeating, "You will survive this," like an empowering chant. She began focusing her mind on something else, Dante empowering her to take a chance on herself.

"Brook, don't limit your ability to fly. Life is about taking calculated risks. You weigh the factors and decide if you're going to take the leap of faith." Dante closed the door behind them as they entered her apartment. Brooklyn took the bags of food, heading to the kitchen.

"What if it doesn't work out?" She grabbed plates out of the cabinets.
"People say when you step out on faith, you don't fall. But it happens. No one wants to talk about that."

"Sweetie, you will never hit a home run from the dugout. Why aren't you going for the new position? This position puts that degree to good use and you're shying away from it." Dante grabbed utensils out of the draw then took the plates from Brooklyn.

"I hear you."

"You hear me, but are you listening and applying it to your life?" Dante stopped fixing his plate and grabbed Brooklyn by the wrist, pulling her towards him. *"Brooklyn Saunders, I believe in you. I believe you are more than capable of handling this new position and all that it brings to your life. I also believe that if it doesn't work out as you hope, you will be able to use that experience to make you a better person."* Dante leaned down and kissed her on the forehead.

Brooklyn had her current position at her job because he had given her the courage to step up and step out of her comfort zone. Right now she was grateful for that. Because of that moment, she was thinking about the beauty in her life instead of reflecting on regrets.

* * *

Dante slammed his fist repeatedly into the torso of the man they'd caught running from Brooklyn's apartment.

"Hey, dead men don't talk," Liang warned, grabbing Dante's arm as he went to deliver another blow to the man, who looked like Dante's personal punching bag as he hung by his wrists from the low ceiling.

Dante clamped onto his throat and demanded, "Where is Brooklyn?"

Liang could see the man could barely breathe, let alone speak. "Dante, step out now!" When he barely moved, she stomped her foot and pointed at the door.

Seething with anger, he released the man's neck and stormed out of the room.

Liang looked at the guy, his chin resting limply on his chest. "I am going to ask you one question. Where is Brooklyn?"

He shook his head, whispering, "I don't know."

"You don't know who hired you? You claim to not know where Brooklyn is. What do you know?"

"I wish I had answers but I don't." His words were drawn out as if it hurt to talk.

Liang placed a chair in front of him, looking up at Dante's handprints around his throat. "You're playing with your life. You either give me an answer or I let him"—she jerked her head in the direction of the door that Dante went out of—"back into the room to rip you limb from limb." Sitting down in the chair, she folded her arms and said, "I'm going to ask you again. Where is Brooklyn?"

"I don't know," he muttered, blood dripping from his lips. "I was paid to retrieve a file and if there was a lady there to grab her."

She jumped up from the chair. "What?"

"I was supposed to grab the file and you," he yelled as the chair clanked when it hit the floor. "I swear that was it. That was all we got paid to do. I don't know where Brooklyn is."

Liang turned, rushing towards the door, with their captive screaming after her, "I swear that's all I know." When she burst into the hallway, Dante grabbed her by both shoulders and stared her in the eyes. "What did he say about Brooklyn?"

"He doesn't know where she is." Liang stepped away from Dante, running her hand through her hair as she walked the hall. "He claims he was instructed to retrieve the file and me if I was there."

Dante walked over to Liang, who was now leaning near one of the basement windows. "You?" The confusion reflected in his face as he spoke. "Are you sure?"

Liang looked at him, nodding her head.

He massaged her shoulders, trying to relax her some. "Did he specifically say you or ..."

Liang knocked his hand away from her shoulders and turned towards him. "Dammit, I didn't screw it up. The boy said, 'I was supposed to grab the file and you.' Who in the hell else could that you have been?"

Dante held his hands up. "I'm sorry, Liang. I'm just trying to process the ramifications of that."

"We can no longer assume that before he died in prison, the deranged doctor didn't hire someone to keep his promise."

"Yes it is a possibility. However, until we get solid evidence, we have to be careful not to let it cloud our judgment."

She went to the little refrigerator, grabbing two waters out. "You're right." She tossed one to Dante.

Dante caught the water, twisted open the bottle, took a sip, then sat on one of the metal chairs leaning on the wall. "Why did Alec go through so much trouble to gain access to Bevik Media when under his other identity, Alex, he owned a successful media company like TriVision? And how is it connected with the crazy doctor?"

"Shit! Dante, we've been catfished." Liang swiftly filled the seat next to Dante.

"What?" Dante looked at her like she had lost her mind.

"Listen, just hear me out." She grabbed Dante's hands, looking deeply into his eyes to convince him she still had her wits about her.

"I'm listening."

"We know Alex and Alec are the same people. What we ignored, once we learned this information, was that the files we were given had two different pictures to represent each name." Liang looked at him as if to say you know they didn't match. Since they weren't looking for either man, Liang only scanned the information for the files, not the pictures. Liang was still upset with herself for not immediately realizing that the pictures didn't match.

Dante popped up from his seat and paced in front of her for a moment. "Tuck must have found the identity of the real person behind the two names, the true mastermind behind the …"

"Exactly." Liang stood. "And that file he sent to Brooklyn holds that information."

"We need to get to Hunter immediately." Dante and Liang both bolted towards the basement door. As they raced up the stairs, the guards at the top of the stairs opened the door with their guns drawn. They put them away once they realized who it was.

The guards stepped back to allow them to come through the door. "I guess we're keeping an eye on our company."

Liang immediately went to grab her messenger bag and their work duffle.

"Yes, but keep your eyes open. This case just got upgraded to a black flag." Dante grabbed his keys and jacket, following Liang out of the door.

Dante unlocked Hunter's truck. "Before you start clicking away, call Hunter to see if he looked at the file. Find out his location. I'll head in the direction of his club, but ..."

"I hear you. We don't have time to waste. If we can confirm the identity behind Alex or Alec, we may be able to gain enough information to track Brooklyn down," she stated, throwing the duffle in the back seat, getting in the truck, and buckling up.

Dante pulled out his cell phone and handed it to Liang before buckling up and taking off.

Chapter Twenty-Six

Hunter sat at his desk, looking at a picture of his friends in the early years. While staring at young Brooklyn's smiling face, he prayed that she'd come home safely. The thought of never seeing her smiling face again overwhelmed him in a way he had never felt before. He'd secretly loved Brooklyn for a while. He'd always kept the picture on his desk because it never raised the alarm bells and revealed his secret to anyone.

Focus on finding her, he thought as he once again tried to make sense of the contents of the files from Brooklyn' house. He shuffled through them until he came upon the one that Liang and Dante had overlooked, the one that had been wedged in the back of her convertible desk. It had a picture paper-clipped to a document labeled "the real Alex aka Alec". The photo was of a woman, with *wifey* written above it. The paper was filed with names and data that he was hoping Vince could make sense of. It took just a few minutes to scan the file to a flash drive, but he kept getting error messages when he attempted to email the scanned document to Vince.

His office intercom buzzed, followed two seconds later by bamming on the door. He opened his desk drawer to grab his Glock as the person tried to turn the locked doorknob. Hunter glanced at the security monitors. After seeing it was Alexis, he put the gun back in the drawer.

He answered the intercom. "Sorry, sir. Alexis demanded to see you. We told her you're busy but she asked to go to the restroom and ran straight for your office instead."

"It's okay. Next time, know that she is not above trickery to get what she wants," Hunter stated.

Alexis continued banging on the door. "Hunter, I know you're in there. What the hell has happened to Brooklyn?"

"Give me a minute. I'm coming." Hunter closed the file on his desk covering it with others before heading to the door. He glanced back at the desk to make sure the file was covered.

He opened the door and Alexis pushed passed him. "What the hell happened to Brooklyn?"

"I don't have any more information than what the news is reporting." He followed Alexis across the room as she bypassed the chairs to lean on his desk.

"Why didn't you call me?" Alexis demanded to know.

"I called LaShawn."

"Well, LaShawn claims you didn't tell her much." She sat on his desk, crossing her legs. "You know more than you're telling us."

"I have no reason to lie." Hunter frowned, not in the mood for Alexis. "Could you please get your behind off my desk and my files?"

She scooted off of his desk, knocking the files onto the floor.

"Dammit, Alexis I don't have time for this. I'm trying to get the answers to your questions, but I can't if you're in here wasting my time." He quickly bent over, picking up the files.

Alexis pouted. "If you'd call and give us regular updates, I wouldn't have to come here."

"Shit, Alexis!" He slammed the files on the desk. The pictures went flying out the file onto the floor. "If I had an update to give, I would have called you, but I don't."

Alexis jumped, startled. "We just want to know what to do to help." She bent over to pick up the pictures. "What are you doing with a picture of Dr. Kane LaPorte and his crazy stalker chick?"

"How do you know them?" Hunter questioned as Alexis handed him the pictures.

"Well, we used to keep each other company." Alexis adjusted her purse on her shoulder. "I'm going to get out your way, but could you please keep me informed?"

He grabbed her wrist as she began to walk away. "Wait." His cell phone rang. Glancing at the caller ID, he silenced it. He was eager to hear her story. "An Alexis escapade is just what I need to hear. All I'm doing is waiting for a call, hoping to get more information."

She looked at him, confused. "Didn't your cell phone just ring?"

"Yeah, but they're supposed to call me on my office phone." Hunter decided he would call his cousin back when he was done with Alexis. If it had been Dante, he wouldn't have done that. He sat his cell on the desk. "Tell me, why did you stop keeping each other company?"

"Despite his girlfriend, we had a good thing going until he took her crazy behind on as a client." Alexis pointed to the picture of the woman on his desk.

Hunter grabbed the picture of the woman. "You're sure this is his stalker chick?"

Alexis grabbed the picture, nodding her confirmation. "Yeah. Her hair was a different color, but it's definitely her."

"How did she interfere with your relationship?"

"I'm going to need a drink for that." She crossed her arms, pinching her lips together.

"I can handle that." Hunter walked over to the door, closing and locking it. "What do you want to drink?"

Alexis sat in the chair, as she watched him walk over to the bar in the back of his office. "One of your special concoctions please."

"What's stalker chick's name?" Hunter inquired as he mixed up Alexis' drink.

"Megan something. I don't remember. It was one thing to have a girlfriend, but girlfriend and stalker chick was a bit much. He claimed her clinginess would end once she got back on her feet and got to a good place in her life."

"Did you really let that stop you?" Hunter tried not to react to Megan's name as he dropped a cherry in the drink.

"No, but fortunately for me he lost his mind, killed somebody in an attempt to track down his foster sister, and ended up in jail before I could do anything stupid. All of that creeped me out because when we first met, he told me my name reminded him of his sister, Alicia Michel, and I thought it was a cute way to engage me in conversation." Hunter handed Alexis the drink, then leaned on the desk near her chair. "Besides, that Megan chick hacked into my damn bank account and took my money. She wouldn't give it back until I promised to stop seeing him."

Hunter stood and got a coaster for Alexis to put her drink on. "Do you know what happened to stalker chick?"

Alexis crossed her legs and leaned towards Hunter. She watched as he moved across the room. "The rumor is her crazy butt was at every trial date. She was probably his pen pal until he got killed in prison."

"Do you know how the stalker became his client?" He sat the coaster on the desk in front of her.

"She came from a well-to-do family." Alexis sipped her drink. "I guess her parents pulled some strings to keep her out of jail for hacking. Instead she had to do therapy sessions with him." Alexis looked at Hunter over her glass before finishing it off then sitting it on the desk.

"Interesting." Hunter figured he'd gotten enough information for Vince to go on. Hopefully it was enough to put all the pieces of the puzzle together. "Well I'd better get going. I want to go down to the station to see if I can get more answers that way."

Alexis jumped out of the chair. "I can go with you."

"No." Hunter had to think of something quickly to keep him from having company. He needed to get Alexis out so he could check in with Dante and relay the information he just got to Vince. "If you could go make a care package for Brooklyn, that would be a big help."

Alexis crossed her arms. "Really, Hunter?" Her stance said, *I'm going with you.*

"Alexis, her apartment has been taped off by cops after this last incident. When they find her, she'll want to be able to change and brush her teeth." He pulled out his wallet. "If you could buy an overnight bag, an outfit or two, sleepwear, toiletries, and anything you think she would need." He handed her three hundred dollars.

"I'm on it. I thought you were just trying to get me out of your hair, but you have a valid point." Alexis headed to the door. "Do you really think she's coming home?"

He unlocked the door. "I'm counting on it. I'm sure she might not want to stay home for a couple days."

"You're right. I can handle it." Alexis folded the money and slipped it into her purse. "It'll make things easier for her when she comes back to us."

"Thanks." Hunter held the door as she walked out.

She turned to give him a stern look. "Don't forget to call if you hear anything new."

Hunter nodded, closed and locked the door, then returned to his desk. He noticed his cell phone lighting up on the desk. He reached for it, missing another call. *I must have accidentally turned the ringer off.* He saw he'd missed several calls from Dante and a few from a number he didn't recognize.

His top priority was to call Vince then call Dante. He knew whatever Dante wanted had to be important for him to call several times but he wanted this information in Vince's hands so he could start digging into it. Hunter knew he had to make it quick so that he could get back to Dante as soon as possible.

Vince immediately stated upon answering, "I don't have any updates for you."

"Well I may have some for you." Hunter quickly told him Alexis' story.

When Hunter finished and asked Vince what he made of it, Vince said, "Hold up, I'm getting an instant message." There was silence on the line for a moment, then Vince's urgent voice asking, "Where are you?"

"My office."

"You and your employees need to get out ASAP. I've been informed trouble is coming your way."

"Thanks. I'll call once I relocate."

Hunter picked up his office phone and called security. "Did Alexis leave the building?"

"Yes."

"Lock up and get everyone out of here. Trouble is heading our way and we don't have plans to be here to greet it," Hunter said as he tried to scan the file over to Vince. He kept getting an error.

"You're sure you want us to leave too?" The head of security moved the phone from his mouth to yell to his team to pack it up and get ready to head out.

Gathering all the papers and pictures, Hunter returned them to the file, sitting it on his desk as he shut down his computer. "Positive."

"Okay we'll be on-call if you need us."

"You know what?" Hunter said. "Why don't you come back in two-to-three hours, assess the damage, if any, and take care of it for me." Hunter figured he'd be too distracted with this latest development to follow up on the club. "Text me if you need my assistance."

"Will do."

Hunter watched the monitors until he was sure everyone had left the building. He grabbed his gun, keys, jacket, the file, and the flash drive before exiting his office. Moving quickly, he went to his car, pulling out into the parking lot and cutting through the alley in order to come out further down the street. As he exited the alley, he realized he left something in his office that he really needed. Plus, he hadn't called Dante back. Hunter maneuvered the car back towards the club planning to run in quickly then call Dante afterwards.

Chapter Twenty-Seven

Frustration was not an adequate word for what Dante thought Liang was feeling. He moved through the street traffic, heading to where they thought Hunter would be. Liang continued calling Hunter from both Dante's and her cell without any success. She hung up after another unsuccessful attempt. "Damn, he's not answering his cell." Dante began to slow down then pulled over less than half a block away from the club.

Liang looked over at him. "What's the problem?"

Dante nodded forward. Several men in black were at the front door of the club. "Why are they stepping back from the door?" he asked. They didn't have time to speculate, as the doors of the club exploded and the group of men rushed inside.

"There's too many of them. Is there a back door?" Liang inquired. "Maybe we can get to Hunter before they do."

Dante started evaluating what was the best place to set his sniper rifle up to take them out as they came out of the door. "There's a back door but by the time we get through it, they would have grabbed him and gone."

"We can't let them take Hunter." Liang reached in the back for the duffle bag with the big guns.

"We're just going to have to play this one by ear," he said, even though he was working through a plan in his head. Dante opened the door just as the phone rang. Liang grabbed his arm, showing him the screen quickly before answering and putting it on speaker. Dante closed the door, keeping an eye on the club.

"Hunter, where are you?" Liang asked.

"Heading home."

"Don't think that's a good idea. You have visitors. Once they realize you're not in the club, the next spot they'll visit is your home," Dante stated, starting the truck.

"Won't be there long, just need to pick up a few things and head out," Hunter replied.

"Unless it's absolutely necessary in our search for Brooklyn, I would suggest you find somewhere else to go. There's no guarantee there's not a welcoming party already there."

Dante imagined Hunter debating the pros and cons as he explained, "If we take the file off your hands, we may also take the target off your back."

"I'll happily hand it over to you," Hunter stated.

Dante backed the truck into a side street and turned around, heading away from the club. "Where are you? Maybe we can do a quick hand-off."

"I'm about twenty minutes east of the club." Hunter paused. "I do have a couple questions. Who is Dr. Kane LaPorte? And why is he pretending to be Alex Michaels and Alec McNier?"

The blood drained out of Liang's face. Shocked, she fumbled to catch the phone as it slipped out of her trembling hand. She accidentally hung up on Hunter.

Dante knew his face probably looked grim also as he picked the phone up and dialed Hunter back. He held the phone in one hand, driving with the other. "Hunter, sorry about that disconnect. Did you say Kane LaPorte?"

"Yes. According to Alexis, the picture in the file that says, '*the real Alex Michaels a.k.a. Alec McNier*' is Dr. Kane LaPorte."

"If that's true, you need to stay off the radar. If it's Kane LaPorte, he's not trying to allow anyone to live that knows his true identity."

"When I googled Kane LaPorte, the picture online matched the picture in the file. But according to the article, he's dead." Hunter paused then muttered, "I don't like the implication of a crazy man who was believed to be dead having Brooklyn."

Dante didn't respond to Hunter almost inaudible mutter, instead he explained, "We're going to find somewhere safe to lay low, but don't access any more information on Kane LaPorte. He has someone on his team that ..."

"His wife, Megan."

"Wait! How do you know about her?"

"She's in the file, too."

Dante kept looking over at Liang, who finally snapped out of her shock. Her fingers were now flying over her keyboard. "Hunter, meet us at ..." Liang read off the address. "I'll have our team look out for you. What are you driving?"

Liang typed in the information as Dante took the turn to head to the safe house. "We'll discuss the rest of the information in the file in person."

Liang and Dante drove in silence, both lost in their own thoughts.

* * *

Hunter agreed to turn the file over, but he intentionally failed to mention that he was going to first stop by the office of one of the apartment complexes he owned so he could email a full copy of the file to Vince. He came up the private elevator and entered the office that he barely used. After he was satisfied that the scanned files were successfully emailed to Vince, he headed out to meet Dante and Liang.

* * *

The atmosphere was intense as Kane explained the new plan to Gus and Megan. At the conclusion, Gus stood without a word and exited the room. Megan was furious. Her face reflected her displeasure. She got up, walked over to the window, and looked out into darkness with her arms crossed. Kane stood and walked over to her. "Baby, we have no choice. If Dante and Liang have that file, they know I'm alive."

"I'm fine with you setting a trap to take them both out. But I don't understand why you're sending me after Aaron's slow behind," Megan stated, sounding extremely frustrated.

"Well, his 'slow behind,' as you said, might be able to lead us to Tuck's vault." Kane smiled, knowing Megan had no clue of the true importance of the information his former ally placed in the vault.

"Why do we need to access that money?" Megan asked. "I can hack some zeros into our account."

"I'm sure you can," Kane replied as he wrapped his arms around her waist, placing a kiss on her cheek before leaning his chin on her shoulder. "But the information that's sitting along with that money can't be hacked into our possession."

"Dammit, I wish I could do that." She pressed against him.

He turned her to face him and stated, "I'd do anything to make it possible for us to live our lives outside the shadows as Mr. and Mrs. Alex Michaels."

She tilted her head, looking up at him lovingly. "We weren't supposed to bring any unnecessary attention to ourselves, but that's all we seem to …"

Kane took her by the hand and led her over to the couch. "Once we execute the last of the people that will recognize me as Kane LaPorte—"

"We can't kill all your old patients, girlfriends! Or my parents, for that matter," Megan interrupted, sticking her hands into the back pocket of her jeans and refusing to sit. "I know that once someone recognized you, you got obsessed with locating the information and getting revenge. But, Kane—"

"You need to get used to calling me Alex again." He sat down on the couch, pulling her down onto his lap. "Kane LaPorte is officially dead. We're trying to keep it that way. The only ones we need to remove are the ones that would want to put me back behind bars." His hand slowly moved up and down Megan's leg.

"Ka—Alex, when we got you out, we were living happily as the Michaels of TriVision. Staying low key, but living the life. I was loving it." Megan didn't understand why he wasn't willing to do what was necessary to maintain that.

He started placing light kisses on her neck. "You know that one call from some stranger in the middle of the night ruined that."

"He's dead," she reminded him, moving her neck away from his lips.

As he nuzzled into her neck, he mumbled, "But the information he held over us still remains with his possessions in Tuck's vault."

She slid off his lap and onto the couch. "We both knew that buying into Tuck's company probably wasn't going to be enough to give us access to that part of his business. But when we decided I'd go in, I just didn't expect …"

"Look, it was a challenge, but we finally know about the vault. We also know we need someone with authorization or who is highly skilled to get in." He turned his body to face her. Taking his finger and turning her face towards him, he stated, "That's why Gus is finding Ryan, your task is to find Aaron, and my task is to neutralize Dante and Liang."

She fussed, "I don't like—"

"Ever since Tuck started asking too many questions, our plans have been going sideways. Ryan was a blessing in disguise with his skill for breaking in to highly secure facilities." His eyes followed her across the room.

"Until Tuck found out what I was…"

"Sweetie, we got this." Kane smiled. "We're in the final leg of destroying the last links to Kane LaPorte."

Megan began pacing the room. "I don't know why you couldn't have just gotten plastic surgery. Then Dante and Liang wouldn't matter."

"Baby, I need to be that man you fell in love with," Kane explained while thinking, *I need her to recognize me.*

"Two weeks. That's all I'm giving you to fix this mess."

He stood, walking directly into her pacing path. "I need you to hang on a little while longer. Then we'll discuss plastic surgery so that you can actually bring me home for the holiday instead of your little beau,

Ryan." Kane knew he needed to keep her focus. It wasn't her hacking skills that got her caught, it was her being irrational and doing something stupid.

"I like the sound of that." Megan smiled. "I guess I should get to work while Gus is working on the other project." She rose to her tippy toes, planting a brief kiss on his lips.

"If you find Aaron, make sure you have Gus help you out. Clearly, Aaron's not as slow as you originally thought. He got away from you before."

If they could procure Ryan and Aaron, it could reveal the location of Tuck's vault. Then he could stop this charade and be with the woman he loved. The only woman he'd ever loved.

* * *

Brooklyn's food was slipped through the slot and onto a ledge. After eating the sandwich and chips and drinking her juice box, she used a screw she managed to loosen from the dresser to try to pry the food window open. After working at it for hours, she managed to open it.

"Dammit," she mumbled as she looked out into darkness. She could hear voices, but she couldn't make out everything they were saying. Brooklyn was losing track of the days. Some days the curtain didn't even open. The only sign of life outside her cell was the window sliding back to put her food in. She peered out of the slot. The next thing she knew, she was being grabbed from behind. Her body slammed against the wall. A knife was placed to her neck, with a warning that nosiness will get her killed. She felt a needle in her flesh. As her body slithered down the wall, she could see him walk through the wall. He almost looked like a ghost going through it but she knew there had to be a hidden door.

When Brooklyn came to, she determined every time the curtain closed, she'd search for the door. She didn't care if they were watching. From the bits and pieces of the conversation she overheard, she was fairly sure they had no intention of letting her get out of here alive. Her mind went to Dante and the moment he reminded her to fight for her life.

Brooklyn had just hung up the phone from one of the most devastating calls of her life. Her mind hadn't even processed what the nurse had told her. The tears began to build up in her eyes as she re-read the information she looked up on the diagnosis. She could hear her office phone ringing in the background. Taking a deep breath, she answered.

"Brooklyn Saunders of ... "

"Brook ... are you okay? "

She thought she had disguised her pain by putting on her professional voice, but Dante had picked up on the fact that something was off.

"It's not a good time, Dante. I'll have to—"

"Every other time I haven't called you in a while, I'm Mr. Nines. Now you're referring to me as Dante. I know something's seriously wrong."
Dante's car door slammed in the background.

Brooklyn grabbed a tissue. "I'm having a bad day."

"I'm down stairs," Dante stated.

Brooklyn reached for a tissue, feeling another moment coming on. "Dante, I ... "

"I'm not taking no for an answer. Either you come down or I'll come up."

There was silence on both ends of the phone. "Fine, I'll come down." Brooklyn hung up, then checked her face before going down to meet Dante.

Her heels click-clacked across the tile of the lobby floor as she walked towards Dante's tall figure near the door. As she neared him, he opened his arms, wrapping them around her. Immediately, Brooklyn broke down crying uncontrollably.

Dante gently rubbed up and down her back until the crying subsided. They completely ignored the onlookers in the lobby.

"I'm sorry." Brooklyn sniffled, trying to pull it together. She stepped back. "I'm fine."

He grabbed her hand and started walking towards the couch in the lobby. Brooklyn told him the devastating news about her health and the results of the biopsy. "I can't stop thinking of all the things I won't have the opportunity to do."

Dante guided them to the couch. "Brook, baby, all we are ever granted is today."

"I know that but ..."

"No buts." He held her hand. "I know the news the nurse told you wasn't good, but don't die before your time. Don't walk around here lifeless and defeated. Regardless of if you're healthy or sick, you have to live your life for today."

The tears flowed from her eyes. "I can't."

"Brooklyn you're a survivor. Don't you dare give up on me now. If life has dealt you these cards, then play them to the best of your ability, but don't let them play you."

"Did you hear what I told you they told me?" Brooklyn had read the statistics and knew her chances were not good. It didn't help that the few people she knew that had the same type of cancer, died within months of their diagnosis.

"Yes, I did. Do you have a battle on your hand? Yes." He lifted her chin and stared into her eyes. "But every day is a gift. It doesn't matter how bad things get, someone wasn't granted that gift today. So every day you're granted is an opportunity for things to get better. Choose to live. Don't you dare condemn yourself to death before your physical body makes its exit."

Her voice trembled as she spoke, "I'm just so scared."

"It's okay to be afraid, but don't allow that fear to end your life prematurely."

Brooklyn hugged him tightly, grateful that today was the day he chose to return to her life.

She faced months of frustration trying to get a follow-up appointment with the doctor. Brooklyn couldn't understand why the doctors didn't think it was urgent enough to squeeze her in. Dante always deposited good seeds in her life, and during that time, he kept her focus on living her life, fighting for it, and not the fact that she might not have the opportunity to experience growing old. When she finally got in to see the doctor and he reviewed the file, it turned out that the nurse had made a horrible mistake when relaying the information.

Dante will come for me. He will make it to me in time, Brooklyn thought as she continued to reflect on Dante's effect on her life.

Chapter Twenty-Eight

Hunter watched Dante and Liang review the file he'd delivered to them for a few minutes before they turned to him with a look that terrified him. Liang grabbed her laptop.

"What?" Hunter asked.

"This isn't good for Brooklyn." Dante stood and Liang handed Hunter the laptop.

Hunter's eyes scanned the screen. "Okay, what do you need me to do?"

"Those are all the properties Kane LaPorte owned prior to death. Clearly his defense didn't bankrupt him. So if you have your contact search these locations to make sure Brooklyn isn't there, we can continue to dig."

Hunter took several pictures of the screen with his cell phone then stood and handed the laptop back to Liang. "I'll check in with you later," he said, heading for the door to give Vince the new information.

"Where are you going?" Dante asked.

Hunter stopped near the door. "To pass the list of possible locations on."

"I want you to pass the information along, but we need you to stay here and help us figure out this file and locate any new properties that may be listed under Kane's alias." Dante muttered almost inaudible, "We also need someone that had no previous history with LaPorte to keep me and Liang seeing clearly."

"Sorry, I assumed that you and Liang would want to do your thing without me in the way." He returned to where they were.

"Normally we would, but this file may lead us to the leverage we need to get Brooklyn back alive." Liang handed the file to Dante, who passed it to Hunter. "We need all the help we can get."

Liang inquired, "Did any of the numbers make sense to you?"

"The only thing I could think of was they were reference numbers. They almost remind me of tracking numbers when you ship something out," Hunter said, looking at the file as he walked over to sit across from Liang at the dining room table.

"You may be on to something." Liang stood, grabbing her messenger bag. "Did you bring your laptop?" She glanced back at Dante as she returned to her seat.

Dante replied, "Yeah it's in the truck."

"After Hunter gets the information to his contact, we'll work on seeing if we can crack this code in the file. You find the addresses of properties under Kane's aliases."

Dante stared at Liang's stressed face. His eyes went gentle as he began to ask, "Are you sure you're—"

"I'm good," Liang stated, interrupting him. "You're wasting time." She cut her eyes over at Hunter as if to say, you too.

Hunter immediately stopped watching the exchange and texted the pictures of addresses to Vince. Dante exited out of the back door and Liang returned to her laptop. When Dante returned, his eyes were lit up like a kid on Christmas day.

Liang looked up at Dante. "Spit it out."

"Let's hack the hacker. That might lure Megan to us. She has to know Brooklyn's location."

Hunter's phone pinged. Hunter read the message out loud. "Word on the street is there's someone willing to pay top dollar for information that will lead them to find Tuck's friend Aaron or the whereabouts of Ryan."

"How about we use Ryan to bait Megan out of the shadows?" Dante suggested as he set up his laptop on the dining room table.

"Only problem with that is we can't be sure if they're looking for him to kill him or to have him break into something. It's probably both." Liang emailed their company's computer hacker to see if he could set a digital trap for Megan.

"Ryan as bait might work. If we can get Megan, we will have something to trade," Hunter stated. "Megan is so dedicated to Kane that it's not likely that she'll give him up easily."

"What if they send Gus?" Liang asked, trying to be cautious.

"Look, let's go back to our tasks at hand. We'll keep the idea of Ryan as bait in our back pockets if he's willing," Dante said knowing it would give him time to formulate an efficient plan to use Ryan as bait.

"One thing you need to keep in mind is Ryan's track record for being sucked in by women," Hunter stated. Every time Ryan got arrested, it was due to an entanglement with some shady woman. "Don't give Megan time to get in his head and convince him you're the bad guys."

They returned to working on deciphering the file. They had been at it for hours. Liang was able to trace the numbers to the special delivery log from Tuck's office. But they couldn't figure out several entries that had the letters TAIV in front of the numbers.

Hunter stood to stretch his legs. "I just have one question. Why would Tuck put his shipping information in a folder that basically contained information on Kane and his wife?"

Dante looked up from his computer. "Yes, yes."

"I assumed it was because this was what Megan was looking for before she went missing," Liang supplied.

Dante got up, walked over to Liang, and looking over her shoulder, he asked, "Did Tuck have anything highlighted?"

"I don't think so," she replied. "But let me make sure." Flipping through the file again, she stopped and slipped one page out of the stack. "He just had this sticky note to check the uncollected TAIV accounts."

"Which are the numbers we still haven't been able to figure out." Hunter glanced at his phone. Vince hadn't gotten back to him, which meant the addresses were a wash.

Dante's computer beeped. He rushed over and looked at the screen. "Whoa! I think I know where Brooklyn is." His fingers flew over the keyboard.

"Talk *and* type Dante." Liang turned away from her laptop to look at him. "I know you can multitask."

He pointed to his screen. "McNier purchased a remote property six month ago," he said as he read the details that popped up on the computer. "My gut is saying that this is the location where Brooklyn is being held."

"You want me to send an update email to the rest of the team?" Liang asked, watching Dante as he nodded his head.

"We need to get over there now." Dante looked over at Hunter. "You're going to have to set this one out. We need you to stay back and keep looking for more possible locations just in case we are wrong."

* * *

Hunter's phone rang. He got up, moving quickly into the kitchen as he watched Dante and Liang check their guns and put on their bulletproof gear. "Hey, what do you have?"

Vince confirmed Hunter's suspicions. "Brooklyn wasn't at any of the addresses you sent over."

"We think we've found her location." Hunter peeked out the kitchen to see Dante talking to one of the men that had escorted him in when he arrived.

"Quick update," Vince said. "It's seems Kane adopted the alias of Alec McNier from the man who helped him fake his death. What he didn't know was that the name is an alias for low level employees of an elite criminal network."

Hunter looked out, not sure why Dante and Liang had not left yet. "That doesn't sound good."

"It's not good." Vince sighed. "They're currently looking for the person that vouched for Kane when he came to Tuck pretending to be Alec McNier."

"That's a problem."

"Tuck managed to send a warning to the Alec McNier he thought he was going into business with." He paused as if he was trying to convey to Hunter the real implications of what he was saying. "I'm going to need to shut you out of the details from here on out."

"Hopefully Dante and Liang will bring Brooklyn home tonight and none of this will matter."

Dante came and stood in the doorway of the kitchen. Hunter held his finger up.

"We don't have time to wait," Dante said through his teeth. "Liang and I need to get over to that property now. But we can't afford to waste time and resources checking out this location if your source is giving you a better lead."

Vince was silent on the phone, no doubt listening to what Dante was saying to Hunter. He said, "Look, I got to go. Let your new friends know to be very careful while digging into Alex McNier. Don't go further back than when Kane faked his death, otherwise you'll know trouble like you've never known before." Vince ended the call.

Liang came in the room, and Hunter looked at her and Dante, both of them poised and ready to go. "Is there anything new we should know?" Dante asked.

"Ummm… well."

Liang stared at Hunter's face as he struggled to decide whether to say something. "Spit it out," she demanded.

"Hopefully it won't matter," he answered, deciding that the information Vince had passed along wasn't vital to them checking the location for Brooklyn. "Go find Brooklyn."

"Liang, stay here with Hunter and find out what he knows," Dante commanded. "I'll take Robert with me."

"Dante, I'm—" He flashed her a stern look and she left it alone. "Okay, I'm on it. Go bring Brooklyn home safely." Dante bolted out of the door without another word. "What you have had better be good," she stated, folding her arms and staring at Hunter.

"LaPorte adopted the alias of the man that helped him fake his death.

Only I get the feeling that whoever faked Kane's death wasn't necessarily the real Alec McNier." Hunter didn't know how much he should tell her. "According to my contact if we start digging into the McNier alias prior to Kane faking his death it could be a very deadly expedition for us."

"Dammit." Liang went back to her computer. "Do you know who really helped Kane fake his death?"

"Who?" Hunter moved closer to her.

"Shit," she exclaimed as she dug through her bag, pulled out her notebook, and flipped through the pages. "Maybe the goon is the beginning of Kane's life as Alec McNier."

"I'm sorry, you aren't making sense." He pulled out the chair next to Liang.

"Gus has to be Kane's help. We need to find out what Kane has over him," Liang explained as she went back to the information she had pulled on Gus. "Even if Dante finds Brooklyn today, we need to shut Kane and his people down."

Hunter took out his phone. "Give me the info you have on Gus and I'll pass it along to my contact."

Liang shared the information with Hunter about Gus. "Whatever Kane was holding against him, I hope that your contact can find out."

"He will."

"If we could take out Kane's muscle, we could definitely slow him down and flip things in our favor," Liang stated, sounding energized. "Let's get back to looking for possible locations for Brooklyn, just in case the location Dante's headed to isn't the right one."

* * *

Aaron couldn't believe he'd finally made it. Tuck had always told him that if anything happened to him, he should come here right away. He had already learned the hard way that Megan had a way of using a computer to track down anyone she wanted to locate. For that reason, he now avoided his home, ditched his car and all electronic devices, and used only cash instead of credit cards. As he approached the door, it opened.

Tuck's wife cautiously looked out at him. "I expected you sooner."

"I didn't want to bring company with me." Aaron stepped past her and into the house.

"I know, that's why Tuck loved you." She closed the door behind him. "You're always careful." He followed her into the living room.

Aaron always appreciated Tuck for trusting him despite his issues. "I'm ready to work."

"Megan is still diligently looking for you. We'll sit tight while certain things fall into place, then we go to work." Mrs. Holder walked over to her desk and turned the security system back on.

Aaron sat his backpack next to the couch and took a seat. "I can—"

"Aaron, I'm not underestimating you. I'll treat you just as Tuck did. Because you take a little longer to process information, I won't bother you with all the details, but I'll trust you to execute the job with the basic information I give. Is that good for you?" She walked into the kitchen, opened the refrigerator, and grabbed two beers.

Tuck always told him to let that thing that people saw as his weakness become his strength. "Yes." People always assumed that he was dumb. Tuck told him not to bother to correct them. So people often spoke freely around him because they thought he wouldn't understand. He appreciated Tuck filtering the information so that if anything went wrong, Aaron would never have to lie. If he was ever questioned, he never had to worry about saying the wrong thing since quick thinking wasn't always his strong suit under extreme pressure.

After opening the beer, she handed it to Aaron. "Megan and her husband will pay for what they did. We just have to make sure that Dante Nines gets the information that Tuck wanted him to have. Once that information is delivered to me, I'll entrust you to get it where it needs to go."

"It would be my pleasure," he stated, taking a sip of beer.

"Let me show you to your living quarters. I'll start giving you the information you need to perform your task in the morning. That'll give you plenty of time to process the data and plan your strategy."

Chapter Twenty-Nine

Dante was relieved that Hunter had provided him a perfect excuse not to take Liang. He couldn't be sure what Liang's reaction would be to seeing Kane in the flesh. With Brooklyn's life on the line, he didn't want to take any chances.

He and Robert walked a half mile up to the house, knowing there was no way to approach in a vehicle without being seen. Fresh tire tracks let him know that the property was being used. What he didn't know was if Brooklyn was there. He hated that they didn't have a female element along. She could have driven up to the house and pretended to ask for directions without raising too much suspicion.

The house had motion sensors. They threw rocks and waved their hands in front of them several times to see if anyone would come out. When no one did, they stormed the house. Robert went through the door first. What Dante saw upon entering made him grateful that Liang was not by his side. The entire layout of the first floor from the living room to the kitchen was duplicated to look like Liang's house the night she lost her husband. They searched the entire house, but no one was there.

"I don't see where they could have been holding her," Robert stated as Dante came from the basement.

Dante pointed to the door next to the curtain. "What was beyond that door?"

"It was a hallway that led out to a back door, and there was an office back there. It looked like there had been a security monitoring system."

"Then she was here," he stated, moving through the room and searching for anything that could help them find Brooklyn. "Who would need a discreet security office by a back door unless they were hiding something or somebody?"

Robert shrugged. "I know, but none of the bedrooms look as if they were set up to hold a hostage. One wall down the hall had a slot, but I just saw darkness when I looked in."

"There's too much space on that wall for nothing to be on the other side of it." Dante walked over and peeked behind the curtain. "Damn!"

"What?" Robert asked as Dante held the curtain back to reveal the room beyond the Plexiglas wall.

Dante tried to pull the curtains back but they weren't cooperating. "Find a way in."

He looked around and noticed a remote on the table. Robert had disappeared into the hallway. Dante pressed random buttons until the curtain moved back. His heart broke when he peered into the room beyond the glass wall. Without a doubt, he knew that glass box was intended for Liang. He stared at the room for a while before Robert pushed through a door in the room. Dante knew he had to keep Liang out of Kane's grasp. They had a chance of getting Brooklyn back alive, but looking at the room at that moment, he knew that Kane wanted to punish Liang. He had no doubt that it would ultimately lead to Kane taking her life.

* * *

Brooklyn didn't like that they were moving her. She felt like she had been in the back of the windowless van for hours with her hands tied behind her back and a rag over her mouth. They'd taken the hood off her head once they threw her in the back. Her thoughts were on what really mattered in life and all the sacrifices she made for work meant nothing at this moment.

The van came to an abrupt halt, sending her body flying into the wall. The door of the van opened and a masked, burly guy stood among the darkness of night and the stars.

You're definitely not in DC anymore, Brooklyn thought as he grabbed her leg, pulling her towards the door. She wanted to kick at him, but her mind was made up—her job was to stay alive until Dante, Hunter, or the police could rescue her. She would fight for her life if it came down to that.

Gus stood her up and dragged her into an old warehouse. Now she wished she had taken her chance with the burly guy outside the van. There was a lot of construction on the lower level. She knew in her heart of hearts that whatever they were building, it wasn't good. This place was whispering death, and she prayed it would not be her own.

* * *

Ryan shifted nervously as he waited in the park. He had been real content with laying low until this blew over, but Hunter talked him into setting up a meeting with Megan.

Megan's shapely body stepped out from the shadows of the trees. "I'm glad you called me." She walked up, hugging him.

Ryan placed a kiss on her cheek then looked around. "I don't know if this was the best place to meet. I feel exposed right here. Let's walk."

"Okay, but not too far."

Ryan walked, trying not to look in the direction of Dante's people. "I'm so sorry. I knew it couldn't possibly be true what they were telling me, but they were watching me like a hawk."

"I'm amazed you got away." Megan stopped walking.

"Yes, I was just waiting for the right moment. Having a talent for breaking in also means you have a talent for breaking out." Ryan gazed at the woman he had thought he was falling in love with and felt a sadness come over him. "Maybe it was a mistake reaching out to you so soon. Maybe, I should …"

She grabbed his hand. "Ryan, if you help me locate and break into Tuck's infamous vault, we can get the information needed to back these people off us."

"How I am supposed to do that?" Ryan asked. "Tuck's dead."

Megan moved closer, looking at him seductively. "But his contacts aren't. There has to be someone running it. Maybe his wife knows?"

"Are you sure doing this will allow us to go back to a normal life?" Ryan asked as Megan played with her necklace, bringing his attention to her cleavage.

"Yes." Megan placed her hands on either side of his face. "Baby, I missed you. Don't you want us back?" She kissed him.

Ryan ended the kiss and took her hands in his. "Yes, but I can't do what you're asking."

Megan snatched her hands away then reached behind her back and pulled out a gun. "I'm sorry to hear that, but at the end of the day you will."

Gus stepped out of the shadows.

"You may want to put that away," Ryan suggested, nodding towards her gun then to the red dot on her chest.

Megan looked over at Gus, who had his gun aimed at Ryan. Dante and his team of eight quickly came out. Robert placed his weapon to Gus' head.

Dante walked over to Megan, relieving her of her gun. "Megan Chambers Michaels, it's nice to finally meet you. Your parents have been looking for you. They'll be happy to know we found you."

* * *

A small crew of men worked to repair the wreckage at Hunter's club. Since the blast had only damaged the doors and the front desk area, he'd be able to re-open by the upcoming weekend. However, Hunter's focus was on Brooklyn. Devastation was the only word to describe what he had felt when Dante returned with news that they'd found where Brooklyn had been held, but not before Kane had moved her to another location. Megan and her goon hadn't given Dante any information on Kane's and Brooklyn's whereabouts. It was frustrating. The only thing they learned was that Kane was holding over Gus's head the fact that Gus had killed a woman with his car and then covered it up. They also learned that he was the one that took out the real Alex McNier. The only thing Megan let slip was they were looking for Tuck's wife, but no one had seen her since his funeral.

While Gus told them how Kane got his hooks in him, it took them a while to figure out that Gus was more scared of Kane than he was of doing jail time. That in itself was interesting, seeing that trying to avoid jail time was what landed him under Kane's thumb to begin with.

Hunter was pissed off when Dante informed him that they had to release Megan and Gus to the authorities. He had Vince do some digging into Gus. Vince informed them a short time later that they would get nothing on Kane's location from Gus because Kane had Gus' family.

It was frustrating to now be back at square one even though they had two people who held the information they needed. The objective became finding properties that were purchased within the time frame that Brooklyn had been snatched. Though Hunter was functioning on fumes, getting some much-needed sleep wasn't an option. He felt guilty sleeping when Brooklyn was still out there. In the last week, they had searched for every suspicious property purchase that was within a three-hour drive from where she'd been held. This week they expanded to a six-hour radius.

A knock on Hunter's office door pulled his attention away from the list of properties on the screen. "It's open," he yelled.

The club manager opened the door, peeking his head in. "I just want you to know everything is set for the re-opening this weekend."

"Good. You'll be running everything on your own for the next few weeks." Hunter glanced at the box holding the last of his personal items. "After today, I'll be working remotely and can only be contacted in emergencies. If you can't reach me, call one of the other club managers to help out."

"Thanks, Mr. Torres. I appreciate this opportunity."

"Just show me I selected the right man for the job," Hunter stated as his manager left the room.

He frowned when he saw Vince's number on the display. There was no way Vince could have checked the properties Hunter had sent him. He literally had just hit send before his club manager knocked on the door. "You got the list of the properties I just sent over?" he inquired upon answering the call.

Vince ignored his question. "Drop whatever you're doing and head to Levi's."

"Why are you sending me to him? You two aren't even on speaking terms."

"Where are you?" Vince asked.

Hunter stood and walked over to his office door, locking it. "In my office at the club."

"Lock your gun up in a safe and head to Levi's immediately," Vince commanded.

"Levi's place is almost five hours from here."

"By the time you get there, I should have confirmation on Brooklyn's location."

"Vince ..."

"Hunter, do you trust me?" Vince asked.

Hunter grabbed the Glock from his top drawer then placed it in his safe. "Yes."

"Then get your ass moving. Levi's expecting you."

"Okay." Hunter emailed the property list to himself then shut down the computer.

"I'll call you back with more details as you drive." Vince disconnected.

Hunter grabbed his gear. Jumping into the car, he didn't fully understand Vince's plan, but he trusted both Vince and Levi with his life. Therefore, he was willing to trust Brooklyn's life to Vince's plan.

Chapter Thirty

Dante felt like the devil had personally came to earth to rip his soul apart and drag him back to hell for all his sins. The two women that meant so much to him were in grave danger. Brooklyn was still missing. Kane was coming for Liang. The decision to keep Liang out of the field was a hard-fought battle. While Liang gave him hell about taking her out of the field for the remainder of the case, he could see in her eyes that she was relieved. He kept three guys with her at all times but felt even that wasn't enough.

He was close enough to almost see the safe house Liang was staying in. He planned to check in with her this morning before heading to the air strip and hopping on a short flight to get to locations on his list where Kane might be holding Brooklyn.

The first thing he noticed when the safe house came into view was that no one was on the front door. He parked out front, pulled out his firearm, and rushed out of the car. The front door opened just as he reached for the knob.

"Dante, is everything okay?' Peter asked after noticing Dante's drawn weapon.

"Why aren't you on the door?" He put his Beretta away and stepped inside. "Where's Liang?" Dante asked after not seeing her in her usual spot at the table in front of her laptop.

"She left with Stephen and Robert after opening the envelop you mentioned when you called her from the office," Peter answered as he returned to the breakfast he'd left in the kitchen.

Dante followed him to the kitchen. "Who brought it over?"

"Bill came over to give Liang an update on Ryan. He said he figured she'd want to see it, so he brought it to her," he replied between taking bites of his food.

Dante pulled out his cell. Noticing the missed call from Liang, he tried to call her back. "Dammit." He jammed it back into his pocket when he got her voicemail.

"What's wrong?"

He held up the envelope he'd brought with him. "This was the envelope I was referring to. What in the hell did Bill deliver to her?"

"I don't know." Peter shrugged his shoulders. "I was on door duty."

"Why didn't you go with her? She's supposed to have three people with her at all times." Dante got a sinking feeling at the pit of his stomach.

"Bill went. He was supposed to relieve me in two hours. Decided he'd start early. I was going to wait until Robert's replacements arrived to let them know what was going on before I left."

"I need to get in touch with someone on that team ASAP. If you can't, turn on their tracker and send another team after them." Dante looked around, praying that Liang left her laptop, notebook, or something. He retrieved his laptop from the SUV then ripped open the envelope that had been addressed to Liang.

It contained a note and what looked like a movie DVD. The note said, *The answers you seek to find a monster can be found here. Just follow the instructions.* Dante loaded the disk into his laptop. A login screen appeared. He glanced at what appeared to be login information written below the message on the note. When he entered it, an icon popped up on the screen. He clicked on it and saw two file folders. One contained a request for fifteen to twenty men to guard an old warehouse. Dante kept looking at the address. It looked so familiar. He minimized the window, pulling up his list of possible properties where Brooklyn might have been taken.

He enlarged the screen to see if there were any other details in the files, then logged into his email to send the file over to the office. As he glanced through it one final time, he realized he hadn't opened the second folder. Dante double-clicked on it, finding a request for a specialized thirty-man team to acquire a target and transport it to a drop-off location. His heart sank when he clicked the link to see who the target was and a photo of Liang popped up.

No longer did he wonder what was in the envelope that Bill delivered. It was bait to draw Liang out. Dante knew looking at the details in the file they didn't stand a chance. Only a psycho would send thirty people after one woman.

From the doorway, Peter shouted, "I couldn't get any of them. Our team is tracking them now."

"I'm pretty sure I know where they're going. It's a warehouse on one of the remote properties Kane bought," Dante said, closing his laptop. "We'll need every available person that's in the area on this. Find out if we can get an additional plane at the air field to be ready to fly into the same general area as this address." He glanced around looking for a sheet of paper, but when he couldn't find one, he pulled out his phone and texted it to Peter. "And see if there's a private airport closer to that address."

"I'm on it." Peter headed to the other room.

Dante put his cell up as he called out, "Hey, what time did Liang leave?"

"About forty-five minutes ago," Peter yelled from the other room.

"Dammit!" He slammed his fist against the table. There was no way the team, even breaking every speed limit, would make it to her in time. Kane most likely already had Liang. The address was nearly an hour away in traffic, plus there was the ten-to-fifteen-minute drive from the private airstrip. Dante headed to the weapons room to pack up for the trip.

* * *

Liang tried to get Dante again to let him know where they were headed. Now she wished she had actually left a message on the voicemail. Since they weren't heading to a cell phone dead zone, she hadn't expected to not be able to get a call through.

The traffic was fairly light for this time of day, but Liang tried to keep an eye out for suspicious vehicles. She looked over the contents of the envelope again.

"Get off at the next exit ramp and turn back around," she stated, pulling out her Ruger. Finger on the trigger, she started glancing in the side view mirror.

"I thought meeting this person who has information on who Kane paid off was important," Bill said, already in the lane to exit.

Liang's eyes carefully scanned their surroundings. "Yes, it would be—if it wasn't a setup."

Robert drew his weapon and angled his body so he could see out the back window. "Why do you think that?"

"Who else knows that the deranged doctor is alive? The story isn't in the news." Liang was mentally kicking herself for jumping the gun. "How would the person know to specifically contact me?"

"You do realize we're nearing the exit we would have taken to reach the address?" Bill asked.

Liang glanced at the clock. "I thought you said forty-five minutes to an hour."

"Yeah, but the traffic was light."

"Well, get off and head back to where we came from," she ordered. "Going anywhere near that address will be extremely dangerous for us."

Bill put on his turn signal. Everybody was on alert for trouble. They didn't notice anything strange. The only car that got off with them was a small compact car and it turned in the opposite direction as they turned under the viaduct to reach the on-ramp.

"Shit, people, we have a problem," Robert announced when a construction truck pulled off the back road and blocked traffic.

Bill glanced in the rearview mirror, then sped around the car in front of him, making a crazy turn onto the ramp. Blocking them at the top of the ramp was what appeared to be a state trooper. Bill slammed on the brakes. He couldn't go straight, and he couldn't go left because of the viaduct wall. The driver stepped out of the fake patrol car, drew his gun, and aimed. Bill threw the truck into reverse but slammed on the brakes as another SUV turned onto the ramp.

"I think we can make it to that access road over there!" Liang shouted as the fake trooper took out one of their tires. Bill maneuvered the SUV off the road, over the gravel, and into the grass. They were about to hit the side road when an eighteen wheeler turned out of the gas station and stopped in front of them. Bill turned the steering wheel wildly, but couldn't avoid hitting the eighteen-wheeler's back end with the right side of the SUV.

"What are you waiting for?" Bill yelled over the screeching tires. "Shoot back at them!"

Liang looked in the mirror. Both vehicles that had blocked the ramp were now following them.

"There's no way I'm shooting out the side window the way you're driving. We're returning fire out the back window." Robert grabbed the weapons bag and unzipped it. Bill lowered the back window as Robert and Stephen took aim.

"This was definitely not the day I expected," Stephen stated as they took out the front tires of both cars. It only slowed them down.

Hitting the emergency beacon in the underbelly of the dashboard would let the office know they were in trouble and give their location. Liang asked, "Are our specialty items in the bag?"

"I think so." Robert went into the bag and handed Stephen the unit.

"Shut the cars down." Liang felt like the eighteen-wheeler was a mile long. They had yet to clear it but the eighteen-wheeler was moving as well.

They loaded on the electro pulse device into the delivery system. He fired twice which activated the units. They headed to the targets and caused the engines of the two cars trailing them to stall. Stephen dropped the unit and picked up his assault rifle.

Liang looked ahead. Once they could clear the truck, they had a good chance of making it to the next exit and onto the highway. "Use lethal force if they keep coming. Let's not give them a chance to—"

"They're multiplying like roaches, people!" Robert shouted as more cars passed the two stalled vehicles. They ducked as bullets pinged off the body of the truck.

"Shit." Liang rolled down her window as the door of the eighteen wheeler opened and an automatic rifle came into the view. She shot at the door until the gun retreated into the cab.

Liang called out, "Guys, I'm going to need something more than this pea shooter."

Stephen passed her a larger weapon. "We don't have enough fire power to handle this."

"I know. If we can make it back to the highway, we'll stand a chance," Bill stated. "No!" he bellowed as barricades came into view at the end of the road.

"Go through them," Liang commanded, still firing at the cab of the truck as they passed it. Turning back into her seat, she buckled up and prepared to crash through the barricades, hoping there was nothing else waiting beyond them.

A pickup truck came off the back road in front of the eighteen wheeler. Liang didn't see it until she felt the impact of it slamming into them and heard crushing metal. Her shoulder hit Bill's as their truck careened on two wheels, mowing a path through the grass. The SUV tipped over onto the driver's side and skidded before finally coming to a stop. Bill's motionless body was pinned against his door. Liang's side of the truck was in the air. She shook him but he didn't respond. She took his pulse. At least he was still alive.

When she unbuckled herself, she grasped the seatbelt tightly so gravity wouldn't make her fall onto Bill. She rotated her body so that her back was propped against Bill's massive shoulder, then she planted her feet against the door and grabbed her gun off the floor, preparing for battle. Not hearing any movement in the backseat, she glanced over her right shoulder. Stephen's body had slammed into Robert's. "Robert? Stephen? You okay?" she asked.

"Robert's out cold and bleeding, but still breathing," Stephen responded. He shifted his body, trying to reach what Liang assumed was either his weapon or the weapons bag.

"Why is it so silent?" Liang asked, noticing that the vehicle that hit them had stopped moving.

Stephen looked out the back window. "I don't know, but we definitely have more company approaching," he stated as he tried to shift Robert to get to the weapons bag. "Dammit the weapons bag is jammed under him."

Liang fired shots through the window in the direction of approaching footsteps while Stephen tried again to get to the guns in the bag.

"Liang," a voice called out from beyond the SUV. "All we want is you. If you put down your weapon, your team lives."

She glanced at Stephen, who moved to the opening between the front seats. "Don't do it."

"Our boss would prefer we deliver you alive," the voice explained from a closer distance. "But he will accept your dead body."

Through the windshield, Liang could see that men aiming AK-47 rifles at the windshield had come dangerously close to the SUV. There were too many for her to take out without getting herself and the others with her killed. She yelled, "Fine, I surrender," then whispered to Stephen, "I fully expect you and the team to come find me."

"Lucky for you," an intimidating Asian man said as he peered down inside the passenger side window. "You're more valuable to us alive. Now put your weapon down," he demanded. "And you in the back seat, keep your hands where I can see them unless you want my men to blow your head off."

Liang placed her gun on the floor and rested her feet on the seat. When the man extended his hand towards her, she reached up and allowed him to clasp her hands in his. With one violent tug that felt like it would dislocate her shoulder, he dragged her out of the window and lowered her into the bed of the pickup truck that had hit them.

"When he hired thirty men to retrieve you, we thought it was overkill, but clearly it was necessary," the man who appeared to be the leader stated before jabbing a needle into Liang's arm.

Chapter Thirty-One

It was eerily quiet as they approached the warehouse. Boots crunching the dirt beneath their feet and the sound of their breathing were the only things Dante heard as he led the team searching for Brooklyn. The air was still as the sun began to set. Despite knowing that anywhere from fifteen to sixty men on the premises, they had not seen a single soul in the thirty minutes they'd watched the building from their hiding places at the top of the road leading to the warehouse. Dante's and his team's nerves got more and more on edge each minute that they continued to watch, wait, and plot strategy.

The team that Kane hired this time to abduct Liang was good. All the gunfire and craziness alongside the highway had been covered up by the fake road construction the team had orchestrated. No passersby saw a thing. By the time Dante's team had arrived, the roads were reopened, the SUV was moved to a side road that was barricaded off to traffic, and Liang was gone. Bill and Robert were unconscious in the SUV. Stephen was bound and gagged in the backseat. All three were being evaluated at the nearest medical center.

Certain that Liang's kidnappers had brought her to this location as well, he split his team up so that once they got inside, half would look for Brooklyn and the others would look for Liang. He led the group in charge of locating Brooklyn. Though the other team was instructed to look for Liang, he ordered them to radio him immediately if they found Brooklyn before he did. He figured she would need to see his familiar face in the crowd of armed men. Otherwise, she could think that they were men that Kane sent to hurt her. Liang knew most of the men on this mission, so that would not be a problem for her.

Dante prayed that the team that had collected Liang had gotten their delivery fee and kept it moving. The fewer bad guys in the warehouse, the better. Doing everything possible to stack the odds in their favor, Dante had a person at his office constantly checking all the mail for any packages specifically addressed to him or Liang. Any additional information they could get their hands on could only help at this point.

He motioned for his men to advance. Weapons drawn, they crept toward the warehouse. A long hallway greeted them as they entered the building. They rushed forward, making as little noise as possible. At the end of the hallway, Dante could look down onto the lower level. The hallway became a catwalk that led to staircases on either side of the room that went down to a sunken area on the lower level. Dante's team would have to climb a small set of stairs to reach the half of the room that was beyond the clear wall that divided the lower level. The area beyond the wall reminded him of the pool room of a gym. Brooklyn and Liang were visible beyond the glass wall, which Dante assumed was bulletproof. As his team spread out, Dante signaled for them to keep their eyes open as they headed to the stairs on either side of the room.

Suddenly Kane's voice filled the room. "Dante, you didn't even wait until I extended an invitation. I should have known better. It's not like you didn't invite yourself to the party the last time."

Dante eye's scanned the room, but seeing no one, his focus returned to Brooklyn and Liang beyond the glass. Liang stood on a platform above a pool that reminded him of a diving board only wider and sturdier. Her right calf had a metal device clamped around it and he assumed so did her left, her hands were tied behind her back and a noose around her neck. The rope that was wrapped around her neck was threaded through a loop that hung from the ceiling attached to a metal lever on the pool deck cross from her where Brooklyn sat in a chair with her hands tied behind her back. It didn't look like she was locked into the platform like Liang.

At least ten armed men poured out of a door on the back wall beyond the glass and pointed their guns at Brooklyn and Liang. Others came from previously-hidden side doors on the sunken level Dante's team was on and aimed at them. "You're the only one allowed to enter through the door, Dante. Otherwise, you will watch both ladies die," Kane's voice cautioned as one of the armed men opened another door in the wall, stepped on the black staircase, and stared down at Dante, who stood at its base. "If you choose to enter," Kane continued, "you may just have a chance to save one of them."

Dante already knew he was going to enter the room. "Fine," he answered. One of the guys lowered his gun and walked towards Brooklyn. He stood her up and removed the chair. Brooklyn kept looking down at her feet, which were tied together at the ankle. Glancing up, Dante noticed that two people were on either side of the room with guns aimed at the staircases leading up to the clear wall.

Dante started towards the stairs.

"Not so fast." Kane stepped into view behind the glass wall, escorted by a security team. He stood on the left side near Liang. Dante could see Liang's mouth moving, but couldn't hear what she was saying to Kane.

Kane pointed toward Dante. "You're not walking in here with that weapon in your hand."

Dante handed it to the person next to him. He mouthed to the person to find the back door. They had looked for an entry point on the back side. Although there was no traditional door, maybe there was a door like the one in the glass wall that they wouldn't have been able to see unless they were up on it.

"I know that's not the only weapon you have on you." Kane walked over and stroked Liang's hair. She tried to move her head away from his hand, but with the noose around her neck, movement was restricted.

Dante turned and handed over his Beretta. He lifted his arms and turned around to show he had no more guns on him.

"Once your team exits this level, you'll be allowed to enter." While his team retreated back up the stairs, he tried to formulate a plan to save both women. The guy guarding the door stepped back as the last member of his team hit the upper level.

"Let me explain to you how this works," Kane stated, stepping away from Liang and heading to the back of the room. "You can choose to save your partner or the love of your life." He turned to face Dante. "If you choice Liang, once you take the noose off her neck it will cause the lever on the front of Brooklyn's platform to go down and the metal grid will rise out of the deck and crush her." Kane used the remote in his hand to display the sharp metal grid raised out from the ground.

Dante noticed that the rope that once laid loose around Liang's neck now looked like a choker until he releases the grid back into the floor. Staring at Brooklyn, he couldn't see anything locking her in place.

"You know what you have to do," Liang shouted, looking at a very distraught Dante.

"Fine. I choose Liang." The sound Brooklyn made beneath her gag broke his heart.

"No!" Liang screamed in shock. He knew that while she didn't want to die, she didn't want to be responsible for Brooklyn's death.

"Not so fast," Kane stated to Dante with a wicked smile. "You may want to rethink this decision. If your intention is to hold the rope to keep it from triggering the grid, I already thought of that. It won't work."

"Kane, why don't you let Brook go?" Dante's mind raced as he evaluated the best way to handle the situation. "You know this is really between you, me, and Liang."

"You're not going to ask why your plan won't work?" Kane laughed as his guard held the door to his escape route open. "I'll tell you. The only way to release Liang's leg is if Brooklyn is moved off of the deck. Her little diving platform automatically releases the clamps on her legs as it moves back."

Kane hit the control and the platform released Liang's calf and started moving back. Brooklyn's face filled with fear as the grid lifted slightly. Kane moved the platform back and the device relocked around Liang's calves. "Or you could unlock the device with the key that is in front of Liang. If you don't take the noose off before unlocking the device, you will end up in the water with Liang hanging above and Brooklyn crushed and sliced up."

"Damn you, Kane!" If Kane was close enough, Dante would have crushed his throat with his bare hands. There was a chance with this contraption he wouldn't be able to save either woman.

"You know what you have to do," Liang repeated to Dante, looking over at Brooklyn.

As one of Kane's men positioned himself behind Dante with a gun aimed at him, Kane pointed to a timer on the back wall that started a countdown and said, "You have one minute to figure it out or it won't matter who you choose. Once the minute is over, you'll have less than a minute to attempt to save one of them."

Dante kept the guy whose gun was trained on him in his peripheral view as the others began to clear the area. Kane moved towards the door. "Liang, it's been a pleasure seeing you again."

"Kane, I hope you go to hell in gasoline drawers," Liang yelled at his retreating figure.

"By the look on your partner's face"—Kane paused, looking back at her then laughing—"You will not be sending me there personally." He blew her a kiss as he exited the room.

There was no denying with this new information, Dante had chosen Brooklyn. He glanced back and noticed over twenty of Kane's men had filled the sunken area of the lower level. When Liang signed up for the job, she signed up to put her life on the line, Brooklyn hadn't. When Kane hit the door, Dante stepped back, grabbing the barrel of the gun of the man standing beside him. He pushed the butt of the gun against the guy's chest, then pistol-whipped him across the face. Racing towards Brooklyn, Dante fired the gun at Kane's security that stood in front of the door. He could tell by the movement of Liang's platform that Kane had hit the button. Dante ran, jumping, grabbing Brooklyn then turning so he would land on his back with her on top. As they started to slide against to floor, he lifted his weapon and aimed at the loop, shooting at the rope. He took several shots at the rope. The sound of Liang's body hitting the water brought him relief, but it was short lived as gunfire filled the room. When they stopped moving, he rolled Brooklyn off his chest and pushed her towards the wall.

"Get in the fetal position," Dante yelled as he turned to his side, using his body to block Brooklyn as he returned fire at the men coming through the door. He cringed as a bullet pierced his thigh.

"Brook," Dante called out to her. It sounded like she was hyperventilating behind him. "Baby, hang in there. Hang in there a little while longer." He kept scooting back little by little to create more distance between them and the back door. "Brooklyn, breathe."

Dante could hear Liang's movement in the water. He had managed to save both of them. However, he knew that if he didn't get help soon, it would all be for nothing. He continued to shoot at the door. He would run out of bullets soon. Glancing over his shoulder, Dante could see part of his team doing battle beyond the wall. If his guys didn't find a way to enter the room soon, the three of them would be dead. Without enough ammunition to hold Kane's men off and with no place to hide, it was just a matter of time until Kane's men would come from behind the door and take Dante, Liang, and Brooklyn out.

* * *

The ride to the warehouse where Brooklyn's was located seemed to take an eternity. Hunter said a silent prayer for her. He owed Vince big time for all of his help. Once Vince's people had showed Gus that they had retrieved his family, he gave up Brooklyn's location.

As they approached the warehouse, Hunter could see people coming out of the building and running around back. It seemed to take forever for him and Levi's convoy to get down the hill. The men in the truck that accompanied him were heavily armed, which made Hunter extremely nervous that something could go terribly wrong. The trucks finally rolled to a stop.

Levi looked over at Hunter's worried face. "What team are you going with?" Levi asked as everyone quickly got out.

"I'll go with the team going through the front door."

Levi handed Hunter a gun and some additional ammo. "Stay behind the team and try not to use your weapon unless you have to."

"Levi ..."

"Let's go get your girl," Levi stated as he exited the vehicle and led his security detail away from the building.

Fifteen of Levi's men moved toward the front door of the building. Hunter followed them, but had a gut feeling he needed to go with Levi. He told the men in front of him to go on, then turned and ran in Levi's direction. Levi had stopped several hundred yards out and was looking at the ground and kicking dirt as the six men with him stood guard. He bent down and pulled open a hatch that was in the ground. He and his men went underground, closing the hatch behind them.

Glancing back at the warehouse, Hunter saw that two huge dudes who looked seven-feet tall had stepped in front of the door to ensure no one could come in behind Levi's team. Hunter crossed the rest of the way to the hatch. He heard a hail of gunfire when he opened it. Lowering himself down into the tunnel, he immediately found himself face-to-face with a gun.

"Mr. Torres, are you trying to get yourself killed?" one of Levi's men asked with a machine gun aimed at Hunter. He lowered his weapon and stated into his communication device, "Torres is on the premises," as Hunter ran towards the gunfire.

Hunter caught up to Levi just as they hit the end of the hall. "What the hell?" Levi glared at Hunter, who was leaning on the wall next to him.

"What's the plan?" Hunter asked. Being in a room with bullets flying all around, they'd definitely need one.

"From what I can see, we need to give Dante some assistance on the other side of that glass. Hunter peered around Levi to see Dante firing at the back door with Brooklyn tucked behind him.

"We need to clear a path to those stairs." Levi signaled for the part of his team to go. "And remember not to have a gun in your hands when our backup arrives."

"Understood."

"Once you enter that door to the other room, go to your right. I'll have a guy come in to the left."

Hunter was grateful they had the advantage of coming up from behind Kane's men. He was sure they weren't expecting anyone to come out of this corridor. "Cool, just keep people off the stairs."

"You're going to be sitting ducks in the room, so make sure your aim is on point," Levi advised as he followed the remainder of his team out. They quickly took out the guys blocking the stairs, allowing Hunter to make his way up.

Hunter came into the Plexiglas room firing at the back door. Three more of Levi's men entered, firing at the men retreating into the back door. As the back door closed, one of Levi's men came in and assisted Liang out of the pool as the other two headed for the back door.

"We have the back secured. We just have to keep them from coming through this door," one of Levi's men said, drawing Hunter's attention to the door they had come in through. Chaos ensued on the other side. On the outside of the glass, there were hand-to-hand battles and shots were still being fired.

Hunter heard Dante say, "Brooklyn, baby talk to me. Are you injured?" Dante brushed the hair off her face. Every time she tried to speak, she just started crying uncontrollable. "Baby, you're safe. I just need you to tell me if you're hurt."

"I have never been happier to see you in my life. I'm sore from you pushing me away like a rag doll, but I'm fine." Brooklyn gave a weak smile as Dante begin untying her.

Dante helped her to her feet and hugged her to his body. Hunter stood back, feeling like the odd man out. He had to stop Levi from shooting two of Dante's men who had managed to make it up the stairs. One headed over to Liang and the other over to Dante. Hunter didn't know if he should approach Brooklyn or leave as if he was never there. They were so focused on each other that he doubted they saw him. His thought were interrupted by someone shouting, "Liang, no!"

Liang ran past her guys, heading to the door.

"Dammit, Liang, don't do it," Dante yelled as Liang opened and went through the back door. He looked at Brooklyn. "I can't let her go after Kane."

"Our team has him cornered in the building northwest of here,"

Dante's guy yelled.

"You're injured," Brooklyn said as Dante detached the strap from the gun then wrapped it around his leg.

"I can't let her go after him."

"I'll take care of Brooklyn. You go after Liang," Hunter said, extending his gun to Dante. Dante took the gun then kissed Brooklyn on the forehead.

"Be safe. We have a lot to talk about," Brooklyn stated just before he took off running towards the back door.

Hunter opened his arms. "It's so good to see your beautiful face again." Brooklyn stepped into his embrace and wrapped her arms around his waist. "BK, don't ever scare me like that again." Hunter glanced back just as the door closed behind Dante.

"Trust me, I have no plans to repeat this." Brooklyn tightened her hold on him, grateful to be alive.

While the rest of Dante's guys ran past them and out of the back door, Hunter pulled her back, tilted his head down to look into her eyes. "Are you sure?"

"I'm happy to be alive."

"Mr. Torres, is everything good?" one of Levi's men who came through the back door asked.

"Yes."

Levi stepped into the room. Gunfire erupted on the other side of the glass as more of Kane's men entered the room.

"Head to the back door," Levi yelled to Hunter.

Hunter suddenly knew the terror Dante and Brooklyn faced being in this room; being shot at with nowhere to hide. Brooklyn broke out running towards the back door with Hunter and Levi on her heels. Levi pushed them through the door. As they neared the end of the hallway they heard, "Drop your weapons and get your hands up!"

They froze in place and turned to see local police and the FBI. "We're safe," Hunter told Brooklyn. Brooklyn visibly relaxed. It seemed Vince's plan to provide them with a little backup worked. As Levi's people were being handcuffed, Levi stood with his hands up. Hunter put his hands up too, wondering when the hell Levi had gotten rid of his gun.

Chapter Thirty-Two

Dante saw Liang racing towards the building where his men had Kane trapped. He knew she planned to make him pay for what he'd done to her and her husband. "Liang, stop." She ignored Dante's plea and entered the building before he could reach her.

Swearing under his breath, he pushed forward, ignoring the piercing pain in his thigh. Through his earbud, he barked to his men to restrain Liang when they saw her. He rushed through the door she had entered moments before. She was nowhere to be seen. Liang was on the hunt and she was excellent at hunting.

"Has anyone got eyes on either Kane or Liang?" Dante moved slowly through the first level of the building. Dark and dank, it was full of containers, crates, and dead bodies—mostly Kane's men. He suspected that Liang had already lifted a gun from one of them. None of his men were on the first floor, which meant they felt certain Kane was somewhere on the second floor. Getting a response that no one had visuals on Kane or Liang was not what Dante wanted to hear.

Kane rushed up the stairs to the second floor. Liang stepped out of the shadows and followed him. She could not let him get away. She knew Kane—he had a plan for escape and it wouldn't be easy to spot. And if she had rushed up the stairs like Kane's men had done, she would have missed it. In the dark stairwell, a pair of heavy drapes were almost invisible against the wall. There was something slightly askew about them. Liang followed her instincts and slowly pushed them aside. The small window behind it was slightly ajar. She peered out and saw the fire escape. *So this is how Kane slipped past Dante's men.* Because it had not been extended down to the ground, she instantly knew that Kane had gone up to the roof. Liang pushed the window open and climbed gingerly onto the fire escape. Leading with one of the guns she pulled off one of Kane's men, she slowly and quietly started up the stairs.

"Are we sure he came up here?" Dante asked one of his men.

He shook his head. "He was spotted on the stairs. His men fired back on us from the stairwell, but eventually we were able to push them back. They've barricaded themselves in that back room. Herman is planning to blow the door. We should be ready to move in five minutes, and then we should be able to confirm Kane's presence."

Dante's gut was burning. Something wasn't right. Where had Liang gone? She should have been spotted the minute she stepped onto the second floor. Had she tracked Kane to another part of the building? He needed to retrace his steps and locate Liang and Kane before something unthinkable happened. "Keep me informed," he said as he made his way back to the stairs. "I need to go check something out."

He stopped in his tracks when he felt a draft coming through what he thought was the stairwell wall. A closer look told him that there wasn't a wall at all in that small area, but rather a set of thick curtains that hugged an open window. Dante cursed himself for having missed it the first time he passed through there, knowing Liang probably hadn't missed it. As he climbed through the window and onto the fire escape, one of his men's voices came through his earbud. "There's a helicopter heading this way. Kane must have found his way to the roof." Shots rang out from the roof. Dante raced up the fire escape, trying to get to Liang.

"I'm not going to let you get away," Liang called from behind the ventilation system where she'd taken cover. "This ends today, Kane." She'd been able to take out one of the three guards that were covering him.

"While I'd love to stay and chit chat with you, my lovely Liang, my ride is almost here." He pointed at a helicopter coming toward them. "I'm afraid we're going to have to pick this up at a later date. I assure you that the next time we meet, the outcome for you won't be pleasant."

Her response was cut off when she noticed Dante climbing onto the roof from the fire escape. She turned and quickly fired at Kane and his men, drawing fire and giving Dante enough time to scramble over the side and rush for cover with her. "Thanks," he said breathlessly.

"I know you mean to stop me from killing Kane, but I need to take him out." Liang wasn't going to back down.

The roar of the helicopter blades was loud. There was enough room on the roof for it to land, but the pilot didn't, probably not wanting to take on hostile fire. Hovering above Kane and his men, he lowered a rope ladder. Kane's men fired at Liang and Dante to allow Kane time to climb the ladder.

Liang panicked. "He's getting away!" She became reckless, rolling from behind the ventilation system to take out another of Kane's men. Dante covered her quickly and took out the last man before he could fire on Liang.

Liang jumped to her feet, and ran towards the helicopter, which was quickly making its way off into the sunset with Kane clinging to the ladder. She tried to fire a shot off, but her gun clicked. Empty. She dropped it and pulled another one from her waistband, but Kane was too far away now. She dropped to her knees, disgusted with herself.

Dante came up behind her and pulled her to her feet. They watched as the helicopter became smaller and smaller. Then the unexpected happened. They heard a whiz sound and an explosion before the helicopter took a nose dive and smashed to bits on the ground. Relief flooded both Dante's and Liang's bodies. It was finally over.

Dante's head was spinning. Things happened quickly after that. His men subdued the remainder of Kane's forces. Hunter, Brooklyn, Levi, and a few of his men managed to slip into another hidden corridor while the local police and FBI were distracted by the huge explosion outside. It was mostly Dante's team and a few of Levi's men that were left to explain the mess to the authorities. Dante tried to convince Liang to slip away in the commotion, but she refused. She wanted to see things through to the end.

Chapter Thirty-Three

Hunter checked Brooklyn into a hotel since they were required to stay nearby for the time being. It was clear by the way she kept asking when they were going to the police station that she was worried about Dante and wanted to provide her statement sooner rather than later in order to help him sort things out with the police. But Hunter wanted to make sure she had time to get herself together first. The ordeal she had just gone through, coupled with her conflicting feelings for him and Dante, seemed to be weighing heavily on her.

He talked her into taking a shower. While she did, he called the hotel boutique to have clothes brought up for both of them. He also ordered room service. The clothes were brought up first. Tomorrow one of Levi's men would bring the overnight bag he had Alexis put together for Brooklyn.

Hunter knocked on the bathroom door. "BK, I have some clothes for you to try on." When she didn't answer, he became concerned. "Brooklyn, are you okay?" Still no response. "I'm coming in," he stated as he cracked the door. She sat naked in the shower, her back against the shower stall wall and her knees curled up to her chest. Her head laid on her knees and she was sobbing softly.

"Ah, baby," Hunter said as he grabbed a bath towel. He shut off the water, wrapped her in the towel, and lifted her out of the stall.

"I'm sorry. It just all hit me at once, and I can't seem to pull it back together." She sobbed into his neck.

"No need to apologize. You've been through a horrible ordeal. It's understandable that you're shaken." Tenderly he dried her off and then bundled her in one of the hotel's robes. "We'll get some food in you and let you get some rest before we head to the station."

"But Dante needs me now, to help straighten things out." She struggled to get her emotions in check.

"Believe me when I say Dante is more concerned for your well-being than his right now. He would want you to take care of yourself first."

"Are you sure? I don't want to let him down after the way he came through for me."

"Absolutely. Look I promise we'll get you to that station as soon as possible. I just want to make sure that you're up to par first. Once we get there, you're going to have to relive everything and you'll need to get your strength up for that."

Brooklyn snuggled into his neck. "Thank you, Hunter."

"For what?"

"For always being the voice of reason and letting me use some of your strength when mine is low." Her voice started to drift.

"Anytime, BK, anytime." He carried her into the bedroom and laid her down. She needed the rest, and he was going to see that she got it. When room service came, he wrapped up her sandwich and placed it in the mini refrigerator so she could have it before they left for the station. While Brooklyn slept, Hunter's mind kept picturing Dante consoling her in the glass room. Dante had taken a bullet for her and saved her life. *I probably don't stand a chance with her now.* His heart ached at the thought of losing her, but with all she had been through, he wouldn't dare try to pressure her in any way. The decision, when she was ready, would be hers to make. He just hoped she would swing his way.

* * *

Dante had been taken to the hospital, where they removed the bullet from his thigh and stitched him up. He and Liang had been separated at the site, and he imagined she was already in an interrogation room. Dante wished she would have let him deal with this on his own, but she refused. They had agreed to tell as much of the truth as possible without revealing the part that Levi and his men played in their rescue. Levi had made it perfectly clear to his men that if they were caught, it was best to keep his name out of the story. Since they wouldn't have made it without his help, both Dante and Liang had agreed. They were pretty sure that Brooklyn wasn't aware that Levi and his men weren't a part of Dante's team, so they were confident she wouldn't cause a hiccup in their stories when she came in and made her statement. Since Levi slipped out during the helicopter explosion and all the men on his team were from a legitimate professional security company, they had less to try to explain away.

Now that he had been treated, Dante was carted off to the precinct and placed in an interrogation room. He nearly laughed when a cocky lieutenant came in and proclaimed, "Your partner, Liang, has told us everything, so there's no need to try and spin us."

"I have no intentions of doing that. I'm just here to provide you with facts to wrap up this case."

The lieutenant sat on the table by Dante's chair. Dante was not intimidated. "And just what are the facts?"

Dante told the lieutenant and his cohorts behind the one-way mirror about receiving the case to find Megan. He shared the details of how it tied in to Brooklyn's work as well as an old case in which Liang's husband was murdered and she was nearly killed. He explained how both Brooklyn and Liang had been snatched and how he was able to find and rescue them. He provided most of the details right up to the rooftop showdown with Kane. The cocky lieutenant made snide remarks about Dante being a rogue and thinking he could do their jobs better than them. Dante did not take the bait, even though he could have clearly pointed out that he was able to find Brooklyn when they had not been able to do so.

"Where is Brooklyn now?" Cocky Lieutenant asked. "We'd like to talk to her."

"She'll be in as soon as she gets some rest. As you can imagine, she's been through quite the ordeal and needs some time to collect herself."

"How do we know you even found her?" In the commotion, no one seemed sure of anything. The explosion had caused a huge distraction. Otherwise they would have not let her leave the premise without at least trying to take a statement.

"Why would I lie about it? What would I have to gain by lying?"

Cocky Lieutenant stood. "I think you should sit tight until we can corroborate your story. Of course, a part of that is speaking to Ms. Saunders."

"Of course," Dante stated.

Liang was also left waiting in an interrogation room. They already mentally prepared for a long night. Luckily, they had the comfort of knowing that Kane was out of the equation.

* * *

At three o'clock in the morning, Hunter and Brooklyn arrived at the precinct. They both were carted off to interrogation rooms. Like Liang and Dante, Hunter kept Levi's name out of the story and told the police how he worked with Dante and Liang on tracking down where Brooklyn was being held.

By the time Hunter's interrogation was over, the authorities had identified Kane by his dental records and opened an investigation on how he had been able to break out of jail and assume another identity. Dante, Hunter, Liang, and Brooklyn were all released before noon the next day with instructions not to leave town.

As the four of them left, Lieutenant Cocky said, "You're not telling us the whole story. I'd bet my badge on it. And how is it that not one of you could say who blew up the helicopter?" They filed silently past him, with no one bothering to answer.

Hunter unlocked the door to his SUV so that Brooklyn, Dante, and

Liang could all climb in. There was a moment of awkwardness as everyone tried to figure out their next move. Finally Dante spoke up. "Liang and I really have to wrap up some loose ends on this case. The sooner we can get this done the better. Liang, can you hang in there a little longer or do you want to get some rest first?"

"I'm good with a quick shower and some coffee," Liang answered. "When I crash, I'm going to crash hard."

"So where to?" Hunter asked.

"Liang and I have a satellite office nearby," Dante said. "Drop us off there." He gave Hunter the address. "We both have a change of clothes there and a shower we can use." He almost choked on his next words, but they were necessary. "Brooklyn, you shouldn't be alone. Stay with Hunter, and I'll come find you as soon as I get things wrapped up."

Brooklyn was exhausted and could barely keep her eyes open. "That's fine with me. If we could go back to the hotel, I would appreciate it. I'm just happy to crash somewhere where no one will come knocking or looking for me."

* * *

Within minutes of stepping into the hotel room, Brooklyn was in bed and deep into dreamland. Hunter poured himself a drink and took long, slow sips until weariness overtook him. He slipped into bed next to Brooklyn, and she immediately snuggled into him. He kissed her gently on the forehead, wondering if this was the last time he would get to hold her as he drifted to sleep.

* * *

Brooklyn woke up hours later feeling disoriented. She quickly gathered her bearings and realized she was snuggled in bed with Hunter. He was still sleep and she watched him for a moment. Her mind bounced between him and Dante. *I'm too tired for this right now*, she thought. *I know I'll have to make a decision soon, but now is not the time.* She snuggled comfortably against Hunter again and fell asleep with both him and Dante on her mind.

* * *

Dante kept replaying the scenario with Kane and Liang. Liang came into the room towel-drying her hair. She sat across from Dante and put her towel around her neck. "What's on your mind?" she asked.

"The helicopter crash."

Stress and tension returned to Liang's body. "Damn. Don't tell me you think Kane is alive."

"I think it's very important that we answer that question." Dante grabbed his phone, texting Hunter to find out if one of his people shot Kane's helicopter out of the sky.

"But they confirmed it was him by his dental records." Liang's face dropped at the implications of what he was saying.

"He faked his death before." Dante stood and grabbed his shirt that laid next to him. "How did he manage to have somebody identify that body in prison as him?"

"Ugh, that is not what I want to hear, but you've got a point." Liang's eyes went up Dante's abs to his face, locking onto his eyes with an intense glare.

As he put on his shirt, he stated, "Until we get confirmation, you should stay at the safe house or with me."

"You sure know how to ruin a woman's high." Liang stood, throwing the towel at him as she exited the room.

Dante yelled after her, "Would you rather just wait until he pops up in your life again?"

He was no more happy about this than Liang was. It didn't play in his favor with Brooklyn. He needed to be trying to win her over, and he couldn't do that and protect Liang at the same time. However, he didn't want to have the insane doctor reappear later and destroy their lives. He hoped and prayed that Kane was truly dead this time and not putting on a show to go into hiding.

Chapter Thirty-Four

In the months following, Brooklyn tried to get her head and heart straight. She thought she had come to a definitive decision while she was kidnapped. Now that she was free, she was back to wavering between the two men. Both Dante and Hunter had been considerate of all that she had been through and weren't forcing her to choose between them… yet. But to be fair to them, she needed to make a decision soon. Rushing back to work and getting back to her normal life didn't help as much as she thought it would. She put in for two weeks off to get away and figure things out, and was granted it immediately. Before she left, she arranged to have dinner with Dante and breakfast with Hunter so she could explain what she was doing and why.

Sitting across a dinner table from Dante that night, she said, "I'm leaving tomorrow afternoon for two weeks. I need some time alone."

Dante sat back in his chair and his eyes swept over her face. "I won't ask why because I already know. Just know that I love you, I want to be with you, and I'm ready to give it all up to be with you. I've seen firsthand what can happen to the loved ones of people doing what I do, and I could never put you at risk again." He sat forward in his chair and reached across the table to grab her hand. "I love you. So while you're off thinking about who you should be with, know for certain that I'm all in. There's no mistake in choosing me because I would give whatever it takes to make you happy."

Afterward, Brooklyn spent the night tossing and turning, with Dante's words running through her mind. Even though he had risked his life for her and had finally said the words she'd waited years to hear, she couldn't call it in his favor. Hunter still had a piece of her heart and she needed to hear what he had to say before she made her decision.

The next morning she sat across the table from Hunter. "I'm leaving this afternoon for two weeks. I need some time alone." She stopped to hear him out.

"Do you need anything?" Hunter inquired, looking into her eyes. "Maybe a ride to the airport?"

She watched him, she could tell he was thinking through what he was about to say. "No, but thanks."

"Look, BK, I'm going to lay all my cards on the table. I love you, and I truly like the person you are. The second part might not seem as important to you, but I've learned that liking someone is just as important as loving them. I know you have a difficult decision to make. While I hope that you'll choose me, I want you to know that if you don't, I'll totally move out of the way. I won't pressure you in any way to change your mind because ultimately I want you to be happy."

A week later, Brooklyn was no closer to making a decision. She had flown into Sedona, Arizona and checked into a resort. She'd signed up for meditation classes, yoga classes, and massages, all in an attempt to clear her head and make her decision.

On a whim she did a search on relationship advice. A site called The SSMD (Single, Shacking, Married, Divorce) caught her eye. She read through some of the content then posted to the site. *I can't believe I'm about to do this,* she thought as she began typing.

Dear SSMD Advisor,

Recently my life has caught fire. If I told you all that has happened to me in the past few months, you wouldn't believe me. I'm still trying to process it myself.

The reason I'm reaching out to you is because the blaze is burning with the most intensity in the romance department. My story is truly one of being torn between two loves and trying to choose which one is the one. One is my rock, and I can rely on him through thick and thin. The other one is my shield who protects me in times of trouble. They both offer me love and support and both have good hearts.

I feel I'm equally attracted to both and love them both. Most women may think this is a great problem to have, but I can tell you that it isn't. I don't want to hurt either one of them and I truly want to be with the one I'm intended for. I just can't seem to figure out which one that is. What would you suggest I do to determine which of these great guys I'm truly meant for?

Sincerely,
Life on Fire

"Now I know I'm losing my mind." she mumbled as she hit the enter key. "I hope you have some skills to get me out of this mess, SSMD Advisor." Brooklyn shut down her computer and grabbed her water bottle. "Time for yoga."

Despite herself, when yoga was done, she rushed back to her room, hoping to find a response. She was in luck.

Dear Life on Fire,

I would suggest you take a moment to look ahead. Imagine your life with each of these men. Will you have to give up any part of yourself or your dreams to be with either of them? Will one of them have to give up a part of themselves to be with you? Which one does your life purpose align with? Look at the things you don't like about them and determine if you can live with those things over a lifetime.

You're afraid to make a decision because you're afraid to make the wrong choice, but there are no guarantees in life. You'll just have to fully commit to the one you choose. The other one can't be your plan B.

Trust your decision,
The SSMD Advisor

Brooklyn knew the minute she read the response which one she would choose. Her heart ached over the one she had to let go. She spent the rest of her time in Sedona alternating between crying over the one she had to let go and looking forward to spending her life with the one she chose.

As soon as she arrived home, she made a call and asked, "Can you meet me later for dinner?" Hunter agreed quickly. She could hear the hope in his voice. They set a place and time.

As she had done two weeks before, Brooklyn sat across the table from Hunter. "Welcome back. How was your time away?" he asked her.

"It was exactly what I needed, thanks." She offered a slight smile but it didn't last long, as suddenly she felt a bit awkward. Hunter reached across the table and took both her hands in his. "It's okay, BK. Just say it and it'll be okay."

Brooklyn cleared her throat. "Hunter, I love you and … I choose you." Relief flooded Hunter's eyes. He pulled her up by the hands and guided her around the table and into his arms. She added, "I haven't told Dante yet, but I promise I will, and you'll never have to worry about me choosing anyone over you again."

Later that day, Brooklyn contacted Dante and asked to stop by his place. When she arrived, he let her in and led her to the living room. Once she'd taken a seat, he asked, "Why?" She cocked her head at his question, but before she could find the words to answer, he said, "I knew the minute I opened the door that I wasn't going to like what you had to say."

"Dante, I do love you, but you shouldn't have to give up anything to be with me. I know you love what you do, and that's the thing that's been between us during the course of our relationship." Tears ran down her face. "We've tried to make our lives fit and they don't. I couldn't live with knowing you had to give up something you love to be with me, and I really couldn't live with you resenting me for it."

"Brooklyn, I could never resent you," Dante told her. "Are you sure about this?"

She stood and looked him directly in the eyes. "Answer something honestly for me."

"Okay."

"Is there any part of you that feels relief that you don't have to give up your work?" Brooklyn's eyes kept hold of his eyes. They told her the truth. "Exactly," she said. "So yes I am sure about this." She walked over to him and planted a soft kiss on his lips. "Dante Nines, I love you and wish you only the best. It's been quite the ride." She walked to the door and let herself out. She hopped in the car and headed to Hunter's.

He let her in, and she walked straight into his arms. "Are you hungry?" he asked as he took her jacket and hung it up.

Brooklyn unzipped her dress and let it drop to her ankles. "Yes, but it's not food I'm hungry for."

Hunter turned to find Brooklyn standing in a red lace low-cut bra with matching panties. "Damn," he grunted.

"I hope that's a good damn," she said as he slid his arms around her waist. He slowly began caressing her behind.

"Yes," he answered in a low, sensual voice before lowering his lips to hers. Brooklyn deepened the kiss as Hunter wreaked havoc on her senses. She thought her knees would give out on her.

"You don't know how much I've wanted this," she said as he pressed her body against him.

Hunter broke the kiss and released her. "Mmm, that was an excellent appetizer, but I think I'll pass tonight. Goodnight, BK!" He kissed her on the forehead.

"Goodnight?" She stood there with her hands on her waist, staring at him while he walked away. "What the hell do you mean goodnight?" Brooklyn asked as she snapped out of it and followed him.

"You've been teasing me for months." He opened the door to his bedroom. "It's my turn to make you wait."

"Hold up, Mr. Torres." Brooklyn grabbed him by the tail of his shirt as he entered the room. "I wasn't teasing you just because. I was trying—"

"Trying to what, Ms. Brooklyn?" He turned and grabbed her wrist. "Use me to ease your frustration now that you've made a decision?"

"You're messing with me, right?" she said as a devilish smile crossed his face and he pulled her closer.

"I just needed to see if your feisty side still existed." He started walking backwards with his hands locked behind the small of her back. "You've been kind of lackluster lately."

"My feisty side is here and ready for you to stop talking and start showing me if all the rumors about you were fact or fiction." Brooklyn put her hand under his shirt, sliding it up until he was forced to release her so she could take the shirt off him.

"I don't know. I'm not feeling the feistiness." He laughed as Brooklyn took both hands and pushed him onto the bed.

"Fine, I have no problem taking control of this ride." She slowly straddled him then leaned over, taking her tongue and circling his nipples as she looked up at him seductively.

He flipped her onto her back. "It'll be my pleasure to feast on you tonight. But remember it's my show." Brooklyn didn't know what it was about his shallow breathing that was turning her on but it was sending a tingling feeling down her spine. She pulled him into a kiss.

"If you say so." She smiled as his lips began making a trail down her body. Brooklyn heard the sound of rip, rip and knew one of her favorite pair of panties was biting the dust. When Hunter's tongue began working its magic between her legs, she was too busy enjoying the feeling to care about anything else. She caressed the top of his head until she found herself grabbing the sheets and gasping for air, with her thighs trembling. His lips began moving up her body as her tremors quieted down. His fingers took over where his mouth left off, gently stroking her. With his weight resting on one elbow, Hunter pushed down one side of the lace edge of Brooklyn's bra, taking her into his mouth. All she could do was moan as she found her body trembling once again under Hunter's masterful touch. Brooklyn arched her back as Hunter's fingers increased their intensity until she lost complete control of her body. Hunter pressed his lower body into hers as his upper body hovered over her recovering body.

"Do you want more foreplay or are you ready for the main event?' he asked, grinding into her then leaning down to kiss her. Brooklyn answered by unbuckling his pants. He reached for a condom then proceeded to show her that the rumors were only the tip of the iceberg.

Chapter Thirty-Five

It was almost eight months since Dante took a bullet trying to save Brooklyn, and five months since she selected Hunter over him. He was frustrated as hell over the current state of his life. Brooklyn was no longer an option for him. Her decision continued to eat away at him.

Having Liang as his roommate again until they were sure Kane was indeed dead wasn't helping his emotional turmoil. They ate together, talked before bed, and watched movies together—all the things he could have been doing with Brooklyn. Since his opportunity with Brooklyn was lost because of the job, Dante now understood on an entirely new level what Liang had gone through when her husband was killed. His situation wasn't as life altering as Liang's had been, but it was devastating nonetheless. Like Liang, his heart hadn't really been into the job since he lost the love of his life. His mind still hadn't fully processed that she'd chosen Hunter. It had him distracted and off kilter.

Liang had taken a leave of absence from work to focus on trying to track Kane down. It disturbed Dante that no one admitted to shooting down Kane's helicopter, which suggested that Kane was on the loose under a new alias. Between cases, Dante followed up on Liang's leads.

Only when he knew that Kane was no longer a threat could he make the necessary changes that would make Brooklyn realize that he meant what he said about altering his life for her. If he could just find out who had sent the disk to his office back when Liang was at the safe house, that could be the break that they needed to track Kane down.

Grabbing his coat to leave for a meeting one morning, he said, "Can I ask you something?"

Liang stood next to the sink taking her last sip of coffee. "What's wrong?"

"I was just wondering if this career is worth our personal lives."

"Look, you and I both know we're not ready to leave the job." She placed the empty cup into the kitchen sink. "How many times have I said I was leaving, then found an excuse to push back the deadline?"

"You think Brooklyn was right." Dante glanced at his watch. They needed to leave soon.

"You had a chance to be with her years ago. You decided that it was in her best interest if you didn't become a couple," Liang said, putting her Ruger into her holster and sliding her jacket on over it. "Don't be upset with her for doing the same."

"Whatever." He grabbed his car keys. "We've got to get going."

"Don't mistake the messenger for the blessing."

"What?" Dante stared at her as if she was crazy, then did a final glance around the townhouse before heading to the door.

Liang walked through the door. "I'm saying that some people enter our lives to deliver a blessing, not to be the blessing. They aren't meant to share a lifetime with us."

"This is a conversation for another time." Dante locked up and they headed out of the building. "Besides, what she and I had was very special."

Liang smiled. "I know. She made you believe that you could actually have love in your life and that you didn't have to—"

"Let's not—"

"No, you brought it up so we're going to talk about it," she said as they got in the truck. "I've been where you are. Only I married my Brooklyn. My first marriage was an amazing disaster. I still love him to this day, but it takes more than love to make a relationship go the distance."

They buckled up and Dante started the truck and pulled off. "Brooklyn and I aren't—"

"Listen, what I'm saying is that in this moment you can't see yourself ever resenting Brooklyn, but I know from experience that it's a real possibility."

Dante cut his eyes over at Liang. The look on her face let him know she was not going to drop the subject. "What happened to you and your first husband? You rarely mention him?"

"Let's just say he made me a better wife for my second go-round. There's a difference between compromise and giving up who you are to make it work. We wanted different things and while we made it work for a while, it eventually imploded. But that's a conversation for another day."

Dante maneuvered through the traffic, watching their surroundings for anything suspicious. "In your second marriage, you made the decision to give up the job to have a family. So how was that different from me giving my job up to be with Brooklyn?"

"Because…" Liang paused to glance at her watch and look at the traffic. "We had more going for us than just love. We worked well as a team and he understood that I might not be cut out to be a full time mother. Since we'd establish I'd give it a try for a year, it felt more like a leave of absence than giving up my career."

Dante knew it would have been difficult for him to transition to a new job, but he was willing to do it. It wasn't like Brooklyn had asked him to. The frustration came in not having the opportunity to at least try. He hated that Hunter was an option for her. If there was no Hunter, he could have convinced her to at least give it a try.

He rubbed his temples, which did nothing to stop the tension headache he felt coming on. Weaving in and out of traffic, he said, "Look, let's save this conversation for another time. What we need to be concerned about now is why after all this time Aaron wants to see us."

By the time they arrived at the meeting place, Dante was rethinking his decision to meet this Aaron character without notifying his team. Was the information Aaron claimed to have on Kane worth taking such a risk? He sat in the last booth with his back to the wall, pretending to look over his menu while watching everyone that came through the front door. Liang sat at the counter ordering coffee and keeping an eye on the area where the staff entered and exited. As the waitress came over to take Dante's order, a lanky, curly-haired guy walked over to the booth. Dante motioned for him to take a seat then smiled up at the waitress as he said, "Could you give us a minute?" He placed the menu in front of Aaron.

Aaron sat down and put an envelope on the table. "Mrs. Holder said Tuck wanted you to have this."

Dante opened the package. It looked like three movie DVDs were inside.

Aaron instructed, "Once you load a disc into your computer, use the top number on the disk label for your account number and the bottom number as your pin."

Just like the last time I received mysterious DVDs.

"Two of them are from Tuck," Aaron continued.

"Have you looked at them?" Dante asked, wondering if those two disks were copies of the ones that had led him to Kane's warehouse.

"I haven't. Hopefully you'll figure out why this information is important enough for Kane to take on Alec McNier's alias that he'd send his wife into Tuck's company to retrieve it." Aaron looked at his watch.

Dante touched the third DVD. "What about this one?"

"That's from Ms. Holder, and no I haven't seen it. She said it was extremely important to check them out within the next two hours." Aaron stood and headed out of the café. Liang left out shortly behind him.

Dante started the timer on his watch. He paid his bill for the coffee then exited the café. Liang was already in the truck with her laptop out by the time he arrived.

"You need to follow Aaron. I was watching him as he got in his car.

When he pulled off, it looked like a black sedan pulled off with him." Liang looked back. "See that silver car that just crossed the light?" Dante spotted it through his side mirror. "That's him," she said. "The black sedan is stuck at the red light." Dante handed Liang the DVDs as he did a u-turn in the direction Aaron was headed.

Liang recognized the tracking number that started with TAIV at the top of two of the DVDs. "This has got to be the information that Kane was after from Tuck's vault," Liang reported.

She inhaled deeply and placed one of the disks in her laptop as Dante tried to keep up with Aaron, who was weaving in and out of traffic. By the way he was taking yellow lights, Dante assumed Aaron knew he was being followed. Liang gasped and when Dante looked over at her, her mouth had dropped open as she viewed the screen.

"Liang I need you to use words. What's on it?" he asked.

The shock immobilized her for a moment. "It … it's about Kane's foster sister." She took a gulp of air. "Alicia Michel is now known to the world as Ms. Michelle Holder."

"Tuck's wife?" Dante said as a red light stopped them. He took the laptop out of her hand to see for himself. When the light changed, he gave it back to her. "If Megan had known this entire time that Kane was just using her to find his sister, I wonder if she would still protect him so fiercely."

Liang loaded the second disk. "This one contains instructions to snatch Michelle and take her to a remote facility."

Dante banged his hand on the steering wheel. "She's his foster sister, for crying out loud. What kind of morbid fascination does this man have for her?" He was now following the sedan, since Aaron's car was no longer to be seen. He assumed the sedan was to busy trying to track Aaron down again to notice that they were being followed.

"That's just insanity!" Liang said as she placed the third disk into the laptop. "Shit," she said at the computer screen.

"What?"

"This confirms that Kane is still alive." Liang looked at Dante as they merged onto the expressway.

"Forward the information to—" A woman's voice coming through the laptop stopped Dante mid-sentence.

"I'm Alicia, Kane's foster sister. He's coming for me within the next few hours. I'm at the cabin Tuck and I shared." Alicia paused. "I'm leery of relocating to a public place like a hotel. Since Kane's team has hit two of my other properties, my attempt to relocate to another property not on his list will take me longer."

Liang took down the address. "Dammit, did this fool get a master's degree in faking his death?"

Alicia concluded the video with a request for them to help.

"Call the office and have them send a team to meet us at the cabin," Dante instructed as he stopped following the sedan and merged onto the exit ramp.

"Kane will not win," Liang said after she placed the call and hung up the phone.

Dante nodded in agreement. There was no way he was going to give Kane a chance to disappear with Alicia or come back for Liang.

* * *

Kane sat smugly in the back of the van as his elite team drove to Alicia's location; the final address on his list. He thought, *If this works out, I'd leave Ms. Megan rotting in jail* for *my crimes. If things don't work out tonight and her parents don't manage to wrangle her off the charges, I will get her out.* Megan's ability to track people and find dirt on them had proved to be very useful. Unfortunately for her, Megan never realized the only woman he'd ever loved was Alicia. He began to think of the counseling session where Alicia had told the therapists her foster parents knew something was wrong with him when they continued to catch him in her room sitting next to her bed just watching her. Kane loved Alicia in a way that they could not understand.

Alicia was thirteen and he was fifteen when his parents took her in. Her presence changed him. He needed to be in her space, to inhale her scent, to touch her skin. It didn't matter that he'd have to sneak into her bedroom at night to do that. At night he would watch the stars sparkle outside of her window, lying very still on the floor until he was sure she was sleep. Some nights he'd just watch her. Other nights, he'd caress her thighs or her arms or touch her hair. It freaked Alicia out. She would immediately popped up and talk to him for hours until his parents would come, find him there, and kick him out. It wasn't until his parents put a lock on her door so that she would feel safe at night that he realized that her talking to him was her defense mechanism against him touching her. His parents didn't understand the depth of his love for Alicia. He was so angry when he turned eighteen and his parents forced him to go away for college instead of staying near home. When he'd come home from break, Alicia always stayed at a friend's house.

Kane remembered the time he came home without letting his parents know. He'd found Alicia at home making out with some boy. He went ballistic. He snatched the boy away from her, throwing him onto the floor and beating him. Alicia grabbed his arm and begged him to stop. As he was swinging to hit the boy again, Kane accidently knocked her onto the coffee table and terror filled her eyes. The boy ran off as Kane checked on Alicia. Their parents were not happy with Kane. But worse than that, the way Alicia looked at him with eyes filled with fear broke his heart. He was determined to prove to her that he loved her and would never intentionally hurt her.

His parents sent him back to school after talking the boy's parents into not pressing charges. When Kane came back home for the holidays, Alicia was gone and his parents refused to tell him where she was. Kane did whatever it took to find her. It didn't matter what college or university she'd attend, he kept finding her. However, once she graduated from college, he had trouble tracking her down. He still couldn't believe his parents always worked so hard to prevent him from being with her. Well, he was coming for her now and no one would stop him.

Alicia Michel, we will be together soon and I will prove to you that my love for you is not sick or twisted, he thought as the vehicle slowed to a stop.

Kane waited for his team to signal for him to come in. This was the moment he had been waiting years for. He was nervous as if he was going on his first date. When he entered the cabin, she was sitting in the living room chair with her back to him and two of his armed men in front of her.

"Alicia, I'm sorry it has taken me so long to get to you." He walked towards the chair, concerned that she had slimmed down so much over the years. Kane rounded the chair to find Liang sitting there.

"Don't be sorry," Liang said as Dante stepped out, taking out the two men standing in front of Liang.

Kane grabbed Liang from the chair as more of his men came through the front door. "I came too far for you to get in my way again."

Liang elbowed him, sending him falling over one of the guys on the floor. Kane pulled out a gun. Liang kicked it out of his hand and hit him in the chest with all her pent up rage. She continued to slam her fist into his body. Kane used his leg to knock Liang over. She rolled and immediately jumped up. They engaged in hand-to-hand combat. Dante continued firing at the guys coming through the door, trying his best not to shoot Liang in the process. Liang's roundhouse kick sent Kane down to his knees. Every time he tried to get up, she'd slam her fist into his face. His blood slowly trickled onto the floor.

Alicia's screams pierced the air as she was being dragged out of the back room. Dante turned, shooting one of the guys that was trying to drag Alicia out the back door.

"Go!" Liang yelled.

Kane used his shoulder to hit Liang. The force knocked her to the ground. Kane started choking her. She grabbed at his arms as he cut off her air supply. Liang noticed the gun was within reach. Her fingers scrapped the ground trying to reach it. As Kane tightened his grip, Liang gasped for air. She finally got hold of the gun, brought her arm up, and fired several shots. Kane's eye bucked. He released her throat and grabbed at his wounds. Liang knocked him back onto one of his dead goons then rolled to her knees, gasping for air. She stood as Kane's body ceased to move. He made no sound.

"Are you good?' Peter asked as he and several others entered the cabin.

"Yeah. Dante may need a little assistance. He went out the back." She walked over to confirm that Kane was dead. To her surprise, his eyes popped open, he grabbed the gun out of the dead man's hand, and aimed at Liang. Liang fired a single shot to his head then said, "I guess I am the one sending you to hell after all."

Alicia stared at Kane's lifeless body. "Is it over?"

Liang looked up to see Alicia and Dante. "Yes, it's finally over."

Liang walked over and checked Kane for a pulse just to make sure. Dante nodded for Stephen to escort Alicia out. The flurry of activity was lost on Liang as she stared at Kane's body. Dante walked over to her, wrapping his arms around her.

Chapter Thirty-Six

Brooklyn had lied. She had told Hunter she wouldn't do this to him, but here she was making a liar out of herself. It was hard to ignore Hunter's heartbroken look when she left his office after telling him she needed to see Dante. She couldn't apologize for what she was doing. This was her life. She had to know she was making the right decision. Life had calmed down and was starting to get some normalcy back to it. As she pulled in front of Dante's place, she could see him waiting at the top of the stairs. There were no words to describe the kind of hold this man had on her heart. Brooklyn sat in the parked car for a minute, took deep breaths, and got out. Dante smiled, watching her hips sway from side to side as she approached.

"Hello, beautiful. To say that I was surprised to hear from you, let alone see you after our last conversation, would be an understatement." When she reached him, he wrapped his arms around her, inhaling a scent that was so uniquely Brooklyn.

"Well you've been on my mind a lot so …" She let her words hang as she entered the door he was holding open for her.

Dante led her into the townhouse. "You stay on my mind, Brook. You know that. Would you like something to drink?" he asked they entered the apartment.

"Yes, a glass of wine would be nice." Brooklyn took a seat on the couch. "So Kane is really dead this time?" She couldn't stop staring and recalling all the reasons she loved Dante as he poured the wine into the glasses.

"Yes. To Megan's chagrin, Kane's entire plan centered around finding his sister, not building a life with her. Now he's gone and she's doing time." Dante handed her a glass of wine, then sat down next to her. "But that's not what you came here to talk about."

"It was creepy watching the interview with Alicia," she said, ignoring his comment. "I don't understand his unnatural obsession with her. What was he going to do? Kidnap her and stare at her whenever he wanted? I just don't get it."

"I'm grateful for that." He took a sip of wine. "If you could understand crazy, then we'd have a big problem on our hands." Dante chuckled, trying to lighten to mood.

Brooklyn laughed. "You are so right about that."

"Brook, baby, what is it that you came to say to me?" Dante took her hand. Brooklyn looked down. Dante lifted her chin up with his finger.

"I love you, Dante, in a way that can't be duplicated. I know we didn't have a typical or official relationship." Brooklyn took a sip of wine, breathing deeply. "We had something so special in those small windows of time over the years when we were together."

"I wish I had taken a chance on us back then, but when Kane threatened to destroy everything we love, I didn't want to risk you ending up like Liang's husband, a casualty of the job that I do." He stood with hope shining in his eyes.

"It's ironic that I ended up in the midst of danger because of your job anyway." Brooklyn took another sip of wine, working up the nerve to say what she'd come there to say.

"I apologize for that."

"You can't take the credit for that. Tuck sending me the file with Kane's picture in it is what drew me into the madness." She attempted to release the death grip she had on the wine glass. "As I told you before, it would have been nice if we could have discussed it and come to the conclusion together."

"Brook, why are you here? Did you change your mind about Hunter?" Dante put his hand on top of her thigh to stop its nervous bouncing.

Her sudden silence was killing him. Finally she whispered, "I don't think you really ever understood what you mean to my life."

Dante sat his wine on the coffee table and sat next to her. "That isn't answering the question I asked you."

"I need you to hear me out before I answer that question." She inhaled deeply then took another sip of wine.

"I'm listening."

"You coming in and out of my life taught me to love, encouraged me to excel, and matured me in areas necessary to have a successful relationship. However, I was obsessed with what I had with you and I wanted to be more than just content." It still amazed her that she was here risking what she had with Hunter for a man that may not have really given up his career. Brooklyn went to sit her wine down, noticing for the first time that there were files and a laptop on the coffee table.

"So are you saying you've decided to love Hunter despite what you feel for me? If so, you already made that decision. I don't understand why you're here."

Brooklyn nodded at the laptop. "Have you gone back to work?"

"I'm not sure I'm going back." Dante looked as if he'd wished he put it up. "This stuff is unofficial."

"Oh." Brooklyn demeanor changed as she stared at the files.

"I'm asking you again. What are you trying to tell me? Have you changed your decision to be with Hunter?"

"When we leave certain jobs, there are exit interviews to give a person a chance to speak freely about the company, positive and negative, to see if there are improvements to be made." Brooklyn knew that's not why she had come there, but those files answered the question that she had really come here to ask. Now she knew he wasn't ready to give up his career. "When we end relationships, we don't always get that."

"This is my exit interview?" Dante huffed, picked up his glass, emptied its contents, and then grabbed Brooklyn's empty glass.

She rested her hand on his forearms as he tried to turn away from her with the glasses. "This is me honoring our love and friendship."

"By breaking my heart again?" Dante looked into her eyes, then shook his head as he headed to the kitchen.

Brooklyn quickly followed him into the kitchen. He placed her glass in the sink then poured more wine into his. She touched his forearm, stopping him from lifting his glass to his mouth. "What I need to say to you is important. I'm saying this not to hurt you but because I love you. Please hear me out."

"Dammit, Brook, why are you slicing me opening again?" He sat his glass down on the counter.

The pain in Dante's eyes crushed her. Brooklyn put her hand on his face. "Because I want to see you happy."

"I want to be happy with you. Are you planning to make that happen?" Dante stared at her intensely for a moment. "I thought not."

"You're not ready for the white picket fence yet. I appreciated you for wanting to try, but if you're giving it up before you're truly ready, you would resent me and our relationship." Having trouble looking in his eyes, she shifted her focus down.

Dante pulled her closer and gently caressed her arm. "I wouldn't."

"You say that now, but I saw you in action. What you do is part of you and Liang's DNA. I don't think either one of you is really ready to retire." Brooklyn refrained from saying that the files on the table proved that.

"We both think it's time to retire."

"Yet what you both really want is a personal life that will sustain what you do. Which is why I'm here. I want to see you happy. I believe you can have that happiness with Liang." The lie rolled off her tongue easily. Brooklyn was shocked at the words that were coming out of her mouth.

Dante stepped back. "What are you saying?"

"I'm asking have you ever considered going the distance with Liang? She's a woman that can handle what you do and have your back if anyone comes after you." Words were flowing out of her mouth, but she didn't even seem to have control of them.

Dante walked around her. When he reached the coffee table, he grabbed her purse.

"What are you doing?" she asked as he stuffed her purse in her hand and turned her towards the door.

"It's time for you to leave." He walked past her.

She stared at him as she spoke, "Hunter and I may not have the intense love that you and I had but we're better suited for each other. He doesn't have to sacrifice part of who he is to be with me. Just changing his work schedule created time for our relationship. But you would have to change your whole line of work to accommodate a relationship. I couldn't ask that of you. You were created to do this."

"Please go." When she wouldn't move, he circled back and escorted her to the door then opened it.

"Sweetie, you don't have to give up what you do, your purpose, to have a good love. You just have to find a love that's a better fit for your life and one that can go the distance whether you work this job ten more years or leave it in six months. Maybe that woman isn't Liang, but there is someone out there that you can go the distance with."

He refused to make eye contact with her. "Okay, I appreciate whatever it is that you think you're doing." Dante fought to keep his emotions in check. "But it's time for you to go home."

Brooklyn tried to get him to look her in the eyes, but he kept turning his head. "I sincerely want to see you happy, even if we can't find that happiness together." She finally grabbed him by both sides of his face. Dante closed his eyes. "You can have love and your career, just not with me. Like you told me, don't limit yourself."

She wrapped her arms around him. He just stood there stiffly. *Maybe this was a mistake,* she thought as a tear rolled down her cheek. Brooklyn was regretting her decision to come see him. All she did was put the dagger deeper into his heart. It was stupid of her to believe that he would actually be able to leave the job behind. Dante doing it unofficially would have just led to him lying to her in order to maintain their relationship.

Her heart was breaking all over again. She knew she'd made the best decision for her life as well as his, even though he couldn't see it now. Brooklyn turned, and walked out the door. As she hit the exterior stairs, tears were freely flowing down her cheek. She said a quick hello to Liang, who was coming up as she trotted down, trying to resist breaking in to a full-fledged run.

Brooklyn was kicking herself in the behind for risking her current relationship for a pipe dream. Sliding into the driver's seat, she wiped her cheeks with the back of her hands then started the car and drove off. Brooklyn exhaled as she tried to gain control of her emotions. When she heard that Kane was dead and Dante had taken a leave from his job, she thought that maybe she needed to reevaluate her decision, despite how much she loved Hunter. Dante's job had been the biggest reason she had chosen Hunter.

She stopped at the mall to walk around and clear her head. She could see clearly that chasing a fantasy in her head had prevented her from truly appreciating the reality that she had with Hunter. She entered the food court, ordered a tea, and took a seat. Hunter deserved better than what she had done. She would now be more considerate of her friends staying in a relationship or doing things that made her want to scream, "What the hell?" They were addicted to love, just like she was addicted to Dante. Now she wished she had taken time to truly get over that addiction and grieve over the relationship before pursuing something with Hunter.

Hunter was an amazing man in so many ways, but like a druggie trying to recreate the feeling of their first high, she had continually compared what she felt for Hunter against what she felt with Dante. If she was honest with herself, it was the memory of what was and the unpredictability of what could be with Dante that kept things feeling intense.

Brooklyn fought back the tears as she realized that she had created the problem and now had to come clean with Hunter. The idea of losing Hunter over this incident devastated her soul in a way that walking away from Dante had not. Part of her wanted to lie to Hunter but she couldn't do that to him; that was not who they were in their relationship. It was her prayer that Hunter would give her another chance. If he did, she would not mess it up. Brooklyn grabbed a napkin and wiped her tears. She was so mad at herself for being stupid and hurting Hunter. When she realized how late it was, she finally got the nerve to head home.

The cell phone rang. Hunter's name popped up on the display and she answered.

"Hey, handsome." Brooklyn rolled up the window.

"I'm just calling to see what my relationship status is." Hunter's voice was overly chipper as if he was trying to hide the torment of the waiting and wondering.

Brooklyn's mind replayed asking him to push back their dinner because she need to see Dante and promising to meet him back at his place later. Recalling his look of sheer devastation and disappointment ripped her apart. "The same as it was when I left your office." She almost choked on fear that she'd lose Hunter. The thought of not ending up with either of them because she was still straddling the fence struck terror in her heart.

"Glad to hear that."

"I'm pulling into the garage. Are you still up for going out for dinner?" Brooklyn parked the car and grabbed the car key, her purse, and cell. She tucked the cell between her shoulder and face, then locked up and started looking for the apartment key.

"How about we stay in?" Hunter suggested.

When she entered the door, she saw two rows of rose petals leading from either side of the door to the living room. Hunter was standing where the rose petals stopped. She smiled as she closed and locked the door. "What is this?"

"You have to come to me to find out." Hunter gave her a devilish smile as he slid his hand into his pocket.

Brooklyn smiled and threw her stuff on the console table near the door. As she walked towards him, Brooklyn suddenly felt nervous. "I'm listening."

"BK, after all the other men you've dated, after all the men you've loved, you've finally made it to me." Hunter dropped to his knee just as Brooklyn reached him and pulled out a ring box. "I love you, Brooklyn, and I want you in my life forever."

"Hunter." Brooklyn covered her mouth as he opened the box to reveal a one carat pear-shaped diamond set in a twisted diamond encrusted platinum band. She squealed a little bit.

"Will you marry me?" Hunter grabbed her hand, looking up into her eyes.

She stood with her mouth open wanting to say yes but remembered what she had just done.

"Whatever happened at Dante's doesn't matter as long as the end result is you want to be with me." Hunter stood, sliding the ring box back into his pocket.

Sadness filled her face as she crossed her arms, stating, "If I hadn't gone there to see if he had given up his job, so I can reevaluate my decision maybe it would be that simply. But I…"

"Listen, I'm willing to do what many good women have done for years and take that leap of faith despite what you've done. My best friend couldn't appreciate the good woman he was with because he kept running up behind his baby mama." He uncrossed her arms and held her hands. "He is happily married to that good woman because she was willing to take that leap of faith."

"That's a beautiful lollipop and gumdrops story but your boy lucked out. Everybody stories don't end so well."

"Look, I'm willing to take that risk to attempt to be one of the couples that the story ends well for. You could have hidden the fact that you were going to see Dante but you didn't."

"Hunter." She sighed stepping back. "While I don't want to lose you, saying yes to marriage after just wavering on my decision to be with you is—"

"Listen," Hunter interrupted. "If seeing Dante one last time has helped you finally accept that I'm indeed the man for you, then I still want you in my life as my wife." He paused. "But you do realize from this moment forward Dante can't be in your life in any shape, form, or fashion, right?"

"Yes." Brooklyn nodded to confirm her answer.

"People may think I'm crazy for proposing to you after you visited your ex but I believe in us." Hunter gazed down at her. "The only person's opinion that I care about is yours."

"Okay," she smiled as he descended to his knee again.

"So Brooklyn, will you be the recipient of a special kind of love that believes no matter what anyone else thinks that we have what it takes to create a great partnership?" He took out the ring box and opened it again. "Will you take that leap of faith and team up with me to be one of the few happily married?"

"I'm so sorry for ever doubting what we had. Yes, Hunter Torres, I would love to marry you." She watched as he slid the ring on her finger, with tears flowing down her cheek. Brooklyn pulled him up into a hug. In that moment, she realized that she almost gave up getting the eighty percent of what she needed in her life by chasing the twenty percent she didn't have. As Hunter lowered his lips to hers, Brooklyn decided to never let him regret taking this chance on her. Now that she was fully committed to her decision to be with Hunter, she was determined to work towards making sure it stayed that way. Dante was now a part of her past that she had to let go of in order to grab hold of a bright future with Hunter. He ended the kiss and tears rolled down Brooklyn's face as she silently promised to spend the rest of her life showing Hunter how much she loved him.

Hunter wiped away her tears and said, "I love you too," as if he'd heard her thoughts. Brooklyn wrapped her arms around him, holding him tightly, and feeling like the luckiest woman in the world.

About the Authors

Chicago natives, Jenetta and Karen Bradley, are sisters and authors.

Jenetta has always had a love for writing and has written and published five fictional books. She also post weekly updates to The SSMD, her online, interactive fictional story of a relationship advisor helping the Single, Shacking, Married, and Divorced (SSMD) while dealing with her own life's ups and downs.

Her younger sister, **Karen,** didn't start off sharing the love of writing. While being a creative mind, English and Grammar were never her strongest subjects. As life would have it, her weakest link would become her saving grace in life. It was during college she wrote her first book to help her cope with the death of her father, the upheaval of emotions, and her changing family dynamics. Writing fiction soon became one of her favorite forms of therapy.

Here's where you can find the Bradley Sisters:

Jenetta M. Bradley
On the Web:
www.jenettambradley.com
Facebook:
https://www.facebook.com/JMBAuthor
Twitter: @JenettaM

Karen D. Bradley
On the Web:
www.ambrosiasands.com
Facebook:
https://www.facebook.com/kdbauthor
Twitter: @ambrosiasands

KAREN D. BRADLEY
TAINTED
LOVE

Asya Brown took a bite from an apple that she wished she hadn't!

When Asya and Vic Webber's paths crossed, her instincts told her to keep him at a distance. She didn't. Vic slowly inserted himself into her life and into her heart. Their relationship became entangled in lies, accusations and manipulations. Even after breaking up, she couldn't seem to escape his madness.

Asya's focus was now all about surviving Vic. The question is, can she?

Terry Johnson refuses to allow the impending storm to keep her from sharing the news of her pregnancy with her best friend. That decision will change her life forever. Terror will shake the very core of her soul as she finds herself in a fight to keep those she loves alive. Before the clock strikes midnight, Terry may lose everything she cherishes in life. She drove through the storm, now can Terry live through it.

Only one of the women will survive to tell the story. Years later, she goes by the name Danya but the memory of that night still haunts her. Danya finds herself coming face to face with her past when she finds out that the man that killed her best friend has been released. She slowly discovers the truth about what really happened that stormy night. Every illusion Danya had about her past and her life will be shattered. She once again finds herself fighting to save her life.

Raven Hunter was perfectly content with her life. But without notification or warning, her life would crash and burn in the fire of people's trifling ways. Raven had no idea love could be such a beast and loved ones could be so cruel. After one of the most devastating events of her life; embarrassed and hurt, Raven shut down and attempted to separate herself from the situation by making some extreme life decisions.

Death has taken the only parent Tara has ever known.
Now a promise made to her dying mother forces her to
spend a summer with the father that walked out on her. At
summers end Tara believes she has made it through only
to find herself, ten-years later, almost full circle. Cedric
has a few people he has forgotten to tell his daughter
Tara about. Estranged for seventeen years his hope is to
win the love of his daughter before she walks out of his
life forever. Unfortunately, his daughter has a prejudice
that threatens his household. In Daddy Mixed Bag, Tara
is completely uprooted and finds herself in unfamiliar
territory full of heartache, disappointment, love, happiness
and laughter as she learns some tough life lessons.

Hearing the word bastard as a child changed something in Winter. Since that day she has fought against whatever was inside of her that accepted the thought that she was inferior. Abandoned by her father, Winter has retained the hope that one day she would learn why. Late one night she receives a call that she thinks will lead her to the answer.

Jeril Monroe has no desire to form a relationship with what he considers a constant reminder of his fall from grace—Winter. A minister with mega church dreams, Jeril is determined to keep the life he's built with his wife, picture perfect. Unfortunately, his mistress was threatening to expose him to the church, his wife was starting to rebel, and Winter was becoming a snag in his plans.

Winter soon learns that truth has many folds and the Monroes' have stories, secrets and issues of their own.